The Motherhood Club

MC

A NOVEL

HOWARD Fiction

Reality Queen

Debbie DiGiovanni

OUR PURPOSE AT HOWARD PUBLISHING IS TO:

- *Increase* faith in the hearts of growing Christians
- *Inspire* holiness in the lives of believers
- *Instill* hope in the hearts of struggling people everywhere

BECAUSE HE'S COMING AGAIN!

Published by Howard Publishing Co., Inc.
3117 North Seventh Street, West Monroe, Louisiana 71291-2227
www.howardpublishing.com

Published in association with the literary agency of Janet Kobobel Grant.

06 07 08 09 10 11 12 13 14 15 10 9 8 7 6 5 4 3 2 1

Edited by Ramona Cramer Tucker
Interior design by John Mark Luke Designs
Cover design by Terry Dugan Design

ISBN 1-58229-487-9

This book is dedicated
to my **Mother**,
who trusted God all her life.

Many thanks to Ramona Cramer Tucker, my brilliant and big-hearted editor; Philis Boultinghouse, a godly example in the mostly hectic publishing world; Janet Kobobel Grant, my patient agent; and Susan Krause, my Reality TV expert. Also to the Red Hat Society ladies for allowing me to grill them over breakfast at the Cracker Barrel and Dr. Phil Higgins for his kind assistance.

I was trying to remember if I had added an egg to my cookie batter when my daughter, Hannah, sat next to me at the kitchen table with that freshman Psych 101 look in her inquisitive brown eyes.

"We're studying empty nest syndrome. Have you heard of it?"

I wrinkled my nose. "Yes, I've heard of it."

She patted my right hand with hers, which gave me the impression I was being consoled for some reason. "So Mom, Mark is already out of the house."

"Yes, I noticed that."

She grew even more serious. "And Jeff is practically gone. He's hardly ever home."

"He has been spending a lot of time at the library," I admitted.

"It's Kelly."

"Who's Kelly?"

"This girl he likes. She works in the reference center."

"Jeff likes a girl, does he? I wondered why he was suddenly fascinated with expanding his mind beyond the sports page."

"You promised I could live in the dorm next year when I'm a sophomore."

I nodded. "That's the plan. I haven't been clipping coupons and inventing creative casseroles for nothing."

"What is it going to feel like when you have no life?"

I gave her a blank look.

"What I mean, Mom, is, what are your plans? For when all of us kids are gone."

The blank look remained. "Goodness, Hannah. I don't know. Maybe I'll take up skydiving or some other low-impact sport."

She rolled her eyes and continued grilling me. "Who are you, Mom? Besides being a mother, a people pleaser, and a domestic goddess. If you were on an island, who would you be?"

That didn't take much thought. "Stephy Daniels, age forty-three. Blue eyed, wiry-haired brunette. Five foot five, one twenty five . . . uh, a hundred thirty pounds. Making lots of coconut casserole dishes, I guess."

She focused in on me like a camera. "Not the outer you. The *inner* you."

Apparently, she and her professor had me pegged for a self-identity crisis.

"Have you considered switching your major to animal husbandry?" I asked wryly.

"Does that have anything to do with scooping poop?"

"Yes," I verified.

"Then absolutely not." She stood up and showed me all those dazzling, straight teeth we paid for, before she made a hasty exit.

I heaved a big sigh, shook my head back and forth a few times, and returned to my duties as a domestic goddess. Checking on my chocolate-chip cookies, I found them to be a perfect golden brown.

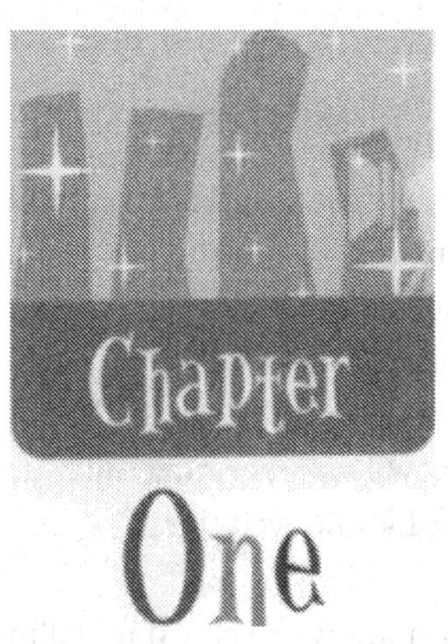

One

Eighteen months later

I didn't think it would really happen—at least not so fast. All three of our children were gone. It was just Brock and I all alone in our big, yellow house.

Still, there was no weeping or clinging to photo albums. My babies all lived within a forty-mile radius and were only a visit or phone call away. I'd been as busy as ever taking care of them the past six months.

After six rings Hannah picked up and breathed heavily in my ear.

"Good morning," I chirped, and she managed a sleepy hello.

I was Hannah's wake-up call. She slept through alarms and earthquakes. Every morning I called her before her first class. "Get a head start on the world! Come on! Get out of bed!"

She moaned.

I imagined her rubbing her eyes and yawning. I could hear her shuffling across the floor in her flip-flops and smiled as I thought of her in her Tweety Bird pajamas (the only kind she wore), brown hair in every direction, as unmanageable as mine.

Allowing her a moment of silence to get her bearings, I stared proudly at the pictures of my children. I heard the hum of the microwave in the background.

"Hannah, you shouldn't do that."

"Do what?" she asked.

"Reheat your coffee. It ruins the flavor."

"How did you know I was reheating my coffee?"

"I'm your mother. I know everything."

"That's what I'm afraid of."

Everything I didn't know she ended up telling me—eventually. I went on to the daily weather report. "How does it look there?"

After a minute she replied, "It's yucky here. Foggy."

Hannah lived in the dorm at Biola University in La Mirada, where I frequently visited and made her bed, cleaned out her fridge, collected dust bunnies, and left goodies.

"The sun is out here," I boasted. "It's another beautiful fall day in Santa Monica."

"That's nice."

I heard her turn on the bathroom faucet. When she was home, sometimes I'd sit on the toilet lid talking to her as she performed her morning routine. We were close.

"Hold on, Mom."

I took a sip of orange juice and waited.

"OK, I'm back," she said, whishing her toothbrush back and forth.

"Brush your tongue, Hannah. It's a known fact that people who brush their tongues not only have good breath and less plaque, but also enjoy better health," I claimed.

She answered with her mouth full. "Well, it's been harder to brush my tongue since I pierced it."

I almost knocked over my glass of orange juice. "You pierced your tongue?"

She whished and spat. "No." She laughed.

"Shock value. How cute." I laughed too.

"But I can if I want. I *am* twenty, you know."

"May I remind you that we are your primary source of income and have the say on your expenditures?"

"My *only* source of income," she clarified. "I haven't been able to find a job."

Honestly, I didn't mind. I'd rather she concentrate on her studies. "Do you have a swim meet this weekend?"

"No, last week was the last one. Why?"

"It's something to do," I said absent-mindedly, then wished I hadn't said it.

"I warned you, Mom. This empty nest syndrome can be a traumatic transition. You need to get a life," she said predictably.

"Animal husbandry, Hannah," I reminded her and laughed.

"I'm not joking. You need a life."

"I have a very fulfilling life."

"What? Picking up Dad's socks?"

"And taking care of you kids. I think I do more for you now than when you were home."

"You really don't have to."

I paused, not sure if she meant it. "Would you like to meet me this afternoon after your classes?" I asked hopefully.

"Sorry. Rachelle and I are going shopping."

"Oh," I said, disappointed. "Isn't she the one with the pierced belly button and nose ring?"

"And tongue. Hey, maybe I can get her to pierce my tongue."

I laughed, but I wasn't sure I liked this Rachelle, 4.0 or no 4.0.

Jeff was next on my call list. At eighteen he was the baby of the family. I loved spoiling him, and he loved being spoiled. The poor child wouldn't eat a peanut-butter sandwich unless the crust was cut off, and he had a dozen other idiosyncrasies that were probably my fault.

Was he driving safely? Was he taking his vitamins? Was he getting enough sleep?

I let the phone ring several times. He always picked up by the third ring, but there was no answer. The answering machine didn't pick up, either.

The basement apartment he was renting was dangerous. It had ancient wiring, inadequate ventilation, and was basically in bad shape. In my opinion, he was too young to be on his own, but since Mark, his older brother, had moved out at this same age, we had agreed to support him in his decision (or try to, in my case).

I called again and let it ring at least eight times.

I called fifteen minutes later and let it ring twelve times.

Jeff was always home in the mornings.

I called one last time, and there was still no answer.

Something had to be wrong.

I grabbed my purse and jumped in my car, speeding down the road in a state of panic. I rang Mark on the way.

"Hello," a deep voice replied.

"Mark."

"Mom?"

"Meet me at Jeff's apartment. I think something is wrong. He's not answering, and I know he's home."

"Wrong? What could be wrong?"

"He's not answering the phone."

"He's probably in the shower," Mark guessed.

"For thirty minutes?"

"Without you yelling, 'Get out of the shower,' it's possible."

I pictured a big grin on his face. I'm sure he thought I was overreacting.

I nearly drove through a red light. "Well, I'm worried. Anything could have happened."

"Like what?"

"Someone could have broken into his place. Or he could be lying on the floor dying from carbon-monoxide poisoning. There's no alarm in that apartment."

Mark was quiet. Then he sighed. "Did you ever think that maybe he doesn't *want* to answer? He has caller ID, you know."

I was on to Mark. I knew *he* ignored my calls sometimes. But not Jeff. Never Jeff. I didn't say it, however.

"Would you please just meet me there?" I pleaded.

"Sure." Mark's voice was resigned. "Whatever, Mom."

When I reached Jeff's place, his car was parked on the street. As I ran down the cement stairs to his apartment, I heard music blaring. I didn't know if this was a good sign.

I banged a couple of times, then used my spare key to unlock the door. Barging in like a fireman, I heard a high-pitched scream.

Jeff was standing a few feet away with a stick in one hand, and the screamer, his blond, blue-eyed girlfriend, was holding on to him like her life depended on it.

"Mom!" Jeff yelled and dropped the stick.

Kelly held on to Jeff even tighter. "I was so scared. We thought someone was breaking in!"

I closed the door and took a deep breath. I was relieved Jeff was OK but surprised to see Kelly there so early.

Jeff broke away to turn the music down, and I followed him.

"When did she get here?" I whispered.

Her well-trained ears heard me from across the room, and she answered for Jeff. "About an hour ago. See, I made breakfast." She smiled.

I noted the buffet on the table and gave a tight smile back.

"Where did you get a key to my apartment?" Jeff asked, baffled.

"I made it the day you moved in," I said casually.

"Can I have it? I could use a spare key."

I pulled it off the macramé key chain Hannah had made in Girl Scouts and reluctantly handed it over. I was sure I saw Kelly roll her eyes.

"Jeff, I thought something terrible had happened to you. Didn't you hear your phone ring?" I snapped.

"Uh." He looked to Kelly for assistance, which really bothered me.

"We heard it," Kelly said.

I purposefully faced Jeff and away from Kelly so he would have to answer my question. "It rang twenty times—at least."

"I had the ringer turned off, I guess." He laughed guiltily.

I was sure that was Kelly's doing.

"Anyway, I'm glad to see you're OK, Jeff." I hugged him. "I'll come by later with some chicken and dumplings."

"I won't be here. I'll be at work."

"I'll leave it on your doorstep, and you can have it when you get home tonight."

He touched my shoulder. "Mom, maybe you should ease up on the meals."

Since when did Jeff turn down my chicken and dumplings? "Why?"

"You shouldn't go to all that trouble. You have better things to do."

This was troubling.

"It would seem to me that leaving food on the doorstep would attract animals," Kelly said, nosing in on our conversation again.

"Animals. What kind of animals?" I replied, perplexed.

He scrunched his forehead. "Dogs. Skunks. Raccoons."

"Skunks and raccoons in LA?"

"Sure," Kelly said, like she was some animal expert.

After a couple of eternal pauses, I said maybe I should go.

There was no objection.

I said good-bye.

Oh, to be a fly on the wall and hear what Kelly had to say.

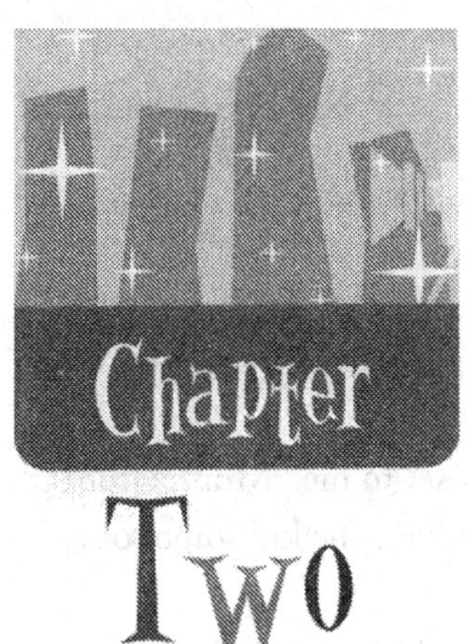

Chapter Two

I stood at the top of the stairs to Jeff's apartment, feeling lost.

When Mark drove up, I ran over to meet him.

"He's fine, isn't he?" he said as he got out of his blue pickup.

"More than fine," I admitted.

"Is Kelly over already?" He ran his fingers through his sun-streaked, surfer-cut hair.

"With a spread that could feed King Kong and his hungry friends." I slumped, wanting to forget the whole terrible mess. "Would you like to have breakfast, Son?"

He looked pensive. I guessed he thought I meant with Jeff and Kelly.

"I mean eat out," I clarified. "Anywhere you want. Ed's Coffee Shop, House of Pancakes. The Disney restaurant would be fun. Remember when you and I went there?" I tried to sound convincing.

His dark eyes narrowed. "That was ten years ago."

I looked up at his six-foot frame. When did he get to be twenty-one? "Or Belisle's is great. They serve sausage patties the size of pizzas."

"I don't have time," he went on. "We're filming a mock shaving commercial at school this morning, and I'm the subject." He beat on his chest.

"Oh, that's why you're unshaven."

When he didn't say anything, I wondered if the comment was meddling.

He took a step closer to me. "Mom, I don't mean to tell you what to do, but you have to give the kid some room."

"What do you mean?"

"You call Jeff several times a day."

I leaned on his truck. "That's an exaggeration."

"I was with him yesterday morning. You called him three times."

"You were there, and you didn't say hi?" I straightened up.

He looked down.

I defended myself. "Well, that was because I wanted to know if he wanted Parmesan on his lasagna, and then I wasn't sure if he was a size ten or eleven in Nikes. Brands vary, you know."

He raised his eyes to meet mine. "Can I be honest?"

"You usually are."

"If you keep treating him like a mama's boy, no woman will ever want to marry him."

And the problem with that is . . . ? I kept that thought private.

"Do I smother you children?" I asked, expecting the answer to be a resounding no.

"You are very protective."

I wanted to choke on that surprising news. "Me, protective?"

"We need to go through our own 'stuff,' you know."

Frankly, I didn't know. I had gone through a lot of stuff alone, and I didn't care for it.

"Mom, you really, really, really need to get a life."

"Hannah said that this morning, too, only she left out the really, really, really."

I remembered Jeff's comment about my having better things to do. It was basically the same thing.

"Listen, I'm late for school." He gave me a compassionate look. "Please don't get your feelings hurt. I hate it when you get your feelings hurt."

I shrugged.

"I'm not leaving until I know you're OK," he insisted.

I didn't feel OK, but I smiled for his benefit.

He lovingly pecked me on the cheek, climbed in his monstrous 4x4, and sped away.

I started my car and sat there for a long time, disbelieving the last hour of unfortunate events.

Finally, no longer able to deny my emotions, I burst into inner complaint.

You change their dirty diapers, stay up with them when they're sick, drive them around like you're their personal chauffeur, and on their sixteenth birthday you buy them a shiny, used car to drive their friends around in. Then the traitors use that car to move out and tell you to get a life.

Why didn't anybody tell me this would happen?

Of course, they had practically stapled a note to my forehead. Everyone from the women in my Bible study, to my bank teller, to the lady at Kmart who was reaching for the Oakland Raiders Bed in a Bag I had claimed for Jeff.

"Just wait," she had said, after I'd pleaded my case and won, explaining that my wonderful son, who'd just moved into his own apartment, was a sports fanatic.

"Your son will get a taste of freedom and, like my son, you'll hardly hear from him," she spewed as she walked away.

I remember thinking, *Well, she's not very nice, and she probably doesn't treat her son very nice, either.*

Now I wasn't sure it was that simple.

I retrieved a handful of Kleenex from my Vera Bradley bag and unleashed a waterfall.

Jeff peered out the window. I didn't want him to wonder why I was still there, so I put on my sunglasses, waved, and drove away, bleary-eyed and shaken.

I had been ushered into a full-fledged identity crisis, just like Hannah and her professor predicted.

Where does one go to have a self-identity crisis?

About thirty minutes later I found myself at the park near my home. There were probably all kinds of people having identity crises there. But as I walked on the paved trail, I wondered. The cyclists, the Rollerbladers, the joggers, and the exercise enthusiasts all looked so happy. That made me kind of happy, until I reached the lake where I had taken my children when they were small. Then the waterfall flowed again. The wadded Kleenex ball came out of my bag.

My tears were interrupted when playgroup moms overtook me with their ultramodern strollers. Five or so women chatted as their younger children fought over the duck food and the older children terrorized the ducks.

I eavesdropped on their conversations, which ran the gamut from motherhood is the most fulfilling job in the world to what a draining existence it is.

"I would love to have one day for myself," a harried mother wailed as her son tugged on her shirt.

I remembered that game. Our mom's group called it One Day.

"One day I'm going to swim with the dolphins."

"One day I'm going to take a gondola ride in Venice."

"One day I'm going to start my own clothing line."

We'd dream. Or at least they would. I never could think of anything interesting I wanted to do, except be a comedienne, which my friends highly discouraged.

They called me Kraft Macaroni and Cheese. I like Kraft Macaroni and Cheese.

But suddenly I wanted to do something spontaneous.

I walked along the lush grass and thought about it. Then I realized if it were a truly spontaneous act, I wouldn't be thinking about it. I'd be *doing* it.

Hmm. If the Society for Barefoot Living had a club dedicated to the experience, there must be something to it.

I looked around before I flung off my tennis shoes and wiggled my bare toes. Then I ran with no particular direction in mind, leaving my Keds where they landed. Holding on to my bag, I tried to capture the sensory experience.

The only thing I captured was wet grass on my feet. I had forgotten about last night's rain. My feet were a soggy, muddy mess.

Panting, and obviously out of shape, I looked up through my tears.

"Would you like to join us?" a lady called and waved me over to a crowded picnic table.

There were at least a dozen women sitting with her. As they greeted me, I was embarrassed by my bare feet. I said hi and smiled at the millinery shop of red velour and velvet and purple plumes bobbing around. They looked so "Broadway musical" that I half expected them to start singing and dancing. I now recognized these elegant ladies as the Red Hat Society—that over-fifty organization dedicated to the art of living.

A white-haired lady in a purple dress and gloves presented me with a red linen napkin.

"Thank you." I dabbed my tears. "Have you ever tried running barefoot on grass?"

"Not after a rain, dear," she answered, amused.

"I prefer the beach," a tanned, smiling woman declared.

Everyone at the table looked in my direction before returning to their socializing.

"You don't seem the barefoot type," the white-haired woman continued.

"There's a type?" I asked.

"Sure. The free spirit, and the 'I need to get rid of some strong emotions' type. Usually, the free spirit run doesn't come with tears."

We knew which one I was, then.

"Have you just been through a wrenching breakup?" she whispered.

I flashed my wedding ring. "No."

"A fight with your husband?" she tried.

"No." I needed to blow my nose, but I had thrown my wad of Kleenex away.

"You can blow if you want," she assured me with a pat on the shoulder.

"Thanks." Since I was blowing into her linen, it was only proper to introduce myself. "I'm Stephy."

"I'm Jane."

I sat down.

"Would you like to tell me what's wrong, Stephy?" she encouraged.

"Now, Jane," a woman with a kind face and dark red lipstick said, "she'll tell us if she wants to."

There was so much to tell.

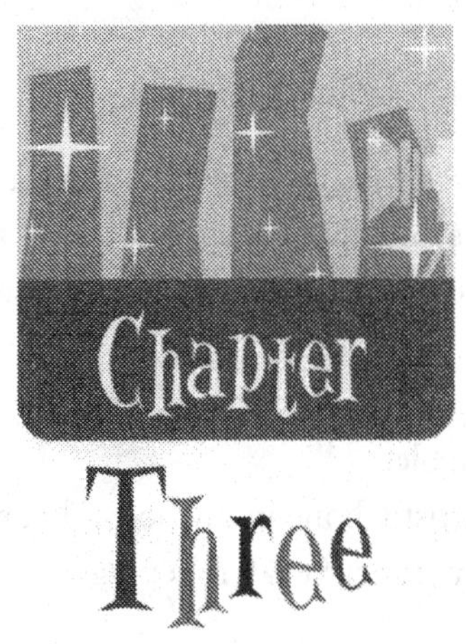

Chapter Three

It all started when a woman I hadn't noticed before came over to me, smiled, and asked if the milk in my fridge was spoiling.

I was stunned—not only because it was a strange question, but also because my milk *had* been spoiling. Every week half of it dissolved into a sour, curdled something that had to be helped down the garbage disposal.

"Yes, my milk is spoiling. How did you know?"

She gave me a knowing look.

"Why would her milk be spoiling?" Jane asked.

"Empty nest syndrome," the other lady touted.

Most of the group looked up. The news filtered down to the other end of the table, where the younger red hats were congregated. "Ahh," they empathized.

Since I had everyone's attention and sympathy, I asked if they wanted to hear my sad, sad story.

Brutes for punishment, they said they did.

I recounted my morning, loud enough so the whole group could hear, and used particularly descriptive adjectives when I got to the part about Kelly and how she was a bad influence on my son. I ended by saying, "So, you see, I have to get a life besides the one I've built around my children. All I ever wanted was to be a mother."

Another "ahh" of sympathy was shared.

I could feel the support of the sisterhood. The advice came pouring in.

"This is an excellent time to take up faux painting," said someone from the end of the table.

"I don't have an artistic bone in my body," I confessed.

"Running is very effective at relieving stress," someone else suggested.

"I have flat feet, and I hate to run."

"You can always revive your career," a distinguished woman in a red, formal business suit advised.

"What career?" I wrinkled my nose. "My job for the last twenty-one years has been stay-at-home mom."

"That's a full-time job right there," someone said.

Everyone agreed that travel was the ultimate freedom for empty nesters.

"Our older son is attending the Los Angeles Film School, our daughter is in a private Christian college, and I'm hoping our younger son will someday choose to get an education."

They nodded, familiar with the sacrifice.

"Besides, my husband can't just leave his real-estate business to go traveling around."

After they ran out of ideas, they went back to talking amongst themselves.

I was distraught. "And to make it worse, my three best friends deserted me for their own ventures." I sniffled.

They had promised close and cherished friendship forever, but then Julie went back to school, Kim resurrected her marketing career, and Cheryl and her husband moved to Florida. I hadn't heard from them in ages.

"I'd invite you to join our club, but you are obviously not fifty," Jane said.

"No, I'm not." I leaned in her direction. "I almost wish I were, though. I could use the companionship."

Jane took my hand. "You know, I'll bet you have a companion right under your nose you may not have considered."

"I don't care for dogs, if that's what you're thinking."

"Not a dog. Your husband," she whispered.

"Of course." I grabbed my hand from her and slapped myself—twice. "Bad Wife," I scolded.

"Your life has been focused on your children, and now you're going to spend the next forty years with your husband," she said.

The next forty years. Wow!

I thought of my earlier conversation with Hannah.

"I have a very fulfilling life."

"What? Picking up Dad's socks?"

Jane waited until I returned from dreamland for the last of her advice. "You need to release your children and nurture your relationship with your husband. Renew your romance. Make the second half of your marriage better than the first."

Somehow I was sure Jane knew what she was talking about. "Yes, yes, I'll do it!"

I stayed and had tea with the Red Hat Society ladies after that.

"You could still join us as a pink hat," the mother of the Red Hats invited me.

"That's OK," I said politely. "I don't look good in pink."

Jane took her hat off and put it on me. "You keep it."

The gesture was so sweet it made me cry. Again.

"And keep the linen too." She smiled.

After retrieving my now-muddy, grass-stained tennis shoes, my next order of business was creating a romantic environment for my wonderful husband of twenty-two years.

I vowed to be the best wife ever. That would keep me busy and happy.

Where could we spend a romantic evening that was something different than dinner out?

Aha. We live in a beach community. What could be more romantic than the beach?

When we were younger, we loved the beach. Brock used to chase me in the sand and surf in my teensy-weensy string bikini. (Well, maybe not that teensy-weensy.)

The last time I had worn a bathing suit was in the bathroom cleaning blinds, and it was a one-piece. Not that I had any desire to go public in any bathing suit. The bathroom mirror had been a grim reminder.

At 4:35 p.m. exactly (I was watching the clock), my husband got out of his shiny, silver Honda and stood in a black pinstripe suit, the epitome of any woman's dream. My dream, anyway.

I ran to meet my lover in a casual, yet elegant, outfit. "Hello sweetheart," I cried as I threw out my arms, preparing to be enveloped.

"Look at that." He pointed and walked past me with his briefcase.

"What?" I followed.

"The paint is chipping off the siding. It's not supposed to do that." He examined it closely.

I frowned. I hadn't been expecting, "Honey, I've been thinking of you all day and I have two dozen roses and a suite at the Hilton." However, couldn't he have saved the home inspection for Saturday?

Oh well. It only proved that romance was drastically needed.

"Get back in the car. I'm taking you somewhere special." I ordered.

Brock gave me a confused look but sat in the passenger's seat anyway. I ran in the house to retrieve the picnic basket I had lovingly put together. By the time I had arranged it in the trunk and was situated in the driver's seat, he was talking business on his cell.

We were sitting on a blanket, surrounded by sand, ocean, sun, and blue skies, when Brock finally got off his cell and looked up, startled, as though we were a care package that had dropped from an airplane and happened to land in this particular spot.

I scattered rose petals from a plastic bag.

"What are we doing here?" he asked.

The question spoiled my fantasy.

He looked around warily. "What's the date today?"

"March seventh. Why?"

"Then it's not our anniversary."

I glared. Our anniversary was months away.

"Phew," he said as I helped him off with his suit jacket and laid it on the blanket.

"Be careful, you're going to get sand in the pockets," he warned.

"You have other suits," I reasoned.

"Did you pick up my suit and shirts at the dry cleaner's?"

"Oh, I forgot." I grimaced and changed the subject. "Hungry?" I fed him a grape like I'd seen someone do in a movie.

He chewed and spit the remnants in the sand. "It's sour!"

"Take your shirt off, honey. Lie down and relax. I'll rub your back."

He stared at me, then slowly took his shirt off and placed it on top of his suit jacket.

I sighed inwardly. I didn't remember having to work on romance.

"Remember when you used to massage mine with Hawaiian Tropic tanning oil?"

"I sure do."

As my fingers and the almond oil worked their magic on his back, Brock relaxed. "Honey, that feels wonderful! And what's that smell?"

The aromatherapy was working.

It was a romantic moment.

I did say "moment."

Then snores mixed with the sounds of the ocean.

An hour later we were back home sitting in front of the TV. Brock had newfound energy, which had everything to do with the football game he was watching.

Thick-skulled, naive little me figured what he needed was some . . . incentive.

I put on the little black number he had given me for my birthday and came prancing into the living room.

"Hi, honey," he said. But who was he talking to? He wasn't looking at me.

Boldly I sat in his invisible four-foot circle that was strictly off-limits while watching sports. But he was too engrossed in the game to care.

I ran his fingers along the sleeve of my velvet dress that I hadn't had a chance to wear, since we rarely went out to dinner at fancy places.

Was it impossible to believe he might be more interested in me than a stupid football game?

I rubbed his temples with my magic fingers.

"I can't see with your hand in my face," he grumbled.

That did it. I stood up. "Have you noticed the dress I'm wearing?"

He glanced at me the way you would a tree as you're whizzing by at 100 mph. "It's beautiful," he said, emotionless.

I held his clueless face in my hand.

"Is it new?" he asked, smash-faced.

"It's the one you bought me for my birthday."

I released his face, and he went back to watching the game.

"Touchdown Packers!" he cheered a minute later.

During the beer commercial he stretched and smiled at me. "I told you that you looked nice, didn't I?" he added, catching on that I wasn't happy.

"You didn't buy this dress, did you?" I accused.

He squirmed. "I *paid* for it."

"But your secretary picked it out."

"You said yourself Peggy has good taste."

Chapter Four

Ten minutes later I stood under the streetlight in my sweats and gulped the chilly night air.

As my neighbor Katie Dillard returned from an evening jog in her velour sweat suit, I uttered a weak "Hello, Katie." (I skipped the warning about how jogging at night can be dangerous.)

Katie was a single, wealthy heiress, with aspirations of becoming a writer. She was energetic, honest, and, most importantly, my only friend these days. Sadly, all my other friends and neighbors (besides my three former best friends) who had called and come over all the time had only liked me for my children.

Katie passed me by, then circled back to stand with me under the light.

"Hi, Katie," I said again.

"Are you OK?" she asked.

"Is it that obvious?" I flared. "Do I have a sign around my neck that says Distressed Woman, Please Advise?"

"I believe the question was, 'Are you OK?' not, 'Are you having a nervous breakdown?'" She untied the sweatshirt from her neck and retied it around her waist.

I apologized. And then, as though it had been eons since I had spilled my soul to another human being, I told her everything I had relayed to the Red Hat ladies . . . with some additional details for dramatic effect.

"Can you believe it?" I asked when I finished.

She tightened her ponytail. "You could use some excitement in your life."

"Please, no more advice," I begged. "I've had enough advice today to start a Web site on empty-nest syndrome."

She smiled thoughtfully. "I don't have advice; I have the solution."

"Solution?"

"I'll just make a phone call, and it will all be better."

"A phone call?"

Katie used that phrase often. Whatever it was you needed, she knew someone who knew someone who could get it for you. She had connections. People in every walk of life who were more than willing to help her out.

At this point I didn't really care to know what she had in mind. The last time she had made a call, we ended up floating in a hot-air balloon over Temecula. She rather enjoyed it. For me it was pure terror.

That night Brock and I did eventually make a romance connection—during halftime. Funny thing, though, it ended the exact instant the third quarter started.

After searching desperately for the remote (hidden under the cushion by yours truly) and turning up the sound, he asked if the sour grape at the beach was dinner.

"Oh, your dinner." I proceeded to the refrigerator.

I took the uneaten contents of the picnic basket, sloppily arranged them on a paper plate, and dropped the plate on the TV tray as the fourth quarter started.

Then I remembered my vow to make my husband happy.

I prepared a warm bath with bubbly salts, and after the game while Brock's tired muscles were being soothed, I whipped up some chocolate mousse.

He was on the bed clipping his toenails when I delivered the treat.

"What are you doing?" I gasped.

"Don't worry. I'm clean, and I'm collecting them in a pile."

That didn't thrill me.

When I looked in the bathroom and saw his wet towel on the floor, I frowned. "How long have you been doing that?"

"Every day since I've known you," he said, enjoying his dessert.

I sat next to him on the bed. "We should talk."

"OK," Brock said, his brown eyes wary.

We were silent for a long time. I think he knew I didn't want to talk about his favorite subjects: work, sports, news, and cars.

"What did you do today?" he finally asked.

"I ran barefoot in the park."

"Uh huh." He shook his head like "you jokester, you."

He gave me a bite of his dessert and went back to smacking his lips.

Suddenly everything about him annoyed me. The way he cleared his throat so often. The way he didn't use the napkin I provided. The way he wriggled around like a little boy.

A few minutes later, as he was reading the newspaper, I couldn't take it anymore. "Would you please read your newspaper more quietly?"

"More quietly?" He gave me a sideways glance.

"Do you have to turn the pages so violently?"

"Violently?" He appeased me with a pat on the knee.

Maybe everything was louder because the house was still. I wanted to scream, "THIS HOUSE IS TOO QUIET! Would someone please put on some heavy-metal music? Can we organize some sibling rivalry here?"

His tone changed. "What's wrong, Stephy? You don't seem yourself tonight."

"I'm sorry," I said, meaning it.

"Did something happen today?"

I couldn't answer. I simply asked him to hold me. After I felt safe and wonderful, I shared about our children.

"Expanding your horizons wouldn't be a bad thing," Brock finally suggested after he'd heard the whole litany.

I stiffened. *Why does that sound like I'm not valuable the way I am? That I need to change?*

And, regarding change. I wasn't very fond of it.

"You can do some filing at my office."

"I want something more interesting than that." I pouted.

"I'm just trying to help."

"I know, and I'm sorry I'm taking everything out on you." I really was. I just couldn't seem to help it.

"That's all right." He put his arm around my shoulder. "I understand this is a hard time for you."

What? Are men exempt?

I thought for a while. Then I said slowly, "So you wouldn't mind if I got a job then?"

"Not at all." He picked a small mirror off the headboard, studied his nose, and rushed off.

"Where are you going?"

"To pluck a nose hair." He burped. "Excuse me," he apologized and beat on his chest with his fist. "I'm telling you, the older I get, the worse my indigestion gets."

A job might not be a bad idea, I reasoned, *or the next forty years could be rather long.*

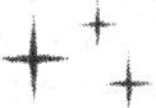

The next day I might have stayed in bed if Katie hadn't come banging at my door.

"What time is it?" I asked, dragging my blanket and bad attitude with me.

"Eleven o'clock," she answered from the doorstep.

She was wearing a corduroy skirt, a silk kimono top, and pointy-toed boots that made her look as though she hadn't decided if she was a high schooler, a Kabuki actor, or a retro rodeo performer.

"Why are you staring?" she asked. "You told me I should dress more casual."

"Well, forget what I said. Trust your own designer instinct from now on."

She invited herself in, took off her sunglasses, and stared in my hall mirror. "Never get dressed with your sunglasses on."

She was obviously in a better mood than I.

I was exhausted from Brock's seismic activity during the night. So exhausted that when he'd nudged me and asked if I was ready to whip him up a hearty oatmeal-and-bran breakfast, I'd glared and rolled over.

A few minutes later he woke me up again and asked if I was trying to kill him.

"Why?" I'd growled.

"Our milk is rotten."

And then I had fallen back asleep, missing half the day. I hated that feeling of having the day pass me by.

I threw my blanket down and stretched.

Katie danced around like she'd had too much sugary cereal for breakfast. "So do you have any plans today?"

"You mean besides housework and my trip to the mailbox?" I flashed a sarcastic smile. "There better be something exciting in there besides Brock's newspapers—like a *Godiva Chocolatier* magazine."

"Get dressed. You have a job interview in one hour."

"A job interview?"

"That means they ask you questions and you answer them, and if they like you, you get the job." She chuckled.

How would she know since she hasn't had a job in years?

"That phone call I was telling you about. Let's call it your lucky day."

"I don't believe in luck," I said.

"What *do* you believe in?"

"Providence."

"Isn't that in Rhode Island?"

"Not that Providence."

Katie had a lot of mixed-up ideas that I was trying to straighten her out on.

"Never mind," she said. "Get dressed. I'll drive you."

I laughed lightly, but she was serious.

Thirty minutes later I was in the front seat of Katie's red BMW, speeding down Santa Monica Boulevard.

Eventually my fear was overtaken by curiosity. "Where are we going?"

"Going?"

I hated it when Katie repeated my questions.

"Details. I want details," I asserted, since it was my future we were determining here.

"It's simple. My friend Mattie does the hiring for the Home Living Channel. One of their production assistants quit, and she's not happy with the caliber of people she's been interviewing. I recommended you," Katie said, all in one breath.

"Based on what? My work on *Jeopardy* or *Star Wars*?" I shook my head. This was ludicrous.

"In this business it's who you know." Katie smiled. "And I know people."

I didn't doubt that, but I did doubt my abilities. "I don't have any experience in television whatsoever. *Nada!*"

Katie screeched to a halt at a red light and turned to me. "The position is entry level, and what they're looking for at this point is someone who is punctual, cheerful, and dependable."

"I'm all those things!" I said, excitement growing.

"Exactly."

Chapter Five

Katie pulled up to the Tenth Street guard gate and checked in. We parked adjacent to the studio.

My eyes widened at the size of the grounds.

"The Home Living Channel rents space in the back lot."

"You've been here before?"

"Of course."

It was amazing to me that Katie had this other, more-significant life.

Golf carts whizzed by. We walked past sound stage three and four and navigated around heavy equipment before we reached our destination.

"They're an independently owned cable station," Katie said, defending the ordinary looking offices.

She thrust open the door, rushed me through the lobby, and escorted me to the tall counter. And then, as though I had just come out of a coma and was incapable of speaking for myself, she introduced me to the black head bent over the keyboard.

"This is Stephanie Daniels. She has an interview with Miss Kinsel."

The young receptionist called Mattie on the intercom. "She'll be with you shortly," she said pleasantly and went back to typing.

Mattie Kinsel emerged from nowhere, dressed, stereotypically, in a navy blue suit and pumps.

She hugged Katie (who was now wearing a smart yellow dress) and told her that she was having a dinner party the following Friday at seven. Could Katie please bring her delicious mushroom hors d'oeuvre?

"Have you tasted them?" The question was directed at me.

"Yes, I have," I said and smiled, because I was the chef.

Katie laughed and said she'd be reading *Hollywood Scriptwriter* in the lobby.

I followed Mattie's pumps out the door and across the dirt into her trailer office. She directed me to a chair. I sat down and noted her frog collection. She had at least one hundred amphibians—glass, beaded, stuffed, and clay, of every shape and size.

I wondered what that said about her personality. Maybe she just liked frogs?

Mattie settled into a big, burgundy leather chair. She looked like she hadn't seen a bathroom mirror all day. "So ya wanna be a production assistant?"

"That's right."

"Why?" Her green eyes were piercing.

How could I respond? Except for, "*I don't know. Because housework is drudgery and my children say I need to get a life.*" Other than that inappropriate answer, my mind was completely blank.

Mattie let out a tremendous sigh and stared at the stacks of paper littered on her desk. "It's lonely being the only one here with brains," she said, thumbing through the clutter. She raised her head slowly. "Since you're a friend of Katie's, I'm not going to beat around the bush."

"Please don't," I said, relieved.

"I'm tired of interviewing bubblegum chewers and people who

don't have the presence of mind to turn off their cell phones in an interview."

Did I turn mine off? Yup. Good.

I could feel her frustration rising. "Star-struck kids, half my age, who want me to introduce them to Brad Pitt."

She knows Brad Pitt?

Mattie pulled off her right earring and rubbed her ear. "Look, this isn't rocket science we're talking about here. I'm tired and overworked, and you are . . . uh . . ."

I tried to help. "Brunette?" (My best answer yet.)

"You . . . you look excessively normal," she finished.

"That's good, I hope." I wrung my hands nervously.

"Stephanie, you're not writing a screenplay, are you?" she cried.

"No."

"You have no aspirations to become an actress?"

"None whatsoever."

"A producer? A director?" She bit her finger. "Do you understand what I'm saying here?"

I sorta did.

"Sometimes I wish I were a zookeeper. That's what I wanted to be when I was seven," Mattie said.

That didn't sound fun to me, but hey, if it did to her . . .

She jumped to another subject. "So how's your skin?"

Dry. Oily. It seemed an odd question.

"Do you have thick skin?" she continued. "Because, otherwise, this business will chew you up and spit you out."

I was taken aback by her honesty.

"These wrinkles weren't here when I started as a receptionist. I was young and cute." She let out another tremendous sigh. "It's the stress that does it."

"Yeah, well, stress can do that," I answered.

"We need somebody right away, Steph. Will you take the job? I can't stand the thought of one more interview today."

"Sure, I think I can do that."

So there I was, a minute later, following the five simple steps to filling out a W-4, thinking it all very strange.

"When do I start?" I asked the redhead who was assisting me with my paperwork, including the confidentiality agreement that basically said if you blab, you lose the family farm.

"Show up at the set at eight tomorrow wearing comfortable shoes and possessing superhuman energy."

She gave me directions.

"Is there anything you can tell me about the job?" I asked, since I had been afraid the question would send Mattie over the edge.

"The pay is lousy, and the hours are brutal."

Brock answered the phone at his office.

"Brock, I have some news," I announced excitedly over all the ringing in the background.

"Look, hon, I can't talk. Peggy is out sick, and the phones are ringing off the hook."

"It will only take a second to tell you this."

"If it's about what you're fixing for dinner, don't worry about it. I'm having dinner with a client."

Katie suggested a linner (late lunch, early dinner). Since I hadn't eaten all day, it sounded good to me.

"Anywhere you want to go," she said.

"Bob's Big Boy. I haven't been there in years."

"Where is it?"

I thought a moment. "On Riverside Drive in Burbank."

We were seated at a window booth, and it was yesterday all over again. I was with my daddy sipping on a malt, feeling it a privilege to be in the presence of the man.

I hadn't been to Bob's Big Boy since I was twelve (the year my daddy died), but everything seemed nearly the same—even Bob, the rosy-cheeked icon dressed in red-checkered overalls.

I ordered the double-decker hamburger and, of course, a chocolate malt. Katie ordered one too. She'd never had a malt before.

"You poor, deprived child," I said.

She laughed. It had been exactly the opposite. She'd been a completely spoiled child . . . at least in the grander things of life.

"Studio people come in here all the time," I informed her as I surveyed the busy restaurant.

"So how do you know this place?" she asked.

"My father was a janitor at Warner Brothers, close to here. We hung out here a lot after my mom died."

That was all I said about it. My childhood was the one subject off-limits, and Katie knew it. She seemed to understand, too, since she had a lot of subjects that were off-limits.

We had been friends for four years now, and I still knew little about the "depths of her soul," as Hannah would say.

Our first meeting had been a strange one, at least for me . . .

It had been a hot summer day at the Beverly Hills post office. My nana (whom you'll meet later) insisted I mail a package from this particular post office because she was trying to impress a friend from high school.

Katie was standing behind me in line, shuffling her feet. I was slightly bothered by it and turned around to give a *can-you-please-stand-still-for-two-seconds* look. And there she was—this woman, a few years younger than I, who was so elegant that I felt like Punky Brewster.

When I noticed she was staring at my socks, I assumed she was a snob. I was wearing blue socks with orange stripes—part of my inexpensive hobby of collecting wild socks. I'd started at the age of ten with my meager allowance.

"Wow, those are really wild!" she said. "I wish I could wear socks like that!"

I sensed that her enthusiasm was genuine.

"Why don't you?"

"Hmm. Why don't I?" she said, like it was a deep question. "I don't know."

I turned around as she went on.

"I am so tired of doing the same old thing," she complained. "Do you ever get tired of eating at Spago's and shopping Rodeo Drive? Everything is getting so commercialized."

"Uh"—I turned around again—"I wouldn't know. This isn't my neighborhood."

It was my turn at the window.

That might have been the end of my association with Katie Dillard, except that I recognized the loneliness in her that I'd felt before I met Brock.

I waited for her outside. "Listen . . . what's your name?"

"Katie."

"Listen, Katie, I can't afford Spago's, but we could have lunch . . . if you want."

"At your place?" she asked, her expression hopeful.

Brock was out of town that weekend, and all three kids had been farmed out for the benefit of my leisure. It was to be the first day I'd had to myself in who knows how long.

"I guess my place. It's very modest," I added.

"Oh, good."

We ended up having the best time doing the most ordinary things—ordering in pizza and polishing our nails in wild colors. Things Katie never did. It was sad that someone with so many opportunities had experienced so little of real life.

We exchanged numbers, but then life got busy.

Two months later someone was moving into the house a few doors down. Being neighborly, I whipped up a batch of cookies and knocked on the door.

"Hey, neighbor!" Katie screamed and hugged me. "I was just coming down to surprise you!"

She had bought the place.

Although Katie preferred our less-prestigious Santa Monica neighborhood, she maintained a residence in Beverly Hills, where she did her socializing with friends I never saw, who might think our neighborhood wasn't good enough.

She was very private about such matters.

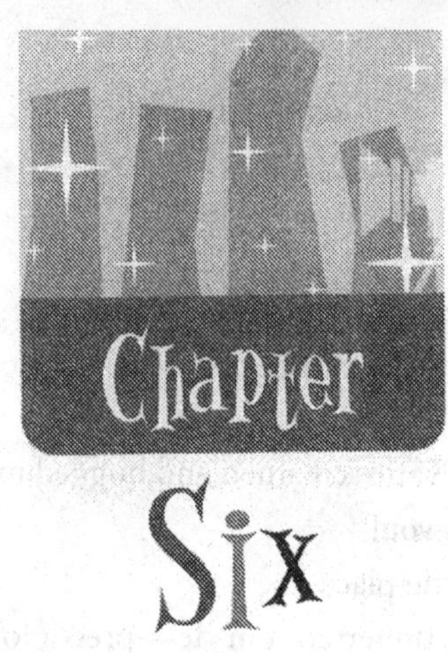

Chapter Six

I never would have guessed it of Katie, but she was a Reality TV fanatic.

After the interview and our linner, I watched Katie shop at fashionable boutiques for the rest of the afternoon. As we drove home, she explained that Reality TV was in, primarily because of lower production costs and high curiosity.

I really didn't care about all that. My brain had been wracked too much for one day. I only cared about *my* job.

"What does a production assistant do?" I asked.

"I'm not sure," she replied. "A little bit of everything, I guess."

It was past seven when Katie dropped me off in my driveway and sped down the block to her much larger, opulent home.

Walking in the door, I realized this was not the house I had left this morning. My living room was a mess, and Hannah and Mark were on the couch, making a bigger mess.

The stereo was blasting.

"Can you turn that noise down?" I yelled.

Mark went to turn the music down. Hannah ran up and hugged me. "Mom, we were so worried about you!"

"Worried?" *They were worried about me?*

"Yes."

I looked over at Mark's clean-shaven face. Guess the mock shaving commercial was over. "So now maybe you'll understand what I go through."

He shrugged. "Hi, Mom."

"Why didn't you call me this morning?" Hannah flared.

"I'm sorry. I slept in."

"I was late for class because of you." She crossed her arms. "And after class you didn't answer, either. Not even your cell. I called Dad but couldn't get him, so I called Mark."

"I had my cell off for my interview."

"What interview?" Hannah asked.

"I got a job."

"A job?" Hannah's brown eyes widened.

"Oh goodie, free samples!" Mark teased. He ripped open a package of Oreos, and cookies and crumbs went flying all over my vacuumed carpet.

I frowned. "No, not free samples."

"Does it involve a thrift-shop discount?" Hannah asked.

"That's very nice of you to think so highly of me." I tapped my foot.

But their responses were understandable. The only job experience I'd had—outside of being a full-time mom, of course—was selling Tupperware and being a cashier at a movie theater in my youth.

"A teaching assistant?" Hannah guessed.

I raised my chin. "You are looking at the new production assistant for the Home Living Channel."

Mark's mouth dropped open. "Mom, I tried to get an internship there last summer. I couldn't even get an interview." He walked closer, as if checking whether the news I'd shared was real.

"I was hired on the spot. What can I say? It must be the charm." I smiled.

He walked away in shock.

So much for that.

"Can we make some Rice Krispy treats?" Hannah begged.

We meant me.

Mark ended up recovering from the shock and wanting a monster meal. (My son eats like a horse, no matter what time of the day.)

Were these the children who, less than twenty-four hours ago, had recommended I get a life?

"Oh, Mom, I left your present in my car," Mark said.

I was still smiling when he came back in the house dragging my present. He delivered it at my feet.

"Thank you, Son. I can see you were so worried you managed to bring your laundry."

"What? I couldn't get out the door of my apartment."

He was so adorable I couldn't protest.

Watching them making themselves comfortable, I realized they had a pretty good deal at home. No chores, no curfews, refrigerator privileges, and Mom to pick up after them. *Hmm* . . .

Brock walked in the door, put his briefcase down, and loosened his tie. "Hi all!"

"I got a job!" I informed him, then kissed him on the cheek.

He raised an eyebrow. "So fast?"

I smiled.

"Ask her what kind of job," Hannah instigated.

"Working at the dry cleaner's, I hope. Did you pick up my suit? The client I met for dinner is from Hong Kong, and he's a suit connoisseur."

"Hollywood. Mom got a job in *Hollywood*," Mark yelled.

Brock stared.

"Not Hollywood," I clarified. "The offices are right here in Santa Monica."

"Can you believe it, Dad?" Mark said, still sounding amazed.

"It's a shock." Brock ran his fingers through his raven hair.

"Katie has connections," I said, trying to read him.

"I don't know if I like Katie's connections." He stood there, unresponsive.

"Do you think maybe you can curb your enthusiasm, Brock?" I added sarcastically. "You're making the goldfish nervous."

"Sorry, honey, I'm just tired."

Normally, if Brock was reading his morning paper (the *Los Angeles Times*), I could turn cartwheels with a giant fire stick in my mouth and he wouldn't notice. Brock also had an afternoon paper (*USA Today*) and an evening paper (the *Washington Post*). And in between he read the *New York Times*, the *Miami Herald*, the *Japan Times*, the *Irish Examiner* . . . you get the picture.

Sometimes I'd say, "There's help for that, you know!"

He would peer up from his paper. "Did you say something?"

He claimed he liked to keep up with things.

In Ireland?

So I was surprised to see him standing at the coffeemaker, no newspaper in hand. After a long silence he said, "You don't have to fix me breakfast this morning."

I'm not intending to fix you breakfast.

And then, after another long silence, he added, "If you don't have time."

Of course that meant he wanted me to.

So instead of leisurely getting ready, flossing, gargling, and taking the time to pick out that semiperfect first-day outfit, I fixed him a bowl of underdone oatmeal. Then I threw on that snappy little ensemble Hannah referred to as my American flag, grabbed my purse, and called, "See ya tonight, hon."

As I headed out the door, Brock caught me. "Wait—make sure you wear your seat belt."

"Thank you, Brock. I've driven before." I kissed him good-bye.

As I started my Volvo station wagon and was backing out of the driveway, he screamed, "Wait!"

Again? I screeched to a halt, and he motioned for me to roll down my window.

"What now?" I asked, a little irritated.

"Watch out. Those brakes can be squishy."

"I know." I rolled up my window.

He knocked.

I rolled it back down. "What now?"

"Can you please not forget to pick up my dry cleaning?"

"Brock, it's three blocks from your office," I wailed.

"OK. OK," he said, finally defeated.

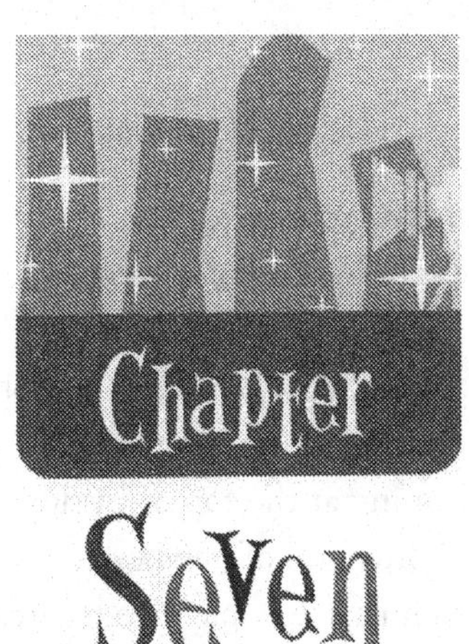

Chapter Seven

According to the Home Living Channel signs, this was the place. The location was a beautiful ranch setting in the hills of Malibu. A place far, far away from my Tupperware experience. I stood for a minute, admiring the beautiful spot.

The location scout had done a good job. *Location scout. Heh! Heh!* I was impressed with myself.

When I reached the sidewalk, I apparently woke up the girl in lime green who was in charge of crowd control.

"You scared me to death!" she shouted.

I flaunted my new identification, which looked like a backstage pass, and said I was looking for somebody.

"Would that be Mr. Blackwell?"

"Is Mr. Blackwell the producer?" I asked innocently.

"No." She looked at me like I was a dingbat.

So I didn't know Richard Blackwell, the fashion critic whose list of the ten worst-dressed celebrities is legendary. I don't read *People* magazine. Even if I had caught her reference to my bad fashion, I probably would have forgiven her because my outfit was atrocious. (This is what happens when your children shop at Guess and you shop at Wal-Mart.)

"Where can I find the producer?"

"Executive producer? Associate producer?"

"Uh. Executive."

She put her fist on her hip. "Look for a stubby, bald guy with a candy bar dangling out of his mouth and a cell phone attached to his belt. He'll be screaming at the top of his lungs. That's him." She pointed in the general direction of nowhere.

Maybe working with nasty people breeds sarcasm.

After wandering around for a few minutes, searching for short, bald-headed men with candy bars and coming up with tall, skinny, baseball-capped ones carrying heavy equipment, I decided to ask. "Excuse me, but . . ."

No one would stop. It was as though their eyes were magnetized somewhere and their bodies were following unthinkingly.

After too many tries I wondered if they would stop if I were younger and cuter. I spotted an empty chair and a megaphone lying near. That would be for the director. I was getting close.

A few yards away I saw someone actually standing still. I high-tailed it to the dumpster, where a thirtysomething man was dropping what I suspected to be garbage into the trash receptacle.

"Can you please tell me where the executive producer is?" I asked.

When he didn't answer, I asked if he spoke English.

His deadpanned reply was that not only did he speak English, but Latin, French, and German.

"I speak pig Latin." I laughed.

He didn't. Laugh, that is.

I coughed. "Anyway, I'm looking for the executive producer."

He seemed very serious, very intent. "Could you give me a description of the guy? I'd like to find him myself."

All I could think of was what I'd heard the sidewalk watcher say: "He's a short, bald-headed guy."

As soon as the words came out of my mouth, I regretted them.

What if this guy was the best friend of the accountant of the producer's second cousin once removed or something?

"That's a pretty weak description," the man said. "Anything else?"

I wasn't sure if I should say it, but as I often did, I crossed the blurred line of tact. "Well, he might have a candy bar dangling from his mouth, a cell phone attached to his belt, and he's probably screaming."

"At the same time?" he asked, looking incredulous.

"Maybe."

"Who are you?" He peered closer.

"The new P.A. I mean, production assistant." (I added the definition in case he was a freelancing janitor, unfamiliar with our lingo.)

"I heard they fired the last P.A.," he said.

"You did?" I thought he'd quit.

He looked at me and whispered in a confidential tone, "Yeah, he put laxative in the short, bald-headed guy's coffee."

"That's highly irregular." I laughed at my unintended joke, and he finally laughed too.

Then the alleged janitor lifted his ball cap and scratched his head. He was as bald as a cue ball, and I felt bad about having been so blunt about the producer's bald head.

When he returned his ball cap, he pulled a candy bar out of his jacket pocket and ripped into it.

Sugar before noon. Terrible, terrible habit.

He then took a cell phone out of his other jacket pocket and clipped it on his belt buckle.

I wonder how tall he is, I thought. *Is five foot five considered short? And aren't producers at least forty?*

My four-minute career flashed before my eyes. I shrank. "You're not going to scream, are you?"

He started laughing—hysterically. "You've got spunk, and you're going to need it around here."

"Can you please direct me to the end of the pier?" I quipped.

He patted me on the shoulder. "We'll keep this between us."

I expelled a gigantic sigh. At this pace I'd be a wreck like Mattie in less than a year.

He surprised me with a personal confession. "I started out as a P.A. In fact, I wrecked the producer's golf cart on my first day."

"Well, those things happen."

"And by the way, if you hear I fire easily, it's true. But only on days when my bagel isn't toasted to perfection." He winked and took a bite of his candy bar.

I smiled excessively.

"I'm Dane Brodie, by the way."

"I'm Stephy. It's so nice to meet you, Mr. Brodie."

We shook hands.

"Dane," he corrected.

"Dane," I said, blushing.

"Let's see if we can set you up, Stephy." He stopped a cute young woman with short, blond hair who was speeding by. "Avril, where is Trent?"

"Trent called in sick," she said.

"Will you show our newbie around today?" he asked, sounding very nice.

Maybe he only screamed during shooting.

"Sure," she replied. But then I couldn't imagine anybody telling the producer no.

"Break her in slowly. We want her to last at least a day."

He seemed to mean it, and that reassured me. Besides, he was dealing with things way more important than a P.A. making a complete fool of herself.

Soon I found out that Avril's title was second assistant director, and I wondered how many producers and directors there were on a set.

"Watch and learn," she told me.

I followed her around like a puppy dog as she talked on her headset, confirmed schedules, and conferred with script editors. Now and then she'd introduce me to someone she literally bumped into. They were all very young and savvy.

"This is Stephy, our new P.A."

"Hi, Stephy," the person would respond and speed away.

I was hoping no one would ask me about my qualifications. I couldn't even manage a one-page resume. I would need a note from my nana.

Dear Fellow Crew Members:

Stephy comes highly qualified. She makes excellent beef stroganoff, and her laundry is really white. She's a great mother and buys me a cat calendar on my birthday.

Love,
Stephy's grandmother

Because I was terrified I'd say the wrong thing, I said nothing all day, except "Nice to meet you" and "Uh huh."

I tried to memorize everything I saw and heard.

For example, a clapper was not the lamp on the commercial from the '70s. And a gaffer, which almost rhymes with clapper (my memory-association trick), is in charge of lighting.

Storyboard is what it sounds like—a kind of cartoon strip that details the shooting.

It was all very new, very interesting, and very bewildering.

Late in the afternoon I received a call from a giddy Katie, asking how it was going.

"It's good," I told her, "but I'll have to call you back later . . . like three days from now." I was joking . . . sorta.

Avril smiled. "I'm glad to know you can talk. I thought maybe you were some kind of monk or something."

I supposed it was safe to speak now.

"Do you have any burning questions?" she asked.

"What are we shooting here?" I asked.

"Are you serious?"

"Yes."

"*Do You Look Like Your Dog?*" she replied dryly.

"Oh."

"Not really. *Dog Wars.* Six mutts, six pedigrees. Qualified trainers. Stiff competition. Who will reign?"

It sounded like a doggy version of Donald Trump's *Apprentice* competition: *Book Smarts or Street Smarts.*

"Dog shows are all the rage in England, you know," Avril informed me.

I didn't know.

My crash course in production ended at six, when the last of daylight vanished.

Avril said to be there at six the next morning for the last day of preproduction.

"Can you tell me what that is?"

"Well, *pre* means before, and *production* means . . . production."

Now that everything was as clear as mud . . .

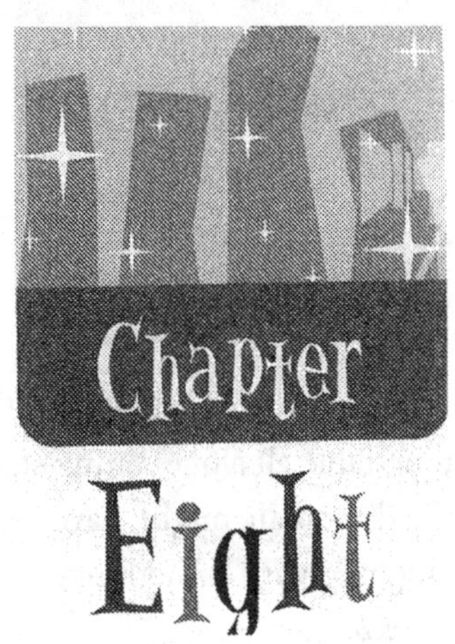

Chapter Eight

Driving home, I realized I hadn't thought about my family all day. I wondered if I should feel guilty.

Nah!

As I parked the car, Brock came barreling out of the house. Before I could set both feet on the ground, he was asking that common male question: "What's for dinner?"

"I haven't thought of it," I admitted.

But now that I had thought about it, I reached the silent conclusion that whoever was home first should start dinner.

We kissed, and he asked about my first day of work . . . but not enthusiastically enough for me. Consequently, I gave a pat answer. "It went really well."

Brock followed me in the house and into the bedroom, where I threw my purse down and took off my shoes. Then he followed me into the kitchen, and we both stood in the middle of the tile, smiling for a full minute.

His helplessness was not appealing.

I turned on the oven and tossed a TV dinner in the center of the rack.

Did I say *tossed*? I meant *lovingly placed.*

It was the middle of the night when I heard a sound. *Crunch. Crunch. Crunch.*

Brock was missing from our bed. I followed the light. There he was, sitting at the long dining table all alone, eating stale potato chips.

Now a more attuned woman might have determined that her husband might be struggling with something.

Crunch. Crunch. Crunch.

"Why are you sitting in the dark?" I asked.

An utterly stupid question.

"No reason," he replied.

An utterly stupid answer.

Flashback to 1983. I'm seven months pregnant. Brock is sitting at our wobbly pine table in the middle of the night. Same crunching sound. Same wounded look.

"Why are you sitting in the dark?" I'd asked.

"No reason," he'd answered.

Three hours later, when we finally reached the layer of brutal honesty, he made his surprise confession. "When the baby is born, you won't pay any attention to me!"

Back to the present.

I turned on the light. "Look, Brock, three days ago the central theme of my life was . . . well, I didn't have one. Can't you at least be happy for me?"

"Why, honey—why would you think I'm not happy for you? I'm happy. Very, very happy."

He looked happy all right. Like Michael Moore hosting a Republican fund-raiser.

I didn't have the energy tonight for a three-hour discussion of brutal honesty. "I'm going to bed," I announced . . . and turned off the light.

The benefit of a good night's sleep cannot be overstated.

At six o'clock I was on the set and ready to start my *real* job.

I had left Brock a bowl of cold cereal, a spoon, a napkin, and an *I LOVE YOU* note with a smiley face on a tray next to the bed. I hoped he would appreciate it.

The same girl who had misled me at the sidewalk was there, this time dressed in tangerine orange. I believe I saw the corner of her lip quiver, took it for a smile, and smiled back.

She apologized for her comment the day before and told me her name was Plum. I was relieved her name wasn't Tangerine. I told her I accepted her apology. (I didn't tell her that her comments about Dane Brodie had gotten me in trouble.)

"You look really cute today, by the way," she said.

I supposed blue and blue was an improvement over the American flag motif.

We got to talking, and I found out she was an intern. "I go back to the Los Angeles Film School in the fall."

"My son goes there," I said proudly.

"What's his name?"

"Mark Daniels."

"Mark? No way!"

Avril was pointing at me, and I waved. It's nice to have friends in high places.

"I have to go," I told Plum.

A man who appeared to be in his midtwenties was walking toward me. The best way to describe him would be Greg Brady, with bigger ears, dressed like a tenured college professor. He locked eyes with mine before saying, "Hi, I'm Trent Powers, production coordinator," and flashing his identification.

"Stephy Daniels, production assistant," I said, flashing mine back. *What a fun ritual.*

"So you're the new gopher," he stated matter-of-factly.

Gopher? I was lost.

"So anyway . . . Betty, we'll need three grande nonfat toffee, high-foam lattes, one venti caramel . . ."

He lost me again.

"Are those coffee orders?"

"Well, uh . . . yeah!" he responded curtly.

"And I am supposed to . . ."

"Drive to Starbucks, stand in line, and when it's your turn, say, 'Hello there, person-behind-the-counter. I'd like three grande nonfat toffee lattes . . .'"

"And pay for it how?"

"See that girl in the red shirt? Ask her for some petty cash."

On my way out I asked Plum how much she knew about production crews and all.

"Specifically?" She twisted a strand of her long hair around her finger.

"Where do I fit in the grand scheme of things?"

"What's your title?" she asked.

"Production assistant," I said, more smugly than I should have.

"Oh, you're at the bottom of the food chain. Anybody living and breathing can boss you around, except maybe me."

Trent came over. "This is not the social hour. We need caffeine!"

When I returned, balancing the gallons of liquid caffeine in a cardboard cup holder, did Trent say thank you?

No!

He said, and I quote, "*There's not enough foam in number four. I hope that won't happen again.*"

Then he informed me that the walkie-talkies had not been handed out. Like I was supposed to know that.

I couldn't even go to the bathroom without being summoned.

"Push the big button!" he kept screaming at me.

By the end of the day, Mr. Personality's charm was killing me. I was completely exhausted.

All I wanted was a quick meal, a hot bath, and the best night of sleep in my entire life.

On my way home I phoned Brock to tell him to expect a *simple* dinner. We would ease into the shared-responsibilities arrangement I had read about in *Working Woman*.

As often was the case, I received his cell's voicemail and refused to leave a message.

For the duration of my drive home, I felt my feet swell.

When I pulled up in front of my house, I saw my nosy neighbor on the other side of the street peering through his window. I cringed. For a whole week I had enjoyed the luxury of stepping onto my own lawn, unaccosted by Simon Amateau.

Simon opened his door and yelled, "Hey, Nature Girl, I'm back!"

He calls me Nature Girl because of my remark in 1989 that the robin in the tree was pretty.

You know, if Brock would only clean the garage out like he promised to do three years ago, I could park my car in the garage and not have to hide from Simon.

I had my iPod in my purse, so brilliantly I turned it on and arranged the piece on my ear, pretending not to see or hear him.

"Nature Girl!" he called again.

Maybe I could beat him to my front door. After all, he's eighty-one and has arthritis.

I walked fast.

Simon walked faster. (His feet weren't swollen.) He tapped me on the shoulder.

"I can't hear you!" I screamed over my noise.

He was not only fast, but smart. "Why don't you take that thing off your ear!" he yelled.

Of course, I did. And of course he had to know what the "thing" was.

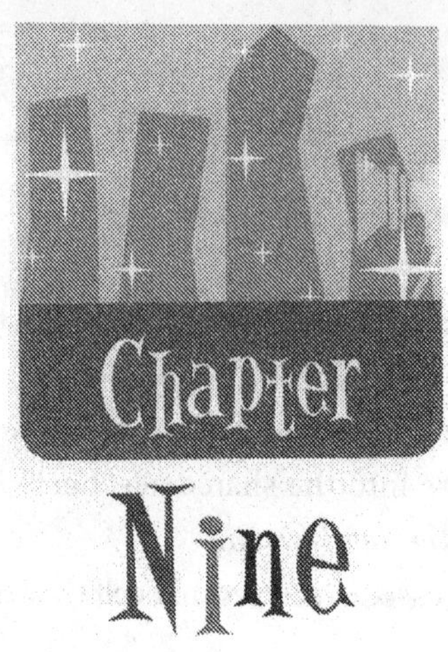

Nine

Having satisfied my chatty neighbor with my bad explanation on technology (how a gadget the size of a sardine tin holds one thousand songs), I stood in my living room, wondering what to do next.

It was then I heard a moan coming from the bedroom. I went to investigate and found the source to be a lumpy, ragged form in the bed.

"I'm dying of the bubonic plague," Brock informed me.

"Do you have a doctor's note?"

"You shouldn't kid a dying man," he uttered mournfully.

I frowned. His brown eyes didn't have that glazed, sickly look. "Bubonic plague, huh? You could have picked a disease from this century."

"OK, West Nile virus. Malaria. Something horrible."

I pressed my lips to his forehead. He was warm. When I took his temperature, the reading was 99.9, slightly under critical.

"Only ninety-nine point nine?" he asked, incredulous. "Are you sure?"

"I'm sure." I shook the thermometer down.

"Can you make me some homemade chicken soup?"

"Sure, I'll get you a can of soup."

"A can? It's not the same as homemade," he whined.

"You're right. It's not the same. Homemade requires a lot of work."

He didn't see the problem.

I dragged myself out of bed after the pesky contraption on the nightstand would not stop buzzing.

The kamikaze moths were still knocking against the outdoor light—that's how early it was.

After a cup of coffee, I checked on Brock. His eyes were fluttering, indicating consciousness.

I felt his forehead. In my unclinical opinion there was no fever.

He opened his eyes. "I'm still dying."

"I don't think so," I replied.

"Feel." His voice sounded pitifully ill.

The actual reading was 98.9. Still, that slight margin was enough to convince him he was at death's door.

"You don't want me to stay home with you, do you?" I'm not sure why I asked when I had absolutely no intention of staying home.

"I might need some help getting to the bathroom" was his response.

Oh, cry me a river, I thought. *When I was sick with a 104 temperature last month, I baked cookies for the youth group and replaced the shelf paper in the kitchen cabinets.*

But I responded like a proper wife. "I could if you really, really need me to." I paused, then added, "But this is only my third day of work."

"I guess I can manage." He moaned again for effect. "Do we still have the cane Mark used in that play?"

The set of *Dog Wars* was beginning to shape up.

People were running around like the sky had fallen. I was afraid to stop for fear of being arrested for vagrancy.

For one celebratory instant I imagined my name being rolled through the credits, until a girl named Shelby with funky glasses and baggy clothes came over and introduced herself. She said she had a degree in political science from Johns Hopkins University. I was tempted to ask her why she was toting plates around for a living instead of straightening out Washington, DC.

But then I had overestimated my job as well.

"Have you seen the mansion where the contestants will be staying?" she asked.

I looked around for Trent, said no, and we walked across the fifteen-acre estate to where the action would take place. Along the way I told Shelby all about my work woes, which were all about Trent.

"Oh, don't worry about him," she said. "He's one continual bad-hair day, and he never gets over it. Mara, my self-appointed slave driver, isn't any better."

When Shelby opened the door to the doggy palace, I wondered if Katie's Beverly Hills hideaway was anything like this.

Shelby gave me a tour, starting with the training room, complete with massage tables, special creams, doggy treats, butt warmers—everything doggy.

"This is a day spa!"

"Almost," Shelby agreed.

I wondered who owned this sprawling mansion and if they would have to tear out every inch of carpet when the shooting was over.

The dog owners' quarters were not so fancy. Basically, the setup was bunk beds and dressers.

Shelby was about to show me the kitchen when a screeching voice came over her walkie-talkie. "Back to work!" She sulked. "Mara says we need cookie dough in trailer two."

While Trent was talking to a group of important-looking people, I stepped in the middle of the grassy lawn and waited to see how long it would take before someone spotted an able-bodied person standing around doing nothing and put them to work.

It was only twenty seconds before I felt a tap on my shoulder and the order came: "You there!"

I ended up assisting at the craft-services table the rest of the morning. (In other words, making sandwiches.)

The bus pulled up the long horseshoe driveway, and the production crew congregated, along with a few lookie-loos who had gotten past Plum's guard post. One scraggly man held a sign, Pit Bulls Have Rights Too! As he was dragged away by a burly crew member, he yelled, "It's discrimination, I tell you. Pit bulls should be allowed!"

That demonstration taken care of, we waited for the hopefuls to disembark.

Avril wasn't that far off, I thought. *This show could have been called "Do You Look Like Your Dog?"*

The basset hound was first—his owner a sorry match with sunken, sad eyes. The suburban housewife with the golden retriever looked happy, loyal—like she didn't have a clue. The owner of one of those long, shiny-haired, skinny dogs needed a haircut.

Then there were the mutts. It was hard to tell with them, except for the ones whose sweaters matched their owners.

I was playing a game my wild imagination had hatched: match the biblical characters with their dog types.

Esther would definitely have a lap dog.

King David a Rottweiler.

Solomon would have too many greyhounds.

"Hello. Is there intelligent life on this planet?" an annoyed voice asked from behind me.

I didn't need to turn around to know it was Mr. Personality himself. But I did anyway.

He stood there, hands on his hips, trying to look intimidating. "Doggie biscuits!" he commanded.

Did this man ever use full sentences?

As I moved through the crush of people, passing out the fancy doggie biscuits, the host, a Ryan Seacrest look-alike, greeted the candidates and presented an overview of the rules. The teams were divided, and a tussle ensued between a wired dachshund and a Saint Bernard three times his size.

"Don't let him get hurt. Rico is breeding stock," one owner screamed. (Like the others weren't.)

Other dogs joined the scrap, and their owners followed suit, literally growling at each other. The tall man next to me elbowed my ear. "Give those people dog biscuits!"

"Laced in Prozac," someone else shouted.

And I always thought these shows of primal emotion were fabricated for the sake of entertainment.

I parked my car and dashed in the front door without being seen by Simon. As I was taking a relieved breath in the entryway, Brock waved to me from behind his newspaper.

"You're obviously feeling better."

He smiled from the couch. "All it took was a little loving care."

"Why thank you, honey, . . . I think."

My grandmother emerged from the kitchen. "I believe he was referring to me."

She was dressed in the kind of dress she usually wore. Flowered cotton, nearly at her ankles.

"Nana," I exclaimed, "what are you doing here?"

"Why, your poor husband didn't have a clue how to use the can opener to open a can of soup."

"Fancy that. Those electric gadgets can be pretty tricky, huh Brock?" I glared at him.

Nana grinned and retreated into the kitchen.

"You called Nana?" I raised my eyebrows in disapproval.

Brock didn't have a chance to answer. Nana was back, waving a rusty, dirty can opener.

"That's the one we take camping," I protested. "It's been in the rain. It's useless."

Brock shrugged.

"Our can opener is on the counter, Nana."

She went back in the kitchen to look. "Oh, there it is. Behind the Rice Krispies box. My, that's a big box," she called.

"Brock, you didn't know we have an electric can opener?" I crossed my arms.

Nana appeared, defending him, as always. "Oh, you know men and old women, sweetie. We can't see what's in front of us."

I did know men—at least mine.

"Anyway, I whipped him up some homemade soup, and I do believe his color is improving."

That's Nana for you. An eighteen-course meal is no problem at all.

Kitchen business settled, Nana led me to the love seat and gave me a comforting hug. "Now, what's this about your Hollywood job? It's not one of those sinful, depraved shows where they swap wives, I hope."

I sighed. "No, Nana. The Home Living Channel is family oriented. Nothing strange."

Brock harrumphed, making me wonder what he wasn't saying.

Nana has to be the most hyper seventy-nine-year-old woman you've ever met. She can't sit still for one full second, unless she's reading one of her cat-mystery books. She bounds from project to project as though life is one big backyard of trampolines. So by the time she took a breath from rearranging my cupboards, it was too late for her to drive home. We insisted she spend the weekend.

She put on a pair of my flannels, and I thought we were all going to bed. Instead, Nana started into old family stories, and I fell asleep on the couch.

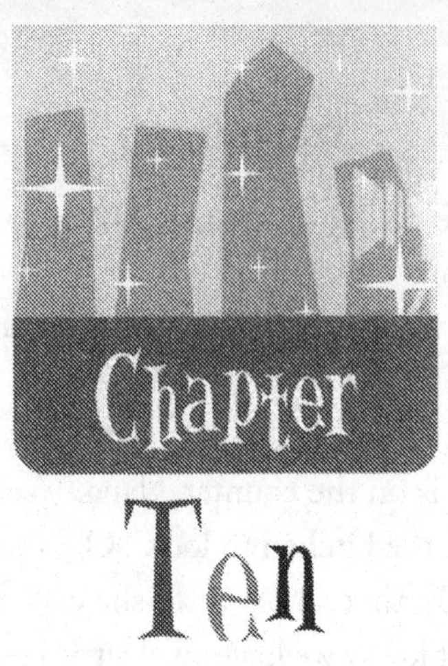

Chapter Ten

Except for church, the long, long weekend was mostly spent watching Nana fold my laundry. I tried to assist, but she told me I was doing it all wrong.

Brock dropped her off at her home around six on Sunday evening. When he came home, I was already asleep.

It was after five the next morning, my new wake-up time, and the only reason I knew that was the *Kee-ya!* sound coming from next-door. Kung fu was Billy Newcastle's latest hobby, and as he explained, predawn was the only time he had to pursue his new interest since he worked nights and slept days.

I would have complained, but he had been very patient with us over the years. He had tolerated an endless stream of youth-group overnighters—toilet paper, silly string, and whatever else happened to land on his side of the fence during the inevitable chases that marked such events.

I cringed, waiting for the second annoying outburst.

Kee-ya!

And then . . . nothing. No more *Kee-yas*! to be heard. The martial-arts demonstration was over.

I squinted at the bedside clock and shook it. *What's the deal?*

Half asleep, I stumbled to the bathroom and flicked on the light switch. "No electricity. That's great!"

I stubbed my toe searching for the flashlight under the bed. I found it, but it was dead. About like I felt.

I could check out that little box in the garage with all those flippy things. If I knew which way to flip the flippy things. And if I had some light.

Locating a candle was a futile undertaking. Hannah had taken every single candle in the house with her, along with lots of other stuff she argued was technically hers because . . . I forget. It was too early to think.

I groped in Brock's dresser and found his glow-in-the-dark watch.

The neon green said it was ten minutes after five. If I hustled, I could still make it to work on time.

I fumbled in my drawers for something to wear. I hoped it would match. Getting dressed in the dark was definitely a handicap. I felt for the tags to be sure my shirt and pants weren't on backward.

All of a sudden I felt bulky. This was going to be a really bad panty-line day.

What on earth?

Horrified, I pulled on the elastic waist to confirm my fear.

I had on Brock's underwear!

Nana, who insists she has 20/20 eyesight, had folded the laundry without her glasses.

It could be worse, I told myself. Brock could be wearing *my* underwear . . . or, worst of all, these could be Hannah's satin thongs.

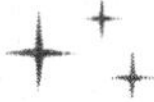

Instead of being late, I was five minutes early. I congratulated myself.

"Good morning, Plum," I said as I approached. "I see you have company today."

I was referring to the fifty or so people behind the yellow tape. Two uniformed males were keeping them in check.

"After yesterday's pit-bull incident, they decided to tighten security," Plum explained. "That's fine with me. It means I get reassigned to something more fun than standing around all day, checking out the cute crew guys."

I wanted to add, "*So you're off Blackwell's worst-dressed neon list now*," but she was being so nice to not mention my greasy hair.

She did, however, mention I was wearing two shoes.

"Two shoes are good," I said.

She stared down at my feet. "Two *different* shoes."

I stared down at my feet too. "Now that's embarrassing. Do I look like a complete idiot?"

"Well . . . yes."

Sometimes I hate honesty. But there was no time to go back home, and no stores were open yet.

I asked for a breath mint while I thought. (Did I mention I dropped my toothbrush in the toilet bowl before I had completed a thorough brushing?)

I stepped over the tape, and the alert guard nodded, making me feel more important than I was. Surveying the diverse group of people disillusioned enough to think they were actually going to see something today, I scrutinized a lady who looked kind. Like the type to buy Girl Scout cookies. Cases of them, in fact.

"Say, I'll bet you're a waitress," I said as I pulled her off to the side so we could chat undisturbed.

"How did you guess?" Her forehead creased in suspicion.

"I love your shoes. You're what . . . about a size eight?"

"Why . . . are muggers particular about sizes?" She laughed.

"No. But I work on the set, and I need those shoes."

She looked down at my mismatched feet. "I can see that."

I smiled faintly.

"Can you get me an autograph of someone famous?" she asked.

"Truthfully," I whispered. "I don't even know the host of the show. My neighbor's pet rat is more famous than I am. How about thirteen dollars for those shoes?"

"Absolutely not," she said with conviction.

"Twenty-five dollars, then." I thought it was a generous offer, considering they were the ugliest shoes I had ever seen in my life.

"I had ligament reconstruction in my right foot. These shoes are custom-made."

She appeared to be telling the truth.

I gave a lopsided grin and considered my options. There were none.

"Make it a hundred and twenty dollars, and you've got yourself a deal!" she offered, driving an insane bargain.

"You have to be joking," I said glumly.

"I'm not," she replied with assurance.

"Will you take a check?"

Baa. Baa. Baa.

The wolf was at the coffee table anxious to order me around. At least he wasn't sending me out to Starbucks this morning. I was thrilled the espresso machine was up and running. The employee behind the counter at Starbucks hadn't been very patient. Then again, I hadn't exactly spoken his language.

"What are those? The latest in grandma wear?" Trent asked flippantly.

Wasn't there some law against telling grandma jokes in the workplace?

Remember last week's sermon on self-control, Stephy, I reminded myself. Today would certainly be a test. "The latest in white orthopedic shoes," I said calmly and eyed the complicated machine.

"After you have your caffeine fix, you'll find a nasty little surprise waiting for you by the front door of the mansion," Trent tucked his shirt in his jeans and walked away.

"I don't get it," I mumbled.

"The pooper scooper is in the shed," he called to me as his form took off down the cobblestone path.

It didn't take long for me to find out what he meant. I knew that with all my animal-husbandry jokes, Hannah would get a laugh out of this.

As I was depositing the stink into the dumpster, I was mauled by a huge dog I later learned was a Bernese mountain dog. Well, not exactly mauled. The slobbery, bulky creature was "jus' givin' me love," as his owner put it.

"Would you take Fish for a walk?" the owner asked. "He's full of nervous energy."

Before I could even reply, the owner handed me the leather leash and jogged away.

Soaked in dog drool, I was as wet as the time Mark tricked me into going on the Big Foot Rapids ride at Knott's Berry Farm. The prankster said we were in line for the Country Bear Jamboree (which is Disneyland, by the way).

On my mush through the grounds with Fish, I realized my lavish footwear purchase was extra, extra wide.

I ran into Shelby. She took control of the leash while I panted. The dog was fine.

"Shelby, are the contestants allowed to boss us around?"

"I think if someone asks you directly, you probably should do what they say, unless it's something outrageous."

I was disappointed to hear that.

"But don't get too personal. Some of the contestants will try to bribe you for extra favors."

"Freshly washed sheets? Shampoo? What?"

"Well not your shoes, for sure." She laughed.

The afternoon was gray and overcast. Every spare piece of ground seemed to be overtaken with someone interviewing someone. Cameras and boom mikes were everywhere.

I inhaled a banana and some kind of finger sandwich, although the food the dogs were eating looked better.

It occurred to me around two o'clock that my walkie-talkie battery might be dead. I hadn't been harassed by Trent for at least an hour. But then I saw that he was ordering Plum around.

I caught up with her at the dumpster doing my old job. "I'll bet you wish you were still manning the street."

"This is nothing. When I was nine, I was a super-duper pooper-scooper at the Rose Parade with a shovel I could hardly lift."

Between being errand girl to the masses, there was some downtime, during which I enjoyed being a spectator.

The villainous trainers put the dogs to work as the owners hovered over them like preschool moms, complaining about everything. Finally the owners were asked to leave.

I was helping in the grooming area, trying to make an Airedale presentable, when the elimination competition began.

"Oh no, they're going to make them work," someone said.

I believe he was missing the premise of the show.

Trent's voice came blaring over my walkie-talkie. My assignment was to comfort a neurotic dog that was terrified of grass.

I located the trembling creature and took her into the mansion. We sat on the tile floor, and I *tried* to sing a lullaby. The terrier mix was afraid of tile as well. She was having a panic attack. The sound of the start gun sent her into a further frenzy, and she took off.

"Good doggie," I cried as I ran after her, because we'd received explicit instructions to speak positive reinforcement in friendly tones, no matter what. Anything that was interpreted as offensive would get you fired.

At the end of the chase, I found her near a puddle of dog vomit.

This is why I have goldfish.

Because of the terrier, I was only able to see the last of the elimination. I don't know why poor Boo Boo was the first to go. I was short on compassion for my canine friends, but the sight of the tiny woman carrying the tiny, coughing Chihuahua tugged at my heartstrings.

"Can I get you something?" I asked pleasantly.

"I'll take some heated soy milk with a teaspoon of molasses and a cinnamon stick," she said as she comforted the little loser.

I was thinking along the lines of a blanket or rawhide toy.

By the time I was back with the dog's order (or her's—I wasn't quite sure which), she was nowhere to be found. It figured.

Then, not surprisingly, it began to rain. Instantly I smelled like wet dog.

Everyone ran around covering what needed to be covered, and then we were let go early.

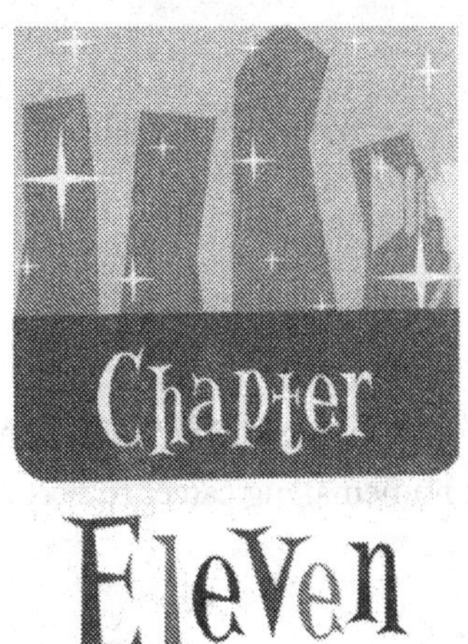

Chapter Eleven

Nothing like a bad, bad afternoon to put everything in perspective.

After phoning Katie on my way home and mostly complaining about my teenage boss, I stopped by Jeff's apartment and told him that I was sorry for pouting.

"I didn't know you were pouting," he said as he searched through his refrigerator for something to eat.

"Well, that's a fine thing." I pouted.

"And what were you pouting about?" He gave me a fleeting glance.

I sat down at his kitchen table but didn't answer. There was a gooey substance on the table, but I didn't mention it.

"If it was Kelly, she's history." He rifled through the cupboard next and came out with a jar of peanut butter.

That's why the place is a mess. The cleaning lady was fired.

"You broke up with Kelly?" I tried not to gloat, but she was so wrong for him.

"Yup." His hazel eyes dimmed, and he didn't say anything more about it.

"Would you like a PBJ?" I asked.

"Sure."

"No crust?"

"No crust."

I was satisfied.

He cocked his head toward me. "So tell me, Mom, is it true you gave up your brilliant homemaking career to become a film director?"

I called Hannah, sure she would fill me in on the details of Jeff's breakup.

"Kelly freaked out when Jeff forgot their thirteen-month dating anniversary."

"Is that right?"

"She was surprising him with dinner and a cake, and he had already made plans to go to a hockey game with Mark."

I propped my aching feet up on the coffee table. "No kidding."

"She frosted the table instead of the cake." Hannah laughed.

That explained the sticky substance on his kitchen table.

"A little extreme, don't you think?" Hannah continued.

"Over the top, I'd say." I chuckled.

Mark phoned later to relate the same story.

He said he was thinking about moving in with Jeff. "The only reason I didn't before was because Kelly drove me crazy."

"That's a great idea!" I smiled.

And then we talked about script edits and all that Hollywood stuff.

Brock wasn't home. I was debating whether to eat a bowl of macaroni and cheese or a Marie Callender's TV dinner when Katie interrupted

my stomach growls. From the looks of her hair, her electricity must have been out this morning too.

"Is the *Hollywood Reporter* story true?" she asked, her blue eyes twinkling with amusement.

"What?"

"I read that you threw a pie in boss boy's face." She laughed and made a face, as if delighted at her cleverness.

I didn't possess the energy to laugh. Plus, I was hungry and tired and didn't find her words all that funny. Tempting, yes, but not funny. "You can come in if you promise we can talk about something besides my issues with adolescent authority." I turned the conversation around to her. "So how's your novel coming along?"

She shrugged as though it didn't matter, even though I knew it did.

"Do you want me to make the mushroom hors d'oeuvre for Mattie's party this Friday?" I asked, thinking that might be the reason for her visit.

"Oh, she cancelled it. She said she may be moving to Antarctica to operate a bulldozer."

"Seriously?"

"Seriously."

I smirked. "Go figure."

A half hour later I was getting ready to wash my face and leaning toward ordering in pizza when the phone rang.

"Hello," I answered.

"Hello, Stephanie?" a nasally voice stated.

"Yes," I said tentatively.

"This is Raymond."

Raymond. Who's Raymond? There was a hint of familiarity in his voice, but I was stumped. "Hi, Raymond. How are you?"

"I'm fine."

"That's good."

I was trying to come up with a mental picture of this guy I knew I knew.

"Well," he continued, "fine except for the dust, airborne mold, roaches, maggots, and—"

"Please stop."

I remembered Raymond now. (Everybody does not love Raymond—especially me.) He was Nana's county health-inspector neighbor—and the reason she wouldn't eat out.

"—vermin infestations." He laughed annoyingly.

So maybe I wasn't hungry anymore.

"What can I do for you, Raymond?"

"It's your grandmother."

My heart began to pound. "What's wrong with Nana?"

"She received an eviction notice today."

I was confused. Nana was never late on her rent, so why would she be evicted? I could have asked more questions, but I didn't feel like hearing Raymond's going on and on. I'd rather hear the details from Nana. "Where is she?"

"She said she was going to her usual 'cheering up' place. Do you have any idea where that might be?"

"As a matter of fact, I do."

Two minutes after I'd hung up, Brock walked in the bedroom. I was slumped on the bed.

"We need to go find Nana," I wailed.

"Let's go!" he said.

Brock would do anything for Nana, no questions asked. Having been raised in a foster home, she was his only extended family too.

Nana was exactly where I expected her to be: on aisle three at Joann Fabric in Pasadena, with a cart full of sale items.

"Nana, are you OK?"

She slapped a scarf around her neck. "You go away a couple of nights, and they hatch a plan. Ever since that new landlord took over the place, his attorney nephew has been looking for a loophole to get me kicked out of my rent-controlled apartment."

There is no rage like the rage of an angry grandma evictee.

It was no secret that the apartment could be rented out for triple the amount Nana was paying.

She handed Brock folded documentation out of her crocheted purse, and he reviewed it. His eyes widened. "It says here that you pack a pistol, Nana."

"Oh, that's just a story I made up to keep the delinquents away."

"And you play loud music all hours of the night."

"Frank Sinatra." She sniffled. "And it's not loud."

Loud is a subjective thing, though Nana *was* hard of hearing.

As Brock read the rest of the letter, I told Nana she was coming to live with us, and that was all there was to it.

"No, honey. I can't intrude on you like that." She blew into her handkerchief. "I'll just find some nursing home somewhere."

A moment of silence.

"You'll do no such thing," I insisted.

"In the meantime, we're going to fight this thing," Brock vowed, genuinely upset.

Since we didn't want Nana driving alone in the dark (even though she stubbornly insisted she could drive), we stashed her new purchases in her already packed trunk, and I hung on for dear life as her low-mileage Buick careened dangerously through the side streets of Los Angeles. Brock, fortunate soul, followed a safe distance behind.

I believe the greatest invention of the twentieth century is the handbrake.

Once we were safely home, Nana sat in our easy chair with a traumatized look on her face.

"How about some Rocky Road fudge," Brock suggested, and in two seconds flat she was rummaging through our cupboards, humming.

I was happy Brock understood about Nana but wondered if it wasn't his stomach that was doing some of the rejoicing.

Nana was so mad that she pulled yarn out of her purse and crocheted a scarf the length of our street. We stayed up past midnight again.

I couldn't have been asleep for more than fifteen minutes when the smoke alarm started beeping pathetically. I was in the process of pulling out the bad batteries when Nana ran into the hall screaming that we should evacuate and search for buckets to carry water from the creek.

"Nana, there is no fire," I said in a soothing tone. "Please be quiet or you'll wake Brock."

Nana's grandma's barn had burned in her childhood, and she'd never gotten over the trauma. In order to settle her irrational fears, I unplugged all the appliances she said were a potential fire hazard. The toaster, the night-lights, the radio, the hairdryer. Everything but my alarm clock.

It was no surprise I woke up the next morning feeling like I had been hit by a truck, trampled by a herd of buffalo, and dragged by whatever could drag a person hit by a truck and trampled by a herd of buffalo.

Pardon my hallucination, but by the time I got to the location, it looked like things were being dismantled and loaded into vans. What was going on?

Shelby came by and said a production meeting was being held. Everyone shuffled over to where Dane Brodie was standing. Whispers and speculation abounded.

"I'm going to make this short and sweet," he told the production crew. He choked up, and someone provided him a can of Mountain Dew before he continued. "An epidemic outbreak of kennel cough is shutting us down. The incubation period is too long to wait it out and continue the show. The dogs are under quarantine."

Most of these people had worked together before in some capacity and were like family. Most everyone was hugging and crying.

The director took over. "The bottom line is this, people. *Dog Wars* is being cancelled."

"Are we shooting something else?" someone asked.

"We'll let you know." Dane sighed. "I want to thank you for the long, hard hours and diligent efforts." Then, head hung low, he walked away.

Shelby and I hugged, and Plum joined us. I said good-bye to Avril and a lot of people I only knew casually.

"It was great working with you," everyone said.

Before I could open my mouth to say good-bye to Trent, he cocked his big head and shrugged. "I'll find something else easily enough."

Could it all be over so quickly?

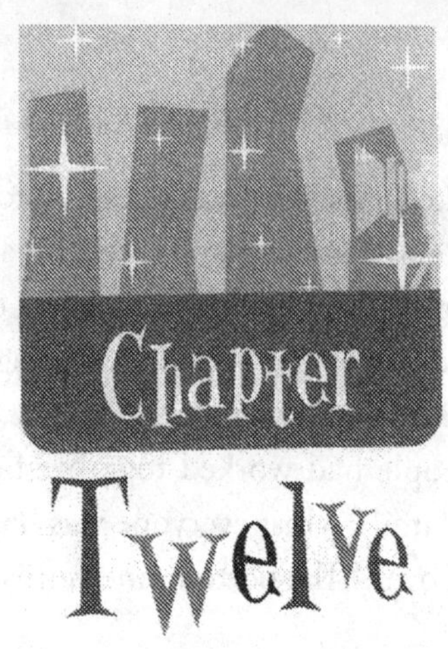

Twelve

I stared at the phone a full minute before answering it.

Katie's worried voice was on the other end. "Is it true? Is it true?"

"Is what true?"

"That *Dog Wars* is being cancelled?"

"Yes, but how did you know?"

"Mattie called me. She's not going to Antarctica, by the way."

"I guess it wasn't meant to be," I said, despondent.

"Well, penguins are no fun anyway."

"I was talking about me, Katie. Maybe I wasn't meant to have a career. Maybe I'm just destined to live an ordinary life."

She paused, then blurted out, "I'm at the mall in front of one of your favorite places—Bed, Bath & Beyond."

"I'm parked in front of my house. Maybe I'll meet you at the mall and buy some root-beer shower gel. That'll cheer me up."

"My, you're easy. My cheering up requires expensive jewelry and travel to exotic places."

I exhaled slowly, imagining Tahiti.

"Aren't you going to help your grandmother move in?" she asked. "When I left an hour ago, she had quite a load."

I turned my head, noting the ancient Chevy truck parked in the driveway. I recognized it as Raymond's and hoped it was not dripping oil.

"Oh my goodness, Katie. I must be blind not to have noticed that heap."

"You should see the heap that came with the truck," she joked.

"Are you talking about Raymond?"

"Does he have a mop for hair, squinty eyes, and long, dirty fingernails?" Katie laughed.

"That's him." My voice cracked.

"And that was what I could tell from a distance. He'd make one scary blind date closeup."

I got out of the car, walked over to Raymond's truck, and cried into the phone, "What on earth are they doing? Brock and I were planning to move Nana's things in storage this weekend."

There was another pause, then, "I don't think she's thinking storage, Stephy."

"Katie, I'll call you later." I clicked off the phone and stuffed it in my purse. Making a mad dash for the door, I opened it abruptly. What I saw made me step back in horrified wonder.

There was clutter everywhere. A mess of boxes, suitcases, and bags of crocheted items (blankets, bears, Barbie clothes), along with dozens of books on crocheting, including *One Hundred Crochet Projects*, *Elegant Gifts*, and *The Wonders of Crochet*.

So it wasn't enough that my brilliant career in the entertainment industry was destroyed by a preventable doggy disease. Now my house was destroyed as well.

"Honey, what are you doing home?" Nana ushered me in and closed the door.

"The show was cancelled." I gave a brief, teary-eyed account.

"That's too bad," was all she said, but then she really didn't understand the significance to me.

"This is a whole lot of moving in, Nana!" I said, having underestimated her belongings by a long shot.

She was busy retrieving her dentures, which had fallen into a box.

I hung my keys on the wall-mounted rack but wondered if there was a point in trying to be orderly.

Raymond came trotting into the living room. "Hello, Stephanie!" he said enthusiastically.

"Hello, Raymond," I answered apathetically.

Katie was right about his fingernails. There was enough dirt under them to fill a hole. I cringed for the obligatory handshake coming next.

One, two, three, yuck.

"Shouldn't you be closing down restaurants?" I laughed lightly to mask my disgust.

"I took time off for Mrs. W."

"Won't you stay for dinner, Raymond?" Nana asked, patting him on the arm.

"I have a restaurant to close down in Chinatown." He stretched. "I'll grab dinner there before I put the schmucks out of business."

Before I could catch my breath, Raymond had left and returned with an industrial-size sewing machine he set near the couch. "I'll be back tomorrow with the rest," he said and was gone.

The rest? What more could there possibly be?

As I stared at my former sanctuary and the flies now circling overhead, I tried to think calmly. Nana had lived forty widowed years in clutter, and I understood that. But I couldn't live like that.

"Nana, we need to get your things in storage as soon as possible."

"Certainly not." She placed defiant hands on her ample hips. "I'm not putting my valuables in a garage that's going to get broken into by hoodlums. Don't you watch the news?"

I sighed. "Brock watches enough news for the three of us."

A few busy hours later, Frank Sinatra's candied voice was booming from Nana's new bedroom (Hannah's room) and the easy-listening station was blaring at the other end of the house. The smell of mothballs permeated the hall where I was standing.

Nana walked up to me, shaking the TV remote. "How do you operate this fancy thing?"

"You have to be in front of the TV," I said.

I was grateful when Katie came by with my favorite root-beer-scented shower gel. "Let's go outside for some fresh air," I suggested.

"Come see the bathroom first," Nana encouraged.

Our guest bathroom looked like Nana's bathroom all right. The burgundy shag rug was the one I recognized from childhood. She opened the medicine cabinet. There must have been two hundred prescriptions in there.

I grabbed a couple of bottles of Snapple from the overcrowded fridge, and Katie followed me outside, where we sat down and relaxed.

"The situation looks permanent," Katie commented.

"Maybe I could pitch a tent in the backyard," I said.

"It gets pretty cold at night." She half-laughed.

"Or move in with you."

"Brock would miss you."

"I'm not so sure."

We stayed outside until it was getting dark. Then Katie slipped out the back gate and I reentered my paradise lost, where my husband was deeply engrossed in the world news, enjoying a bowl of homemade beef stew and cornbread.

I walked around to the side of the couch. "Brock."

"Hi, honey. I didn't know you were home already."

I kissed his cheek, despite my irritation. "Whose car did you think that was out front?"

He didn't answer.

"Didn't Nana tell you *Dog Wars* was cancelled because of kennel cough?" I asked.

"Oh, I forgot to mention it," Nana said, walking by.

Two hundred prescriptions she remembers to take; the critical details of my life she forgets.

"You're not working anymore?" Brock scratched his head.

"No."

"That's too bad," he said . . . and stunned me by not mentioning anything more about the state of our house or my job.

The next morning I showered, dressed, and stumbled into the kitchen. Nana was straining the city's energy supply again. It seemed she had every electrical device on in the house, including the oven, which she said was for heating and eating.

Apparently, electrical appliances were only a fire hazard after midnight.

I moaned at the lack of counter space.

Nana took the moan as pangs of hunger and fixed me a farmer's breakfast, which I ate to spare her feelings, since I tended to skip breakfast.

"Brock sure enjoyed his breakfast this morning before he went to the office," she said as she hand-washed our dishes (she had filled our dishwasher up with a supply of toilet paper).

"You fixed this for Brock?"

"That's right."

That ought to send his cholesterol reading soaring.

Not knowing what to do with myself, I made a cup of tea. I went to throw the tea bag away.

"Oh, no, honey," Nana insisted. "You can't waste a tea bag."

"We have plenty, Nana."

"Oh no. That would be a waste."

First my house, then my tea . . . now my sanity.

I was halfway down to Katie's house when I remembered it was Wednesday and she was at her writing class. By the time I got back to the house, Nana was busy taking over the hall closet. Even Simon, who was busy hoeing his garden, only had time for a casual wave.

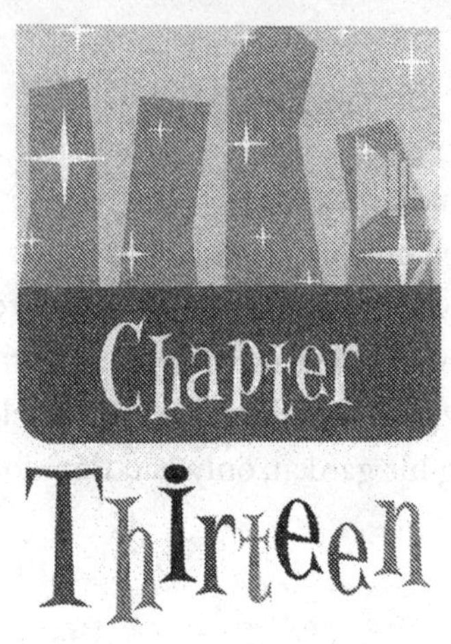

I drove to church to see the good-natured church assistant, Lily Dunn. She always needed help with something or other, and I needed to help.

I poked my head in the front office. A woman I didn't recognize was sitting at her desk.

"Hi, where's Lily?" I asked.

"She's on medical leave." We looked at each other briefly, and she returned to folding the bulletins.

"What's wrong with her?"

"She broke her leg."

"Her leg? Why, that's terrible. Last week she had the flu, and now this?" I shook my head sympathetically.

She blinked.

"I'm going over to Lily's house this very minute with some flowers," I said determinedly. "Besides, she has my best casserole dish."

"So you're the one."

We locked eyes.

"The one?" I asked, confused.

"The one who left the casserole on her doorstep."

"Why, was there something wrong with my casserole?"

She smiled wryly. "The skunk seemed to enjoy it."

"The skunk?" I asked.

"The skunk she tripped over when she broke her leg."

I winced. "Oh dear."

"You know, leaving food on doorsteps isn't a good idea," she said.

The words sounded annoyingly familiar.

"Was she sprayed?" I dared to ask.

"Thoroughly," the woman replied.

I felt bad, extremely bad.

"You look like you could use some help."

"No, thank you." She went back to folding.

"It's not like it's origami!" I snapped.

"No, it's not," she said quietly.

I knew I was behaving badly, so I softened my tone. "How about the food bank? I can straighten up some shelves or something."

I'm sure her patience was wearing thin by now.

"There must be something for a woman with a servant's heart to do around here!"

She peered up at me with a condescending look.

I was feeling, to be honest, totally and completely useless. "Flies that need swatting in the kitchen perhaps?"

Wouldn't you know it? She had a fly swatter in reach.

"Here you go!" She rolled her eyes, and I knew I had overstepped my boundaries. But pride kept me from apologizing.

Admittedly, it was good therapy. After a few hundred misses, I got the knack of the swatter and was feeling a sense of accomplishment. I zapped a bomber and dropped it in the trash. "Yes, yes, yes! You are so good!" I danced around.

Pastor Tom stepped into the kitchen.

I stopped midswing. How long had he been watching me?

"Barbara thought . . . you could use some counseling," he said.

I turned five consecutive shades of red.

"But you look pretty happy to me," he observed correctly.

"Cheap entertainment." I laughed. "I don't know when I've had so much fun!"

He cocked his head, amused. "Imagine the pleasure a one-dollar fly swatter can bring. And here I bring my wife things like flowers and candy to cheer her up."

"Nana, did you ever feel like you weren't needed?" I asked as she made me tea from a used tea bag and I turned down the blaring radio.

"That's why I have pets," she said.

"Oh no, the goldfish!" I gasped, remembering my idea of pets. "I need to feed them."

She smiled. "I already did."

"Nana, at least let me feed my goldfish."

"Well, all right, dear."

As I was feeding Charlie and Sam, who I suddenly realized didn't know me from a guppie, Nana mentioned that Raymond had called.

"He's coming by with the last of my things."

"Really." I stiffened at the thought of that man.

"Where should we put the birds?"

"I didn't know you had birds."

"Raymond bought them for me after . . . after . . ."

"Muffy was hit by the car?" I finished her sentence.

Her eyes dimmed in sadness.

Muffy had been her latest feline in a long line of felines that she had spoiled to utter queendom after I had moved out of the house (Nana had raised me after my parents died). Muffy had been an extremely rare Chocolate Point Siamese.

"Someone is sitting on your doorbell," Nana announced.

"I'm not expecting anyone."

"Oh, that must be Raymond!" Nana rushed to the door, and I followed unenthusiastically.

Raymond was wearing a leather jacket and big black boots like policemen wear. He was carrying a birdcage.

"I'm a chicken," the pretty bird squawked.

"Nana, I'm no linguist, but did your bird just say, 'I'm a chicken'?"

"That's right," she said nonchalantly. "Raymond taught Stuart Big to say that."

Raymond smiled, showing all his bad teeth. He delivered another birdcage . . . and then another.

I pulled old newspapers from Brock's mounting pile, thinking of the droppings and hoping for warmer weather so the birds could reside on the patio.

Raymond walked past me, this time with a box he placed near the kitchen door.

Nana rushed over. "What do we have here?"

"A surprise," he said, reaching into the box.

She squealed in delight as the furry little head of a kitten appeared.

"I thought O' Malley would be a good name." He handed her to Nana.

"Hello, O' Malley," she whispered with a tremendous smile.

Then she walked over to me and dropped the kitten in my arms.

Holding O' Malley out of scratching range, I had a sinking feeling there were more furry creatures to come.

Raymond pulled out another. "He looks like a Sylvester."

As soon as Nana loved him up and put him back in the box, she pulled out another, a black and white. "Oreo would be a good name for you."

I was flabbergasted to find one, two, three, four, five kittens in all.

"The poor things were abandoned on the side of the road,"

Raymond said, shaking his head, though I didn't believe it for a minute.

Down the street in Katie's living room, I sank in her Italian leather sofa and whined. "My house is a zoo. Raymond just delivered five kittens and three birds to my already overwhelmed house."

"That's a lot of fur and feathers," Katie said.

"I don't want pets. I have disastrous happenings with animals!"

"Why?" Katie asked calmly.

"Let's review the history of the Daniels' pets." I curled my upper lip.

"What pets?" she asked and stretched.

"All this occurred before your time, Katie."

She leaned forward to listen.

"Let's see . . . Our first pet was Miss Kitty, a cat I truly loved." I felt teardrops forming in my eyes. "It makes me sad to think of her."

"How sweet. I never had a pet."

"She was gassed in the garage," I said, remembering.

"How?"

"Mark had started the van in the garage when I got distracted with a phone call. Neither of us knew Miss Kitty was in the garage until it was too late."

"I'm sorry."

"So was I. Believe me." I sighed.

"Miss Kitty was replaced with Hardee, the turtle. Mark was playing with him on the lawn and he wandered onto the street and a car ran over him."

Katie appeared horrified.

"Yes, it was all very traumatic. In fact, that's why we didn't object when Nana dropped Mousy on our doorstep Christmas morning, a week or so later. Hannah determined Mousy was a gift from God. And, of course, convincing the child that we couldn't afford the operation when she insisted God wanted Mousy to have it didn't work."

"What operation?" she asked.

"Mousy's leg was partially detached when the dog that followed Jeff home playfully slapped her around a couple of times. The dog was an incontinent Great Dane with bursitis, who died before his time."

"Oh dear."

"Did I mention the hypoglycemic ferret Jeff bought with his allowance? Jeff gave him a bath, and the result was an accidental drowning." I played with her frilly pillow. "After that, when the kids mentioned pets, I ran the other way."

"So tell Nana the animals have to go."

"Nana couldn't live without them now. And besides, the kittens are only about four weeks old."

Katie caught my eye. "Well, it sounds like you can't live with her."

"She took care of me after my parents died, and I know at times *I* was hard to live with . . ." I put my head in my hands. "Katie, I need to get Nana her apartment back. Do you have any lawyers in that secret network of yours?"

"Not any that work for free," she said bluntly.

I closed my eyes.

"I could lend you the money, though."

"You will not. Besides, Brock has an attorney friend he's checking with."

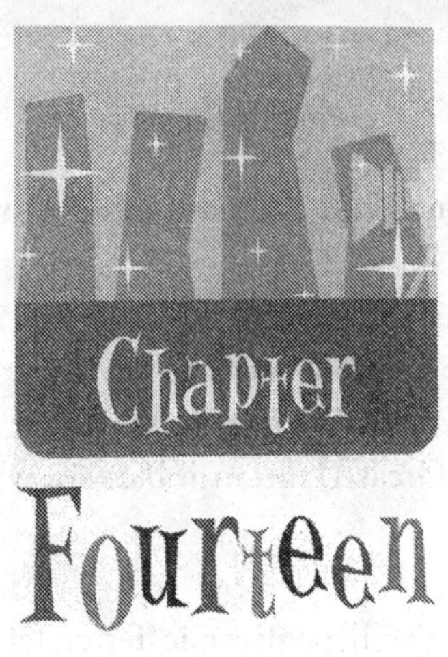

Chapter Fourteen

Sunday afternoon after church all three of my children showed up for dinner, unfazed by the upheaval to my once-organized abode. Apparently, I had wasted a number of years placing things in their strategic spots. Food was the only thing that mattered to my family.

Could I blame them? On the scale of cooking skill, I was a solid seven. Nana was off the charts.

Admittedly, I did have a flame of jealousy over the goings-on about Nana's cooking and the fact there was only a slight mention about my losing my job.

My attempts at pouting were taken as indigestion, and at that point I excused myself. I wandered out to the backyard and sat mournfully on the bench, staring at the petunias Nana had recently watered.

Brock joined me on the bench and gave me a regretful look.

Maybe he wasn't as thick as I thought.

"Hi," he said.

"Hi," I answered.

"It's nice to have all three kids at one table again," he said. (The ultimate icebreaker.)

"Especially Jeff." I chuckled. "I like him better single."

"He seems a little down to me," Brock observed.

Nana stuck her head out the door. "It's time for dessert."

I was sure Brock would pounce at that opportunity. Instead he put his hand on my knee. "I feel like I haven't seen you in a week."

"I feel like *I* haven't seen me in a week."

"What are you feeling, Steph?"

"Ordinary," I replied.

"Ordinary?" he repeated.

"I really liked having a job. Even though it was hard and I was being bossed around, it felt purposeful and at the same time spontaneous." I leaned my head on his shoulder. "Brock, can we please do something spontaneous?"

He was quick to respond. "Let's go out and buy an Alfa Romeo. That would be spontaneous." He laughed, but only as a cover-up.

"I do believe men and women tend to think differently," I said, brushing his hair with my fingers and thinking him superficial.

"I'll settle for a Mazda Miata," he said.

There was a pause.

"What are we going to do about Nana, Brock?"

"I talked to my attorney friend, Johnny Peacock. He's willing to give us a deal. Instead of a seven-hundred-dollar retainer, he'll only ask for five."

"And that's a deal?"

"You bet. And that's just to write a letter."

Things didn't look good.

"Basically, he said that our chance of winning is about zero to none. Landlord-tenant law is a tricky business, and when you involve tricky lawyers, it only gets trickier."

Before I said something mean and irreversible to Nana about the kittens clawing my nice cherry cabinets, I needed to get out of my house.

Katie agreed to go with me to the Monday morning Bible study. She attended with me on occasion, when I nagged, since she was not a churchgoer.

I had been in every Bible-study group our church offered, and even led one at one time, but now I felt disconnected from these ladies—today, more than ever. I tried not to show it for Katie's sake.

The room was packed so we sat in the next-to-last row and were handed an outline titled, "How to serve your husband with a happy heart."

"Sorry, Katie," I whispered. "I didn't know they were having a special speaker."

"It's OK," she reassured me.

The long-necked woman stood at the podium and arranged her bifocals. "We all know those little annoyances can wear on you. Your husband leaves the toilet seat up or puts the toilet-paper roll on wrong, and . . ."

Bless her heart—I'm sure she thinks she's touching on an original subject, but this is the last thing Katie wants to hear about.

"Or leaves his toenail clippings around," the woman said a minute later.

"That does it. I'm never getting married." Katie's blue eyes were wide with disgust.

I didn't say a word.

"The key is finding humor in it," the speaker continued in a monotone voice. "Humor is a wonderful way to relieve tension."

A woman from the audience raised her hand. "My husband just bought an expensive boat without telling me. What's the humor in that?"

"Refer to number three on your worksheet. 'Human beings are not perfect.' And that includes husbands."

I pointed out the typo to Katie. "Human *beans* are not perfect."

It took a minute, but Katie finally got it. "I guess not."

My subtle laughter, being charged with emotional and physical exhaustion, quickly turned into disruptive, hysterical laughter. Heads turned, but I couldn't stop. I told Katie we'd better leave or we'd be labeled sacrilegious.

"*You'd* be labeled sacrilegious," she clarified.

We sneaked out of the study and stood in the sunny parking lot. Katie could have said something negative about the meeting, but to her credit, she didn't. It was one of the things I loved about Katie. Although she claimed she believed in God, she had never said straight out that she had a personal relationship with Jesus Christ. And I'm afraid I wasn't being a good example lately. Katie once said that other Christians she knew acted too perfect, as if life wasn't real. Well, I was here to demonstrate that Christians are real . . . foibles and all.

"Do you want to go shopping?" Katie suggested.

"No."

"What then?"

I thought, lengthily. "I think I'll take up the bagpipes," I said finally.

She gave me a strange look.

"I always wanted a Celtic wedding," I explained. "My father's family was from Scotland, and he loved bagpipe music. But Brock and I eloped because we were so poor at the time."

"When I was seven, I went to a bagpipe museum in Northumberland," Katie said.

I had no idea where that was.

"In England."

"Uh huh."

"Did you know women used to get their fingers cut off for playing the bagpipes?" Katie informed me.

"That's a myth, don't you think?" I stiffened my lip.

"I don't know. But who wants to find out?"

We smiled.

"Anyway, it would mean I'd have to shave my legs to wear the kilt," I said, half-joking.

Katie looked at me strangely again. She waxed at spas.

"I think I'll go home and explore my other talents," I said, resigned.

"Such as?"

"Good point, Katie. Maybe I'll just go home."

It's always disconcerting to walk into your own living room and find it has been turned into a laundry center, complete with ironing board, iron, and a laundry cart (the commercial kind you find in the laundry room of a hotel).

I dropped my purse in agitation. More disconcerting than the disorder was the fact that my entire wardrobe was in the living room.

"What are we doing here, Nana?" I asked as patiently as I could.

"Oh, I was finding something for you to wear to your meeting and I got carried away."

"Meeting? What meeting?" I asked, animatedly.

"Someone called for you about a meeting."

"What? When? Where? But more importantly, who? Who called about a meeting?"

"Let's see," she said, tapping her wrinkled forehead.

"Think, Nana, think!"

I ran over just in time to grab Sylvester, who was trying to make his way up the laundry-cart pole, and deposited him in the kitchen behind Jeff's old baby gate. Brock had put the gate up to partly solve the roaming-animals problem, but apparently, the gate was no deterrent to this escapee.

"The Home Living Channel," she said, finally remembering.

"When? When is it?" I cried.

"Ten o'clock tomorrow at the offices."

I grinned.

I phoned Brock and Katie and Hannah and Mark and left Jeff a message, then skipped across the street and stood on Simon's lawn. "Hey Simon!" I called, knowing he would be within earshot.

He came out in red sweats, sipping on one of his vegetable drinks. "Hey, Nature Girl!"

"I may be a Hollywood girl again soon!" I yelled.

The news was too good to keep inside.

Chapter Fifteen

Shelby and I were the first to arrive. We were sitting at the far end of the conference table chatting nervously when Trent Powers moseyed in with his shirt half-tucked in, looking like a driver's license picture, only worse. He was like thunder arriving in the middle of a nice, sunny day.

I turned to Shelby and grimaced.

She whispered, "Ignore him. He's not your boss anymore."

I planned to try. "What do you think this meeting is about?" I asked her, partially because I wanted to know, but mostly to give Trent the impression we were involved in deep conversation and didn't want to be disturbed.

"I don't know," she said. "It's never happened before. Usually Dane doesn't call meetings in the office with the underlings."

It was difficult to pretend we didn't notice Trent when he was heading in our direction and swishing his coffee all over the place.

Of all the empty chairs he had to pick from, he set his tailbone right next to me.

"Hi," I said.

"Hi," Trent said.

"Hi." Shelby threw up her hand in a mock wave.

"I wonder where everybody is." Trent looked around.

I had no idea.

"I think some of them thought we were meeting in the studio," Shelby said. "But they're shooting in there. This is more comfortable than the risers anyway."

There was an awkward pause. I yawned.

"If I knew the gophers were invited, I might have brought some grass and roots," Trent said out of the blue.

How I wish I hadn't left my copy of *Snappy Comebacks to Second Grade Insults* in my dresser drawer.

"Why don't you ever make these insane comments in front of your employer?" Shelby asked snidely.

"It's called discretion," Trent replied and gave a sly smile.

A flash of naughtiness occurred to me, and I couldn't resist. "Oh, no, Trent!"

"What?"

"Is that a sprig of parsley between your front teeth?"

His eyes bulged like golf balls and his chipmunk cheeks turned red. Without a word he rushed out of the room. Most likely to find a mirror.

"That was funnier than him falling in a manhole," Shelby said, and I agreed.

We were still laughing when some crew members came bounding into the room. They gathered around the coffee table exchanging casual, friendly greetings. It was so unlike the mad pace of working on location.

I noted they were mostly wearing jeans, T-shirts, and tennis shoes. I was overdressed in my freshly pressed, outdated suit.

Plum walked in, wearing a candy-pink cotton shirt, hip-hugging denim, and black pointy boots like Katie's.

"Plum, over here!" Shelby called.

"Sit here in Trent's spot," I begged, and she sat down as though the chair had cooties.

Shelby related Trent's comments to Plum.

"What a goof!" she said, then went into a description of her new roommate's peculiar habit of sleeping with the lights on.

By the time Trent returned, there was only one seat left—at the head of the table.

And even he knew not to take that seat.

He leaned against the wall, and I *almost* felt sorry for him. It was obvious to me he was the sort of kid to be chosen last for the softball team.

Plum caught me eyeing him. "Can't you just see him on a karaoke stage?" she whispered. "Thank you! Thank you very much!"

The egomaniac apparently mistook my stares. Cleverly he inched his way down to our end of the table until I could feel him standing directly behind me.

Dane Brodie walked in and sat down in the big chair at the head of the table. He thanked everyone for coming. A petite woman with long acrylic nails set a Starbucks cup in front of him. "Is it a triple?" he asked, the dark circles under his eyes exaggerated under the direct lighting.

"What we need in this office is an espresso machine," Trent whined.

Dane took a breath. "Here's the scoop, people. We need a new show."

The room was quiet.

"I don't care about your titles today. I want to hear what you have to say." He took a sip of his drink and continued speaking. "Now we know most of the people watching Reality TV are women. We have some other great shows we're working on, but *Dog Wars* was aimed at that untapped daytime crowd, and that is the slot we're looking to replace—and fast."

Every breath was magnified in the silence.

After no one said anything for a minute, Dane added, "We're

looking for a theme that's not overused. That's hard in this market, I know."

Obviously no one wanted to be the first.

"Anything that comes to mind," he prompted.

Not surprisingly, Trent was the first to brave a suggestion. "How about a Noah's Ark version of *Survivor*?" He went on in cockamamie detail how the ark would be built and how the family would care for the animals and do silly elimination rounds.

As soon as Trent took a breath, Dane slammed it down with an "I don't think so."

"I wonder what he expected to do with all the floating bodies after the flood," Shelby teased.

One of the prop men wiggled in his seat. "How about a show about people with unusual occupations—like elephant trainers and smokejumpers?"

Dane looked to the woman who had black-rimmed glasses and wore her hair in a neat bun. I assumed she was legal counsel.

She responded promptly. "That would definitely present a liability problem."

"A Siegfried & Roy tiger mauling would make for bad publicity, don't you agree?" Dane raised his eyebrows.

"Oh," the prop man said.

Danny, a gaffer whom I'd only met briefly, called his show idea *Truly Embarrassing Moments*. "We could do a reenactment of people's most embarrassing moments and have the viewing audience vote for the best."

"I don't see the social value in that, and I believe we're forgetting our target audience," Dane reminded the group.

"How about a housewives' special edition?" Danny offered.

"Moving on," Dane suggested, I thought, rather mercifully.

There were a few good suggestions but dozens of outrageous ones, many of them tried and failed.

I was falling asleep and thinking to myself, in a brainless sort of way. That's when I must have scratched my nose or my head. Somehow I must have given the impression I wanted to say something.

Dane directed his eyes at me. "Stephy."

I tried not to faint.

"Stephy, were you going to say something?"

"Well, I do have an idea," I said.

Do I have an idea?

Trent mumbled some irreverent comment under his breath.

"Go on." Dane woke me from my daydream.

"My show would be a show about . . ." I hesitated a second too long.

"Nothing! A show about nothing," Trent interrupted. "I think that's been done."

Everyone roared, but I was only motivated by the put-down.

"As I was saying"—I glared at Trent—"my show would be about a woman with no experience in television who is given the opportunity to produce a Reality TV show."

"I believe that's my job," Dane said dryly.

I continued. "She would be given the staff, the resources, a budget, and would be filmed as she created the show."

"You have me intrigued. Go on." Dane leaned forward.

"Yes, go on," the woman in the attorney suit said, boosting my confidence.

I had myself intrigued. "It would, in essence, be a Reality show about a Reality show. The cameras would follow her on her day-to-day activities. Sort of an up-close-and-personal of a woman trading homemaking for a crack at producing."

Hey, I thought to myself, *that's pretty good.*

"Why not? Home Edition does *How'd They Do That,*" a voice down the way noted.

A man in a golf shirt added, "It wouldn't require much intervention. We could get by with a consulting producer to save you the hassle."

The decision makers looked at each other.

Trent took over, uninvited. "You could give her a big office. And, and . . . ," he stuttered. His brainwaves misfired.

"Throw in a maid," Avril suggested.

I liked her suggestion. So did Dane.

Trent interrupted, "The byline could be: The day-to-day glories of an unfulfilled woman meeting her dreams on the highway of . . . uh . . . success."

"That's good, Trent." Dane nodded. "Very good."

"The family members could be included. Their reactions to her new career. You could interview a teacher from the past." Trent went on like it was all his idea.

"This is going on the top of my list I'm taking with me tonight when I meet with the station owner," Dane declared.

So I'd contributed *something*, I thought. But I doubted the idea would go anywhere.

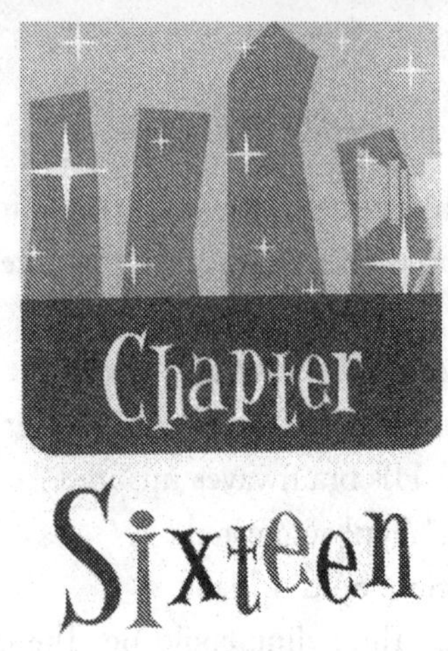

Chapter Sixteen

"Who are you, and what have you done with my Nana?" is the question I wanted to ask the beady-eyed stranger standing in my living room.

"I'm here to make your day!" he said.

I doubted it.

My missing Nana (not known for her sales resistance) came out of the kitchen and handed a glass of Ovaltine to the flashily dressed intruder.

"Honey, this is Rex. He's going to give us a special gift for a few minutes of our time for a demonstration on . . . what is it again, Rex?"

"A vacuum cleaner," he said after gulping the Ovaltine and wiping his brown-milk mustache.

"He's a dead ringer for cousin Roger Baldly's adopted boy, Pete, I tell you," Nana informed me. She then turned to Rex. "The poor man shot himself in the head."

He gulped.

". . . with a nail gun." she clarified.

He pulled on his nerdy tie.

"It was purely accidental, of course," she added.

"Yes, of course," he said.

There seemed to be an unnatural amount of untimely deaths on Nana's side of the family, mostly due to industrial accidents (many of them involving ladders and portable construction toilets).

I plopped down on the sofa, closed my eyes, and resigned myself to a sales pitch. When I opened them, Rex was pouring water in the basin of the so-called vacuum.

He asked if I would mind getting off *my* sofa.

"Well, all right," I agreed, but unhappily.

He removed all the cushions and proceeded to vacuum the upholstery, coming up with a brown, vile liquid that looked like the chocolate river in the *Willy Wonka* movie. It was a nasty shock for all of us. Especially me, since it looked so clean to the natural eye.

I looked at him with an embarrassed grin as he "vacuumed" the only five-by-five square of carpet not buried under Nana's things.

I would be hard-pressed to say I didn't need this equipment, considering it drew an even greater amount of offensive brown liquid.

"This is no ordinary vacuum cleaner. It is an air-filtering system as well," he said and smiled.

My willpower began weakening at that point, particularly when he went into gruesome detail about germs hitchhiking on our shoes and how all that kitty hair could make us ill, and we could develop emphysema. And when he shone a thousand-watt light bulb on the thick dust particles, I was convinced that I was living in Tokyo on a stage-five smog-alert day.

But as he droned and droned and showed me attachment after attachment, the chrome was blurring together and I was losing my patience. So when Nana left to fix dinner, I begged the man. "The price, Rex. What's the price?"

He had been avoiding the subject with vague language. Now he shrugged and finally quoted some outrageous price.

I shook my head fervently. "Absolutely not!"

"Let me see what I can do," he said.

"Are you going to check with the manager in your suitcase? I'm not going to buy it," I said with expression.

"You aren't?" He seemed genuinely surprised.

"I'm not even close to being a prospect. You, Rex, have wasted your time as well as mine."

"Even if my kids have to go to Community College instead of Stanford?"

"That's right."

He wrung his hands.

"What is my special gift?" I asked.

He presented a box of Milk Duds. "King size," he said, trying to impress me.

I opened the box and threw a couple in my mouth.

"Seriously, I gotta tell you my mother needs an operation."

"Good-bye, Rex," I said, devouring the cheap chocolate and pointing to the door.

"Say good-bye to your grandmother," he said as he gathered his wares. As he had packed the last of them, he added, "I sell a microwave coffee maker too."

"Rex, did I mention my favorite play of all times is *Death of a Salesman*?"

He frowned. "That line is highly overused."

"All your lines are highly overused. Good-bye, Rex." I uncharacteristically slammed the door in his face.

Nana came out of the kitchen. "Where did our nice young man go?"

Brock, the champion of perfect timing, showed up a minute later as I was discarding shoes by the bagful after our lesson on germ warfare.

Nana stopped me as I was about to discard the white orthopedic shoes. "Those are cute," she commented.

"You can have them," I said.

The evening might have been a total loss if Mattie hadn't called and asked if I could start tomorrow as the office P.A.

Feeling a mix of excitement and fear, I knocked on Mattie's trailer office door.

"Come in," she said.

I eased the door open.

She greeted me with a handshake. My hand felt wooden.

"Thank you for coming in on such short notice."

"I'm happy to do it," I said.

She directed me to the same chair I'd sat in during my interview. After I sat down, she plucked cat hairs off my sweater.

"It's from my grandmother's cats," I explained. "I'm so embarrassed."

"No reason to be embarrassed," she said. "I'm the one who should be embarrassed."

"Why?"

"My miserable demeanor the other day."

"We all have those days." It certainly was the truth.

"Some of us more than others," she said, and then tossed her black hair. She'd had it cut short since my previous interview. "Is it hot in here?"

"It's actually a little chilly."

She struggled to make herself comfortable. "My dream vacation used to be Tahiti."

"Mine still is." I smiled.

"But now I dream of vacationing in an ice house."

"Really?" *To me that would be too close to cleaning out the freezer.*

"Did you know there's a hotel in Sweden made entirely of ice?" Mattie fanned herself with a magazine.

I was catching on. *Hot flashes.*

Soon I would be in that "special time of life," as many grandmothers referred to it. (Nana preferred Erma Bombeck's frank descriptions, which I won't go into.)

"Anyway, enough about me."

I was selfishly relieved.

"I'm sure you're wondering about your job."

"Yes, I am," I croaked.

"Basically, this job is pretty much the same as your old job, only in the office. It entails running errands, making coffee, and copies. Anything you can do to assist our consulting producer, Trent Powers."

"Trent Powers? Is he related to Trent Powers?" I knew that sounded dumb, but I couldn't help but ask it. "I mean, I know a production coordinator named Trent Powers."

"That's him. He was promoted about twenty minutes ago." Mattie shook her head. "He's a confident young man; I have that to say about him."

I stumbled over my next words. "Can, uh, *may* I ask how this came about?"

"Dane Brodie is wild about his Reality TV show idea. Well, you were in the meeting yesterday. You probably know more about the show than I do."

"What show is that?" I asked apprehensively.

"They're calling it *Reality Queen*. Get this. A reality show about a reality show." She chuckled. "Cute idea, don't you think?"

"Very cute." I could feel my anger rising.

Mattie's intercom buzzed. "Would you excuse me, Stephanie? It's my mother calling from Pocatello, Idaho. If I don't talk to her right off, she'll call back in five minutes and say she's the president of NBC or something."

I nodded and exited the trailer in a haze. Seeking privacy, I called Katie from the roomy, handicapped bathroom stall.

"Remember my great Reality TV show idea I told you about last night?" I cried as soon as she picked up.

"Of course," she said.

"Now all the sudden they're calling it *Reality Queen*, and Trent Powers is being credited as the brain child."

"*Reality Queen*? That's a cute name for a show," she admitted.

"Katie!" I spouted, watching my feet shuffle back and forth across the tiny blue tiles.

"I'm sorry," she said.

"It's absolutely criminal!"

"Absolutely," she agreed.

"How did Trent's dirty fingerprints get all over *my* idea?" I pulled too much toilet paper from the roll and wiped my eyes.

"I don't know," Katie said.

I heard the bathroom door open but ignored it in my fury.

"I intend to do something about this!" My voice echoed in the bathroom.

"Like what?" Katie asked.

"I don't know."

I whipped some more toilet paper off the roll as someone banged. I walked over to the door and could see the overhang of Skechers.

"Hey you! Don't you know that stall is reserved for handicapped people?" the voice belonging to the shoes reprimanded me.

I was hugely embarrassed—again.

"I gotta go, Katie," I whispered and stood there, not knowing what to do.

My conscience banged on the stall again.

I opened the door, slowly, guiltily. "Shelby. It's you!" I said, relieved.

She howled in laughter.

"You scared me!" I accused my friend.

"I'm sorry," she said, and we hugged as I recovered.

"We're going to be working together in the closet down the hall." Shelby said.

"We are?"

"Yes."

I was relieved to hear that. "So I guess you heard all that verbatim."

"Only the, 'I intend to do something about this!'" she mimicked.

"I just don't get how this could happen," I said.

"I'll tell you how. Trent weaseled his way into having dinner with the bigwigs and massaged your show into his own creation. From what I hear, they're in a tremendous hurry. Open auditions are being held tomorrow."

"It's so unfair!" I leaned against the wall.

"Why don't you tell Dane your thoughts?" Shelby asked.

"Confronting him would be basically calling him an idiot."

"Forget about it for a while," she said. "I'll introduce you to our hole-in-the-wall office."

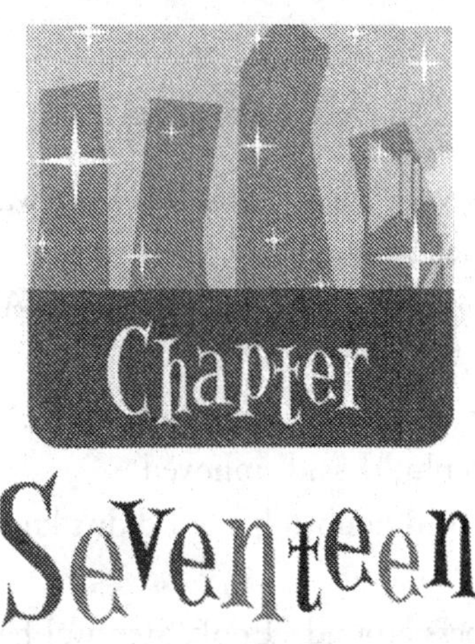

Chapter Seventeen

Our dinky office space was divided by a six-foot partition. My cubicle had a desk and a phone. Shelby's had a desk, a phone, a computer, and a large monitor.

I had barely arranged my purse under my desk when Trent walked in with a self-satisfied smirk. "Ah, my personal gopher," he said, raising his eyebrows.

I shot a look of disdain he failed to acknowledge, then asked if we could speak privately.

"In my office." He led me to his bright, spacious office with a polished mahogany desk. "Sit down." He leaned back in his executive chair. "Are you unclear on your assignments?"

I kicked the inside of his desk with my big toe.

He looked around, searching for the source of the noise.

"I simply want to ask you a question, Mr. Powers."

"Shoot." He tilted his head importantly.

"Whose idea was *Reality Queen*?" I asked, directly.

He leaned forward, scratched his heart-shaped chin, and clammed up.

"We both know the show was my idea, Trent!" I said passionately.

"You say it was your idea; Dane thinks it was mine. I'm going with Dane." He toyed with a shiny, silver pen.

"I'm not going to make an issue of it, Trent. All I'm asking for is some respect."

"I have nothing against you personally, Betty."

"My name is Stephy," I said, annoyed.

"Really?" He looked doubtful, like I didn't know my own name.

"Yes, really."

He shuffled papers around. "Look, Stephy, I have a game plan. In five years I'm going to be Dane Brodie."

This man was a pompous jerk with illusions of grandeur.

"And I'm in your way?" I glared.

He scratched his head. "I appreciate this Hallmark moment, but I have a job to do and you have a job to do, and my job is to tell you what to do."

The intercom buzzed and Trent said, "Deliver it to my office."

A man with a dolly dropped three boxes in the corner of the office.

"You can start your new job by setting up my new computer," Trent said casually.

I faked a look of self-reliance.

"I have something very important to do." He grabbed his army green cloth briefcase and exited his office.

I moaned. Hannah had given me a lesson on her computer once. "Mom, the minimize button is the –, and maximize is the little window thing at the top." We never got past that.

But I was determined to assemble this computer from scratch. As every other newspaper article said, there was no future in this technological world without computer skills.

Two hours later I was still following the six simple assembly steps. I would never again chide Simon about not understanding current technology. I vowed to be more patient with Nana about the VCR.

I prayed.

Ultimately I made it. Everything worked!

I neatly stuffed the Styrofoam, plastic, and paper back in the boxes.

The one simple step left was the registration. No biggie. An alphanumeric code to type in. This should be a breeze.

Fifty tries later I was hanging on the edge of the cliff of insanity.

Think of a blue ocean, I told myself through another few tries.

I kept plugging that code in, certain it would work this time, even though I knew that one definition of insanity was doing the same thing over and over again and expecting different results.

Purple flowers.

Stars against a backdrop of velvet sky.

I graduated to a luxurious villa with an ocean view on Tahiti at sunset. It didn't work. I was a wreck. Shipwrecked on the island of high-tech madness.

I was frantically pressing those keys when the office offender walked in around 2:30.

"Do you need some help there?" he asked. I detected a measure of pleasure in his voice.

"No, I'm fine!" I said calmly as I fought with the code.

"Move over," he ordered.

I relinquished his chair and watched him plug in the sixteen-digit alphanumerical code and press Enter. "There, all done," he said, beating his chest like Tarzan.

I defended myself. "I tried that."

Trent placed his greasy finger on the monitor. "You probably hit *B*, and it's an eight. It's bifocal time!" he chided.

He was probably right, darn it. From here on out it was a slippery slope to old age.

He caught my attention with a throat clearing. "Now you can assemble the new espresso machine. It's sitting in a box by the coffee counter. I have important business to attend to."

How many purchase orders did he sign today?

The espresso machine was also a hideously complicated piece of shiny chrome. However, I managed to assemble it beautifully. I deserved an award.

"I have the machine set up," I said, practically running into Trent's office with the news.

He was playing solitaire on the computer.

"Just testing it out," he said. And then he stared. "I didn't think you'd have a problem."

Was that a compliment?

"I'm sure you spend a lot of time in the kitchen."

I was too exhausted to come up with a one-liner.

He squirmed in his chair and then, like a child who just bought a new snow-cone machine, asked me for a single latte, high-foam. "And surprise me with the flavor."

I couldn't blame him. I remembered my Easy Bake oven. I'd baked three cakes that first day.

As soon as he tested that one, he ordered another, more complicated, drink.

When he ordered his third, I started to blame him.

As I was leaving, I said good night as a courtesy.

"Be at the Embassy Suites Hotel at 9 a.m. tomorrow for *Reality Queen* open auditions," he told me. "Someone just called in sick. Consider this a promotional opportunity."

It was late when I hung my sweater in the closet and surveyed what used to be my house.

"How was your day?" Nana asked, adjusting her hand-crocheted apron.

"Fine. Where's Brock?"

The question was answered before Nana could respond.

Either Eddie Van Halen was tuning his guitar, or Brock's

electric guitar had been miraculously resurrected from its tomb in the garage.

"I haven't seen that in a long time," I said from the doorway. I was actually thinking, *I haven't heard that in a long time, thank you, Lord.*

"I know. Nana got it out for me," Brock said, grinning. "She thinks I'm immensely talented."

I did mention that Nana is hard of hearing, didn't I?

"Listen." He strummed away.

I wasn't sure if he was playing "Stairway to Heaven" or "Amazing Grace."

Trying to decipher his instrumentals was somewhat like looking at one of my children's kindergarten finger paintings.

"Is it a bird?"

"No, Mommy."

"A plane?"

Only this was:

"Guess, honey."

"Is it 'She'll Be Coming 'Round the Mountain'?"

"Stephy—you jokester, you . . ."

"'The Old Rugged Cross'?"

"Go on. You know what it is."

Brock had tried out for the worship team at church once. Unfortunately, he'd dislocated his shoulder skiing the day before they were intending to render their decision on whether or not he was accepted.

The worship leader had told me that God works everything out for good, and then winked.

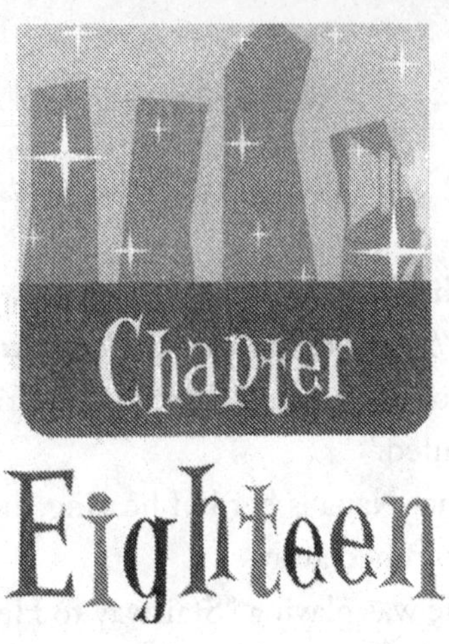

Chapter Eighteen

I made my way through the crowded parking lot to the front door of the Embassy Suites Hotel, where I showed my official-looking identification through the glass. The security guard nodded and let me in.

It was a nice hotel with a beautiful lobby, and I thought how I would like to spend a romantic getaway weekend with Brock here . . . someday.

The faces on the other side of the plate glass peered in curiously. Where did all these women come from on such short notice?

I felt important as I followed the signs to the room where the open auditions would be held.

The cameraman was setting up, and Trent was sitting on the other side of the table across the room. As I approached, I noticed he looked pale and suspected he was still feeling the effects of yesterday's java fest.

"Would you like some coffee?" I asked, almost laughing.

"Water is fine," he said.

"Where's Dane?"

"He has bigger fish to scale."

Fry, not scale.

"I'm running the show today." He pulled out his most recent company purchase: a laptop.

A pretty woman in a teal linen dress walked up to the table at that exact moment. "Uh hum!" She cleared her throat.

Since Trent had absolutely no manners, she introduced herself. "I'm Susie, the casting director today," she said with an English accent. "And *we're* running the show."

I made my way over to the table where the hotel had laid out pastries, coffee, tea, and ice water.

Susie followed me. Searching through the tea bags she found a packet of Lipton English Breakfast Tea and wrinkled her nose. She touched the side of the flowery teapot, as if checking for the temperature.

I'd been to high tea with Katie once at the Beverly Hills Hotel, where I'd had a bit of trouble swishing the tea back and forth without clinking my spoon. I'm no expert, but I knew the English liked their water to the point of boiling.

"It isn't very hot," I commented, sipping on my own brew.

"I suspect I'll never get used to your way of tea," she said. "But then you might not get used to driving on the right side of the street."

"The left, you mean."

We laughed.

Her down-to-earth manner was refreshing. I could see us being friends.

She looked over at Trent, who was listening to his cell-phone messages and laughing mechanically.

"His mum is having trouble starching his underwear, I'm guessing." Susie flashed me a smile.

I tried not to laugh.

"Is he for real?" she whispered.

"Completely."

We giggled.

It was an hour or so later, and the contestants were now standing in the waiting room next-door. A twentysomething woman was assigning them numbers, and I was trying to figure out my job since Trent hadn't said.

The security guard standing off to the side was getting an earful of female conversation. As expected, there was a self-appointed leader among the group, giving everyone advice. A few were knitting. Reality TV gossip seemed to be the main topic. There was no mystique about it. You walked in off the street and you were a candidate.

Milling around, I picked out a few favorites among the two hundred or so participants.

"Can you put in a good word for me?" a voice said from behind me.

Someone had put something in my back pocket, but when I looked around, I wasn't sure who. I examined the bookmark printed by a child. "Pick my mommy!" it said and had a big yellow sun.

I tried to make conversation with my twentysomething coworker, who was holding a clipboard, but it was hard since she had the personality of a stick figure.

I checked back in the boardroom, where Trent and Susie were arguing over the questions they would be asking.

Back and forth I wandered, between the big room and the waiting room.

In my last trip to the big room, I saw the shaggy-haired cameraman was having trouble with his equipment. Trent went over and said he could fix it for him. The cameraman, not wanting to relinquish control of his camera, pulled on it, and Trent pulled on it. During their tussle the camera fell and broke.

The cameraman looked sick for a minute, then asked, "What do you want me to do?"

"Get the thing repaired," Trent ordered.

"So now what?" I asked as the unhappy cameraman gathered his broken equipment.

"As soon as Susie gets back from the bathroom, you can call the bonbon eaters in," Trent said irreverently.

Oh good grief.

The women in the waiting room were huddled by the exit, as though waiting for an elevator to the special sales floor of some divine department store.

The silent security guard took over. "One at a time," he yelled.

"When I call your number you are to go to the red *X* in the big room and wait for instruction," the stoic woman with the clipboard droned.

The first contestant, Maria Castlegate, was allowed in.

"Why should you be the Reality Queen," Susie asked the rumpled lady, who looked like she had been driving all night and had slept in her car.

"Because it's been my lifelong dream to be a famous actress in Hollywood," she blared louder than a beauty-pageant contestant.

"Maria, it says here you live in Texas. What did you do? Jump in the car five minutes after the casting call was posted?"

"Basically, yes."

"Is your family with you?" Susie asked.

"My husband is watching the kids."

"How many kids?"

"Five."

There was silence for a moment.

"Wasn't it a strain on your family? I mean, all this way for a three-minute audition?" Susie asked, sounding concerned.

"Three minutes? Is that all this is going to take?"

"Thank you for coming," Susie said.

I led her out the door. She was shocked she hadn't been chosen. I was shocked that she was shocked.

"I don't even think that was three minutes," she muttered.

I shrugged.

"Could you direct me to the nearest pawnshop? I'll have to hock my wedding ring for gas."

How sad, I thought.

I always wondered how they got through several hundred auditions in one day. I soon found out. In ten minutes we had gone through ten women. All of them definite *nos*.

It took all the way to number seventeen before there was even a reason to stay awake.

As soon as she walked in the room, she started singing "Sugar Pie Honey Bunch" and snapping her fingers in rhythm.

"Stop! Stop!" Susie said. "Has someone given you the mistaken impression that this is a singing competition?"

"I'm good at it."

"And I'm good at flower arranging, but I don't do it in line at McDonald's."

The candidate didn't seem to get it.

"*American Idol* may be your best bet," Trent threw in.

"But I'm over twenty-eight," the woman argued.

After that I was asked to announce to the ladies that there would be no singing.

By the time number thirty-two emerged in Disney-character pajamas, only forty minutes had passed. It seemed more like forty years.

"Why are you wearing pajamas?" Susie asked.

"Excuse me for thinking you might want something different," the contestant screamed and threw one of her slippers in the direction of the judges.

The reason for the twenty-foot barrier between the red *X* and the judge's table.

"Describe your typical daily routine," Trent told the thirtysomething, pretty, rosy-cheeked contestant.

"I start by feeding my family eggs from free-range chickens . . ."

She went into her remarkable routine. How she gave her husband and each of four children individual attention; packed healthy lunches before sending them on their way and starting her cleaning detail, which involved homemade cleaning products of vinegar, lemon, and baking soda.

As she went on, her recounting began to sound more like a complaint. Trent started making violin music over her complaints, infuriating Susie.

"Stop it!" Susie demanded. "You absolutely do not deserve to be here!"

The woman started sobbing.

"I meant him!" Susie said and hit Trent's arm lightly with her fist.

"Ouch, that hurts," he complained.

The woman stood there, wiping her tears with her sleeve.

"Thank you, but you're not exactly what we're looking for, Linda," Trent said after a minute.

"It's Laura," she wailed and stomped out.

"Stephy, can you get me a cup of coffee? *Black*," Susie stated.

Trent nodded. "Me too."

The Swiss attire might have been a clue that Emily was not your typical housewife. The yodeling was confirmation.

"Did you take your training in Austria or Germany?" Trent asked sarcastically.

"No, *Yodeling Made Easy* on CD. I highly recommend it."

"I believe we made it clear there was no singing in this audition," Susie said, nearly exasperated.

"Well, yodeling isn't technically singing." Emily went into an explanation about how yodeling was technically more difficult than opera singing.

"We're going to have to pass," Susie said.

Emily's cheery disposition remained intact. She threw pieces of chocolate on her way out. One landed in Trent's coffee and splashed his nice white shirt and tie.

The next contestant walked in as Trent was making a huge deal about it. "Club soda will take care of that stain," she said.

I don't mean to be vindictive, but it was funny.

"We're taking a lunch break after this," he whined.

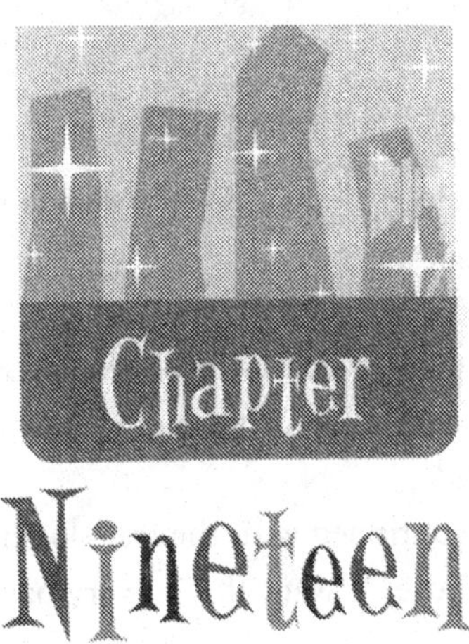

Chapter Nineteen

The scheduled madness started up again at 1:30.

Humor was desperately needed. We'd seen enough weird.

Trent laughed at the tall, skinny woman's PMS jokes, but Susie said they were in poor taste and she ought to be ashamed of herself.

"Do you do casting for *Last Comic Standing*?" the woman asked, holding her card out.

That didn't fly very far.

"Next," Susie called.

Auditions continued with the gothic mom, who looked like she was auditioning for the ugliest bride in California in her black velvet dress with too much cleavage. I hoped she didn't dress her children.

A few acts down the road, the double-jointed housewife tried to wow the judges with a demonstration on how easily her fingers bent into grotesquely unnatural positions.

"I have a cousin who can do that," Trent said, unimpressed.

At that point I was asked to announce that there were to be no shows of talent whatsoever.

I watched in disbelief as at least half of the women threw their numbers in the basket and left.

"Now look what you did!" the stick-figure girl admonished me.

"Hey, can we help it if they don't understand the definition of *housewife*?" I retorted.

The numbers were reassigned.

Those who had auditioned and were being considered as finalists congregated on one side. The fortysomething women yet to audition were on the other side.

And the games continued with the frail-looking housewife sharing her answer in prose. "I want this so very bad. If I don't win, I'll be sad."

I bit into a prune pastry.

When she was gone, Susie said it might be a blessing that the clumsy cameraman broke the camera.

Obviously Trent's spin on the story.

The lady from the Bronx talked faster than Trent highly caffeinated. "I just moved to Los Angeles last month, and when I read my horoscope last week and saw your casting call yesterday . . ."

When she was dismissed, Susie moaned. "This is getting ridiculous."

The twin housewives were told only one of them could be chosen as a finalist. They started fighting about who would be better at the job. In the end they decided it would be best if neither of them applied.

Good decision, ladies. Blood is thicker than fame.

"Can we take another break, please?" Susie asked.

I shared the bad news. "There are only three contestants left."

"Three? As in one, two, three?" Susie flinched.

"One, two, three." I held up three fingers.

"I'm glad you can count," Trent said.

I ignored that.

Susie looked shocked.

Could it be that putting out a casting call twenty-four hours ahead of time did not allow for the proper preparation . . .

I stuck my head out the side door for a whiff of fresh air, but my lungs were blasted with tobacco smoke.

"Sorry to disturb you," I apologized to the janitor.

After hacking up a storm, I went into the waiting room. It was saturated in sweat, dispelling the myth that only men sweat. The perfume and hair spray only worsened the stench.

Thankfully, two of the remaining three contestants were fairly normal. Otherwise, I'd be asking the desk clerk if her mother wanted to produce a Reality TV show.

With the auditions concluded, Susie and Trent braved the waiting room. They announced the five finalists (there were originally supposed to be ten) who would return at 9:00 tomorrow morning to meet with the executive producer.

The chosen were beaming with gratitude.

Everyone left, except one woman with an enormous purse, who lingered way beyond her welcome.

Susie said good-bye to me. Trent left. The solemn young woman grabbed her clipboard, and the security guard helped her out with her box.

"I'm closing up shop," I said to the woman with the purse as I edged toward the exit.

She ignored me.

"I'm leaving," I said.

I flicked the light switch.

She didn't move.

I left the light on for her.

So what are we, Motel 6?

I rolled out of bed cranky, feeling like my life was some distant island I was watching from the middle of the ocean.

Brock was still asleep. He didn't use an alarm, claiming he had an internal clock.

I shook him. "Honey, get up. You'll be late for work."

"I'm not going in today. I'm going to work on my craft."

"Craft? What craft?"

"My music," he replied sleepily, as though it should be obvious. "I've been thinking, Steph . . ."

Uh-oh, we were heading somewhere. Hopefully not a garage band.

"The real-estate office is running well without me. I'm going to hang around today."

"And do what?"

"Jam."

"Jam?"

"Like, play my guitar."

Dane was behind the table conferring with Trent and Susie when I arrived in the big room at the Embassy Suites Hotel.

We had a new camera and cameraman. His name was Jack, he was wearing a tie-dyed T-shirt, and he was sociable, but not intrusive.

The five hopefuls were seated on steel chairs in the hall filling out applications.

It was much quieter today, almost a letdown from yesterday's excitement. There was no security guard—only the serious girl standing around with a clipboard.

I felt like I should be doing something more, but with Trent not ordering me around, I was almost lost.

It was maddening how subdued he was around Dane. I could see how Dane could be fooled by him.

Before they called the first contestant in, Dane discussed the evaluation forms Trent and Susie had filled out the previous day. I drank the Peach Snapple Iced Tea I had brought with me, and when that was gone, I studied the neutral wallpaper, half listening.

Trent and Susie disagreed on the first contestant, Edora Pickle, in many respects. The one thing they did agree on (besides her name needing to be changed) was that she was unruffled by pressure.

"Seven children, and she's calm as can be," Susie said, amazed.

Dane gave a respectful, "Would you show our first contestant in, please?" A far cry from Trent's, "Let the bonbon eaters in."

Edora was dressed in all green, like a . . . should I say "dill" pickle?

Dane asked me if I wanted to sit down at the table too. It was a nice gesture, and I thanked Dane for it. Unfortunately, the chair was on the other side of Trent.

Susie presented the opening question. "Why are you interested in producing a Reality TV show?"

"My hope is to let women know that they can achieve whatever they set out to."

Our panel looked at each other and gave an approving nod.

The rest of her answers were good, but textbook.

"Definitely the best we've seen today," Trent said and was ignored.

It was rather obvious, since she was the only one they'd seen (and a direct steal from *American Idol*'s Randy Jackson, by the way).

As Edora was telling us how she could handle every situation that came along, attributing this trait to the relaxation techniques taught by her psychologist husband every Saturday in his warehouse office at 257 Crenshaw Boulevard in Los Angeles (plug, plug), she looked down at the floor and screamed.

Dane jumped up. "What?"

"A spider! A spider!"

Dane came to the rescue with his newspaper.

"Oh, go home and put on a rain-forest tape," Trent said, and I almost laughed.

The chirpy brunette was next. I'd witnessed her behavior as she made fun of the other participants. I did not like her.

"What sets you apart from the rest of the candidates?" Dane asked.

She squirmed nervously. "I'm very organized."

They hesitated. It was a flaky answer.

"So do I have a chance?" she blurted out, unnecessarily revealing her insecurity.

"Everyone has a chance," Dane replied.

"I have to have this! I have to!"

No one quite knew what to say.

"If I don't, I'll die. My husband trivializes everything I do. I want to show him I can do something that requires more thought than . . . than . . ."

She was digging a deep hole for herself, without the judges saying a word.

"If I don't have dinner ready when my husband gets home . . . ooh, it makes me mad when I think of it. I'm ordering pizza for dinner."

"I'll pay for it," Dane said, void of expression.

"OK," she said, taking him up on his offer, and surprising all of us, especially Dane, who, I'm sure, was joking.

He walked over to her, pulled out his wallet, and handed her a bill.

Susie sighed and whispered, "She's making us look bad. She didn't make such a bodge job of it yesterday."

"What?" Trent asked.

"She wasn't as daft as she is today."

"Daft?" he asked.

"A sad sack."

There was still no recognition.

"Trent, she was not as bad yesterday as she is today," I said.

"Why don't you speak English?" he grumbled with his head down as Dane returned to the table after encouraging the brunette's exit from the room. We all shared a heavy sigh.

"So these were the cream of the crop?" Dane couldn't believe it.

"There was worse yesterday. Trust me," Susie said.

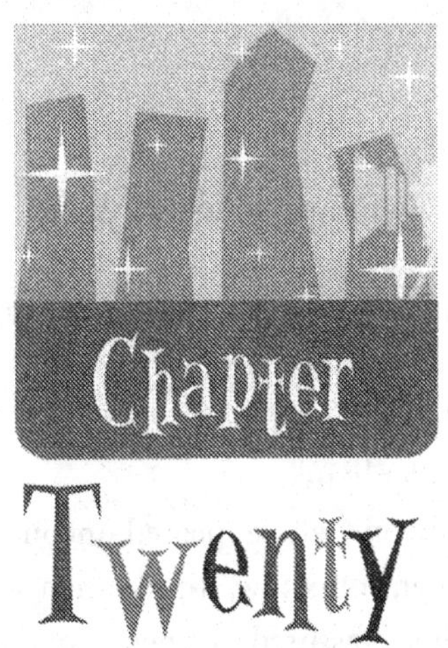

Chapter Twenty

"Let's get this over with," Dane strongly suggested as they started up again.

Number three was a woman with no distinguishing features. If I were doing a sketch for the police, I couldn't tell you much about her, except she had two eyes, a nose, and a mouth.

Dane took a sip of the acidic coffee and moaned. "You start this time, Trent," he uttered.

The next sound was Trent's ego shattering the atmosphere. He wasted no time with formalities. "Is there anything that would prevent you from starting right away?"

She looked suddenly nervous. "Yes."

"Explain."

"Well, there is a teensy problem."

"Just what is your wee little problem?" Susie asked.

She bit her nails. "Lice."

"Lice? That's completely horrid!" Susie erupted.

"We thought we were rid of them once."

"How comforting," Susie commented as Dane shook his head back and forth.

"I don't have lice. Mine are completely gone. It's just that my six-year-old—"

"You understand we can't take that chance," Dane said, scratching unconsciously.

Susie was scratching.

My scalp was suddenly itchy.

Trent was the only one who appeared unconcerned.

"I'm a good mother, you know," the woman said.

"Of course you are," I assured her, because no one else would.

As soon as the door shut behind her, Susie let out an "Ewwww! Let's get someone in here to vacuum the carpet."

Even though the woman was lacking in common sense, I felt sorry for her. Our clean, suburban middle-class family was once visited by the plague. And it came from that nice little girl whose mama was always scrubbing her white carpet too.

It took all of three seconds to realize that our next wannabe Reality Queen had an agenda. "Global warming is causing bad things to happen." She showed us a battery-operated hair dryer I thought was pretty cool.

"I'd like to demonstrate the greenhouse effect for you now." She pulled a plastic sandwich bag from her hemp drawstring pants and turned on her hair dryer.

This should be interesting.

"Where did you get these women?" Dane asked, addressing his question to Susie.

"Would you mind turning off your hair dyer?" Susie yelled.

"What?" she asked over the noise.

"Turn off your hair dryer, please!"

The woman obliged. "Will I be on TV?" She asked hopefully, smiling at the camera.

"I don't think we're the Reality TV show for you."

"Please leave," Dane said, fed up.

"Maybe you could do your little demonstration at the movie

theatre down the street where the penguin movie is playing," Susie suggested, and then added, "I love the penguin movie!"

"Ya gotta respect the penguin," I stated, trying to be funny.

As the woman walked away, Trent said, "Go tie yourself to a tree next time."

I wished that Dane had heard our insensitive clod-of-a judge's remark, but he was sighing heavily about this time. Possibly wishing he were in another line of work. May I suggest zookeeper?

"Bring in the last one," Dane said wearily.

Well-manicured, well-mannered, well-dressed, and size six, Rhonda Zeck was the epitome of the perfect housewife and answered everything precisely.

The judges were smiling soooo big. They thought the hunt was over. Rhonda was asked to leave the room.

"She's good. She's really good," Susie exclaimed.

"Good," Trent said.

"I think we've got our woman," Dane concurred.

They went on for a few minutes.

"Can I say something?" I piped in, not able to let it alone.

Blank stares.

"I think she's lying. I don't think she's a housewife at all."

"What are you? A lie detector?" Trent sneered.

"I just don't think she is," I responded.

"Maybe we should listen," Susie persuaded.

Dane took off his hat and scratched his head.

"Why don't you ask to see her photos?" I suggested, knowing I was climbing out on a limb.

"Call her back in," Dane yelled. When the woman entered, he began, "Rhonda, may we see pictures of your lovely children?"

"Pictures of my children?" She looked suddenly ill.

"What are your children's names again?" Susie asked.

There is something about catching people off guard that crushes all their defenses.

"OK, so I'm not a housewife," she admitted, no contest. "I work at the hotel." She flung her hair. "I had you fooled."

"No, you didn't," Trent claimed.

Was she planning on renting the children?

"Yes, I did." She strutted out, then turned around when she reached the door. "Uh, since you're not going to choose me, do you mind writing a note to my boss?"

With that, the auditions were concluded.

"I'm through with this. How about a bite to eat?" Dane suggested. "We need to discuss doing this by audition tapes."

I grabbed my purse and started walking away.

"You too," Susie said and touched me on the shoulder.

Trent gave a face like he had swallowed something sharp and gigantic.

"I hear the filet mignon in the dining room is pretty good," she encouraged.

"No thank you," I said.

Devouring the last bite of one of Nana's cinnamon rolls, I went on with my recap of the auditions.

Nana looked completely confused. "So she was drying her hair?"

"No, Nana. She was an activist with an agenda, and I guess she thought there could be publicity."

"I was on the agenda once. It was nineteen fifty-one, and I had to wait until the council meeting was practically over for my two cents on . . . now what was that?"

She took my dish and left.

Brock, who was sitting at the table with us, seemed entirely disinterested in my life, which made me entirely annoyed.

I accused him directly.

"I'm not disinterested. In fact—"

"In fact, what?" I snipped.

There was a lengthy pause.

"I'm so interested, I'm thinking of venturing into the world of Reality TV myself."

"How so?"

He showed me a clip from one of his newspapers. "They're filming a local Christian talent show in Orange County called 'Song of the Lamb,'" he said as I read the evidence. "I was talking to our keyboard player this morning."

"Your what?"

"Our new keyboard player. You know, Jeremy from the youth group."

I tilted my head back and looked into his dark eyes. "It's hard not to know him with LOVE tattooed across his knuckles."

"Anyway, he said he's interested in doing the show, and so is Jeff."

"Jeff? You're supposed to be talking him into quitting UPS and going to school full time, not playing in your boy band." I exhaled slowly. "And you, Brock, have a business to run."

"You tell me I work too hard," he defended.

There was an uncomfortable silence.

"I hired a new real-estate agent today, by the way," he informed me.

"It's a slight hop, skip, and jump from working too hard to not working at all."

Chapter Twenty-One

I jammed the copier for the second time—after hole-punching when I meant to collate and stapling the reports backward.

Earlier I had sent a fax to China (intended for Studio City), and when I changed the fax machine's ink cartridge ("*Just follow the simple instructions*," the receptionist said), I got ink all over my hands.

In spite of the fact that I was still on the low end of the learning curve, I was loving my job.

With the exception of my most adolescent boss.

Trent dropped a memo of chastisement on my desk. The memo read:

> *To: My Production Assistant*
>
> *Re: Barista Training (Barista: a person trained in the art of expresso preparation.)*
>
> *The difference between an expresso, cappuccino, and latte . . .*

Blah, blah, blah. I laughed because he had spelled *espresso* wrong!

The pregnant receptionist asked me if I would watch the front desk while she took a potty break. After I adjusted the chair to my shorter height, the phones started ringing off the hook.

In the middle of the chaos, Trent showed up with a "Yo Dude."

Dudette to you, buddy.

"I need you to type something *right now*," he said authoritatively.

It was obvious where he'd spent his lunch hour. He was unevenly tanned from his fake bake.

"Trent, the phones," I stated, over the noise. "Can you please wait a minute?"

"It will only take one itty-bitty second of your precious time," he said in this whiny voice, with his lip out a mile.

I sighed. "Before you start crying, I'll do it." I situated my fingers on the keyboard.

"Are you feeling stuck as a housewife? Unappreciated?" he started dictating.

"Who, me?"

"No, not you. This is the casting call for *Reality Queen*. In fact, put that at the top. In caps. Got that?" he said snidely.

"Yes."

I was grateful all the ringing had finally stopped.

"Are you conscientious, creative, and a good communicator?" He continued dictating from a yellow lined sheet. Then he stopped. "You spelled *conscentious* wrong."

"No, I didn't. Want to check in the dictionary?" I was hoping to avoid an argument and get the harassment over with.

"I'm a college boy, and you are maybe a high-school graduate, but you know better, I guess."

"Can we continue, please?"

He rolled his eyes.

I wanted to roll mine.

"Prepare a three-minute audition tape showing your current living space and telling us why you should be given the chance to produce a Reality TV show. Must be twenty-five to fifty years old and live in the Los Angeles area," he said like a radio announcer.

"Slow down, please, Trent."

He didn't. "Send your audition tape to: *Reality Queen* Casting, eighty-four ninety-three Santa Monica Blvd. Include your name, address, and all contact information. Deadline is April twenty-second. No exceptions."

The ringing started up again.

"Trent, I have to answer these phones!"

"Who's stopping you?" He laughed and pushed me and my rolling chair aside.

"I'll just send this to myself and have my hamster send it out to twenty million people." Then he took over my computer, pushed a few buttons, and left.

Now all the lines were ringing at once.

At that exact moment, a suited executive caught me with a dumb look on my face. "The ring-a-ling sound. That means, 'Answer me. Answer me.'"

Something was wrong with Nana. She had been quiet for over an hour and was rearranging her prescriptions in the cabinet.

"What's wrong, Nana?"

"I got a card from the drugstore saying I have some photos that need picking up."

"That's no problem. I can pick them up," I offered.

"I've been avoiding picking them up for weeks. Most of them are of Muffy."

Nana loved that cat.

"Every time I think how that precious creature got hit by a car," she continued, "it has me all torn up inside."

"Now you have the kittens."

"They are sweet, but they're not Muffy. She was very special and . . ." She couldn't go on.

"I really am sorry, Nana."

Katie and I drove by Nana's North Hollywood neighborhood on our way to the drugstore.

"Stop the car!" I ordered Katie when I realized what I'd seen. "That was Raymond coming out of Nana's old apartment."

Katie parked the car. I put on some sunglasses and turned around warily.

Raymond got into a white Lincoln and drove away.

"Come on, Katie. I want to see something."

We walked a block and then peered in through the window of Nana's old apartment, which was now obviously Raymond's. The bachelor pad was badly decorated in tattered corduroy and cheap wood veneer. A giant TV took up half the living room, and sports memorabilia and trash took up the rest.

"That sneak stole Nana's apartment," I howled.

"You could easily see the man was no good," Katie said.

"This makes me furious. I'll bet he even had something to do with her getting kicked out." I peered closer. "Hey, wait a second. That's Muffy."

"Who's Muffy?"

"Nana's dead cat."

"Are you sure?"

"I'm positive. You don't see a cat like that very often. And look, there are Muffy's kittens."

"Maybe he liked your grandmother's cat and got one like her," Katie speculated.

"Highly unlikely. Muffy is a rare purebred."

Muffy sat on the windowsill.

"No, it's Muffy. I can tell by her markings. It's Muffy."

When we got back home, Katie joined Nana and me for water that was tea in name only.

"Look at these pictures of Muffy," I said, as Katie looked on, concerned.

"She was a beauty, all right." Nana pet Oreo, who sat on her lap.

"What happened that night, Nana?"

"I asked Raymond over to fix the garbage disposal because that landlord never did a thing. I suppose he left the door open. Muffy was an inside cat, you know."

"Did you actually hear a car hit her?"

"Not really. But then, you know I can't hear very well."

Nana's blue eyes clouded as she told me how Raymond came in and told her it was something she didn't want to see. "He's considerate in that way."

"I'll bet," I replied.

Later I told Katie we had to get Muffy back. "Raymond's going to have to advertise the kittens somehow."

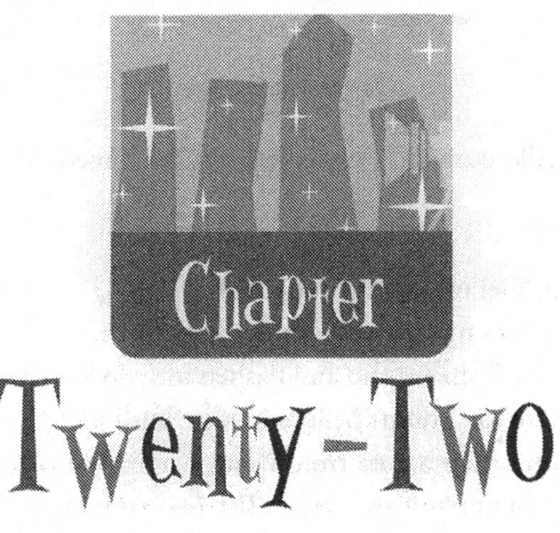

It was on a Monday, a week later, and I was back in my younger, faster, more exciting world again.

Shelby was staring at the psychedelic screensaver on her iMac when I swung open the door to our office.

"Why are you sitting there staring?"

"I was expecting a slew of audition tapes for *Reality Queen* to log in by now, but there isn't even one," she said.

"That's strange."

"I know. I don't get it. Even our lowest-rated show, *The Muffin Hour*, got three hundred audition tapes the first week. And that was to dress up like a walnut and recite the ABCs."

"Where's Trent? I thought he'd be in here whining about his coffee by now."

"He's in a meeting."

"With Dane?"

"No, Dane is trying to negotiate the purchase of some property in Studio City. Trent is with Matt Cirillo, vice president of nothing, who likes to pretend he's Dane."

I felt a hand on my shoulder.

"Mr. Cirillo wants to see you in his office," one of the secretaries said.

"Me?"

"He said, 'Get me Trent's gopher girl.'"

"I guess that's me, then." I clenched my teeth.

"Good luck," Shelby said and flashed me a look of sympathy.

I wanted to say I didn't believe in luck, but I let it go.

I sat in the chair across from Matt, whom I now recognized as the rude man in the suit who said, "*The ring-a-ling sound. That means, 'Answer me. Answer me.'*"

"The situation is this," he said, wasting no time.

"Yes."

He paused, obviously not knowing my name.

"It's Stephy," I said.

"Stephanie," he repeated.

I sat miserably as I waited for him to continue.

"Even a simple error can be costly."

It took me a second. "Are you trying to tell me I made some sort of an error?"

"I call hundreds of tapes delivered to the wrong address an error," he stated.

"What?"

"An hour ago I received a call from the recording studio down the street. It seems the owner got back from vacation to find his secretary had accepted delivery of *our* audition tapes. He was threatening to have them returned to sender until I offered him an appearance on one of our prime-time talk shows."

"I didn't know we had a prime-time talk show."

"Exactly."

"I don't understand."

"The casting notice had the wrong address. You blew it!" he yelled.

I thought for a moment. "Mr. Cirillo, that information was dictated to me."

"Yes, I know. Trent showed me the original. But it was you who transposed the numbers."

I felt a mixture of anger and confusion.

"This is not a big job, Stephanie. You can go down the street and work for a T-shirt shop and make the same pay."

"So you're saying I'm fired."

"That's right."

He picked up his phone, which I guessed meant he wanted me to leave.

I imagined a more temperamental production assistant screaming, knocking over a few plants, and storming off. Instead, I meekly said, "Good-bye," and left.

"Where do I send the flowers?" someone asked as I passed.

Shelby had already heard Trent's inaccurate version of the story. She asked for mine.

"Trent dictated it to me, but I guess I should have known it was the wrong address."

"How could you know? We use more than one address here."

"Trent was in here earlier shredding a yellow sheet of paper," she said, as though it meant something.

I hardly heard her. "I better leave before Trent and I have a confrontation, and then I *will* deserve to be fired."

"Mind if I come see you after I get off work?" Shelby asked.

"Try me on my cell. I'm not sure where I'll be." I shuffled away in a daze.

"Come in," Mark said. His hair looked tousled, like he needed a shower.

I had been driving around for over an hour.

I sniffed the air.

"It's burnt popcorn." He invited me to sit down.

It was my first visit to Jeff's apartment since Mark had moved in. I resisted the urge to pick up the clothes scattered everywhere.

"Where's Jeff?"

"At your place, practicing with the band."

That explained why no one answered at home.

"Do you think they have a chance to make it on that music show?"

He grinned. "About as much chance as a meteor landing on Alvarado Street during a July snowstorm."

After a long pause he asked me if I was on my lunch hour.

"No." I explained.

His dark eyes narrowed. "I would fight it, Mom. You can't let him get away with it."

I was already choked up and weepy over the thought of my future. I changed the subject. "So, do you know a girl named Plum?" I asked, realizing I had failed to mention it before.

"Sure I know Plum. I like her a lot."

That was that.

I didn't have to worry about Mark and girls. As he likes to say, he dates his snowboard in winter and his surfboard the rest of the year.

I was feeding scraps of my uneaten sandwich to the pigeons on the pier, but my body was in another time zone.

I still could not believe I had been fired.

Every time something good happens, something bad happens too.

Shelby appeared out of nowhere.

"How did you know I was here?"

She adjusted her funky glasses. "I called. Remember?"

"Oh, yeah."

"We have a job to do," she said.

"What?"

She pulled me along the pier, all the way to the picnic tables.

It finally dawned on me that she was hauling a plastic bag around with us.

"What are you doing with that bag?"

"We're going to put Trent's note back together again."

They couldn't put Humpty Dumpty back together.

She pulled long pieces of shredded paper from the bag and laid them in a pile.

"There are too many strips, Shelby."

"We can do it!"

Despite my doubt, she started separating the yellow from the white. I reluctantly joined her.

Fifteen minutes later she yelled, "Here it is. All of it. Wrong address and all!"

We did a high-five.

"But wait. How should we handle this?" I asked.

"Let me worry about that after I tape it together." Shelby pulled a roll of tape out of her purse while I stared at the evidence, trying to make a moral decision.

And then a gust of wind raced through, and I helplessly watched my decision blow away. Shelby chased the flying paper around, but I knew it was useless.

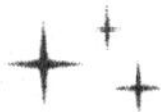

Brock and his band were in the garage practicing when I got home.

He didn't ask about my day. Therefore I didn't share my latest bad news.

Plus I was mad he had cleaned out the garage for his band but wouldn't do it for me.

Nana was humming a happy tune in the kitchen.

I took a shower, ate dinner, watched *American Idol*, and went to bed feeling sorry for myself.

Halfway through breakfast the next morning, Brock looked disturbed. "Aren't you supposed to be working?"

"I was fired," I said matter-of-factly.

"Impossible."

"For a typo I didn't commit."

"What happened?"

"Really, Brock, I don't want to talk about it." But I did, so I told him my sad story.

"That's a bad rap," he said in musician talk.

Nana was watching me intently.

"Did you get all that, Nana?" I didn't feel like having to repeat it.

"Something about a soda jerk, pigeons, and liposuction." She scratched her head.

"Not exactly," I said.

"Say, aren't you going to be late for work, sweetie?"

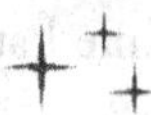

A couple of days later, Shelby called when Nana was rewashing the dishes I had already washed. "You have to apply," she said first thing.

"Apply. Apply where?"

"For *Reality Queen*."

"I was fired, remember?"

"Exactly. That makes you eligible."

"I don't get it."

"It's simple. You're not an employee, so you can apply."

"Apply for my own show?"

"It's not your show. Trent stole it, remember?"

It boiled my blood to remember.

"Look, Steph, I was in on a meeting this morning. Our priorities have shifted with this new show Dane is fast-tracking. An independent firm is going to handle the casting for *Reality Queen*. No one in our office will have anything to do with the selection."

"Would it be honest to apply?"

"Why wouldn't it be? You wouldn't be breaking any rules."

I was deep in thought.

"And you could choose me to be on your team. Choose me please, please, please!"

"Choose me too," someone yelled in the phone.

"Who's that?" I asked.

"It's Plum. She's filling in at the front desk. Claire is having her baby."

"Hi Plum!" I yelled.

"You better make a quick decision," Shelby encouraged. "The deadline is the day after tomorrow."

Chapter Twenty-Three

"Mark said he's coming over with some newfangled equipment," was the first thing Nana said when I walked in the door and kicked my sandals off. "A ranch hoarder or something."

"A camcorder?" I guessed.

"That's it."

I wonder how Mark knew I wanted him to do my audition tape.

"He said Pear called him and you should be—wait. I wrote it down."

She ran over to her note and read her scrawled handwriting. "Then the dweeb could make you complicated coffee drinks."

"I think I get it now, Nana. Thank you."

"That's good, because I sure don't."

After three agonizing minutes of thinking about my audition tape, I told Nana I was going down to see Katie.

Katie had the blinds drawn, so I couldn't tell if she was home. I peeked through a crack in the blinds. I checked the doorknob and walked in with the mail I had picked up from her mailbox.

"Katie, your door is unlocked!" I called. "Katie!"

"Come on up. I'm in my hovel!" she yelled.

The hovel was Katie's working space where she did her writing.

Reaching the top of the plush carpeted steps, I scanned the room and saw that she had redecorated. Something she did regularly.

The mustard-colored room was a hip Internet café, bright and contemporary, with mosaic-tiled floors, and a blinking sign, Katie's Café. The walls were decorated in French posters.

Katie offered me some java from her espresso machine.

"I think I'll just sniff."

"So what do you think about my hovel?" she asked.

"It's cute. I like it better than the rain forest with all those fake bugs on the wall and freaky bird sounds."

"Nana was over here yesterday. You know what she said?" Katie grinned.

"I can't imagine."

"'This isn't one of those feng-shui rooms, I hope.'" Katie laughed. "I told her it was a Russian tearoom—joking of course. And she wanted to make me some hot borscht."

I wrinkled my nose. "What's that?"

"A Russian winter favorite. I had it once in St. Petersburg."

"You world traveler, you!"

"Not lately," she said.

"Speaking of world travel, there's a travel brochure in your mail." I dropped the pile on her coffee-bean-shaped desk, with the brochure on top. "So are you going on that cruise?"

She grabbed the brochure and hid it behind her back.

"Let me see that." I grabbed it from her and did a double take. "A cruise to Cabo Nas Lucas. How fun."

"Cabo San Lucas." She laughed. "It's obviously a misprint."

"Well, OK." I set it down.

"If you must know, Stephy, it's a cruise for dyslexic writers."

"Are you going?"

"I don't know. I drive myself crazy reversing letters all alone. I don't know if I could handle a group of us." Katie crossed her eyes.

"You shouldn't make fun of yourself."

"You have to laugh or cry." She frowned.

"Katie, you're an independent woman. So what if you have dyslexia?"

"Please don't give me the speech about how Fannie Flagg is dyslexic and Leonardo was a dyslexic genius."

I paused. "I didn't know they were."

"Sure. And they speculate that Albert Einstein and Thomas Edison might have been also. Oh, and Cher."

"Cher. How did she get in that group?"

"So you came over to talk about my challenged life?" She sighed.

"No, my own challenged life. I was fired!"

"I already heard that from Mattie and was waiting for you to tell me."

I filled her in on the rest. "So should I apply?"

She looked at her coffeepot clock on the wall.

I rubbed my eyes. "I can't believe I'm considering this. Taking the chance of being humiliated in front of forty million people."

"More like one hundred thousand," she assured me.

Katie looked at the clock again.

"But, then again, the chance of me being picked would be utterly fantastic," I said.

"Stephy, would you think I'm a horrible person if I pulled a Mars on you?"

"What's a Mars?"

"A man's way of dealing with highly emotionally charged subject matters: you're in the middle of spilling your guts, and he pulls the plug on you. It happens sometimes on dates."

That cracked me up. "Please, yes. Pull the plug!"

"I'm sorry. I just think this deserves more than two seconds of thought, and I have a hair appointment."

I secretly hoped she would try to convince me to do the audition tape.

"I'll make a deal with you," she said, as if reading my mind. "If you do your audition tape, I'll go to the writers' conference."

"How about I go on the cruise and you do my audition tape?"

"No way." Katie smiled. "I haven't been on a cruise for a couple of years."

"And I haven't been on a cruise ever."

News travels fast.

There was already a traffic-flow problem in my living room when there was another knock on the door.

I invited Simon in.

"Dandelions." He smiled wide and presented me with weeds.

I fondly remembered making chain necklaces from the stems as a child—blowing the puffballs and watching them dance in the air. When I'd found out they were weeds, I'd cried.

"For tea," he explained. "They'll give you energy and clean out that liver of yours."

"That's what I need, all right." I stood there with the bunch, waiting for him to leave.

We were getting ready to film my audition tape. Jeff was assisting Mark with the lighting equipment, and Nana was telling him his job. Hannah was figuring out my makeup shades. My whole family was at my house, except Brock, the stinker. (He had called me from the music store, asking if I thought it was a "good idea" for him to buy a new guitar.)

This wasn't a good time for extended conversation, and with Simon there was no other kind. However, he seemed intent on staying. I had to say something. "How's that dwarf maple of yours doing, Simon?"

"Very well."

He was craning his neck in the direction of Nana. I finally caught that he wanted to meet her.

Nana wasn't paying any attention to us.

"Come here, Nana." She walked over, gripping her handkerchief.

Mark nodded like a bobblehead doll from across the room, appearing rescued.

"Simon, meet my grandmother, Amanda Witherfall."

"Honored," he said and lowered his silver head in a bow.

"Nice to meet you," she said indifferently.

Now that Raymond was out of the picture, she needed a new friend. And maybe not only a friend. A love match. I was suddenly positive that these two entirely opposite people were meant for each other. Don't ask me how—it was just a gut feeling.

"Nana was a young Rosey the Riveter in her day," I offered.

"Ah, World War II," Simon reminisced.

Was this the beginning of a conversation?

No. It took two to talk, and Nana wasn't talking.

I supposed if Nana had been interested in men, she would have shown it before now. But she'd always said no man could hold a candle to her Walter.

Be charming, I commanded Simon in my mind.

Simon wiped the sweat off his brow.

"You know, Nana, Simon knows most everything about everything—except maybe technology." I laughed.

Nana tried to.

I thought some fascinating, intelligent fact might speed things up. According to legend, my grandfather had been an intelligent man.

"Take that Roman emperor. The one who was single-handedly responsible for changing the calendar." I remembered Simon telling me about this one last week.

A smile spread over Simon's tanned, wrinkled face. "Ah yes, Gaius Octavius, grandnephew of Julius Caesar."

"If Simon says." I chuckled and hoped for more.

Nana yawned.

"Emperor Augustus," he continued, sounding nervous.

"Did you say Augustus?" Nana asked, all of a sudden fascinated.

"That's right."

"Why, Augustus was my grandfather's name . . ."

And off they went to the kitchen. (Nana has this thing about family names.)

Hannah assaulted me with makeup brushes. I looked in the handheld mirror, unsure.

"You need scads more blush than that," she said and flung more powder on my cheeks.

"I was under the illusion that the face I had was fine," I answered meekly.

"Just let me do my job!" Hannah pulled an eyelash curler out of her makeup bag.

A few minutes later Hannah said my hair and makeup were complete. "Mom, don't be disappointed, but I have to go."

I tried not to show my, uh, em, disappointment.

"I have to go too," Jeff said. "Can you give me a lift to my apartment, Porsche?" (Porsche was Jeff's nickname for Hannah. Hannah's nickname for Jeff was Mom Hog.)

"Exude confidence" was Hannah's parting advice.

When the room was quiet, I asked Mark the painful question. "What do you think of Hannah's handiwork?"

"It's great," he said.

I was surprised to hear it.

"If you're looking for the Phyllis Diller effect," he added and furrowed his brows.

"That's what I thought."

"Mom, if you want my advice?"

"I do."

"A lot of these people apply for every show under the sun. They're going to get tapes of people doing all sorts of stunts. Your selling point is that you are pretty normal."

He had a point there.

I dipped a Kleenex in Vaseline and removed the makeup. I fixed my hair the way I usually did for the camera, in a messy bun.

A few minutes later I was settled on the barstool, embarrassed by the clutter in the background. Mark said the disorder would also be a selling point, and I was trying to figure out why.

"Let's do a run-through," he said, bending the camera in position.

I must have looked panicked, because he paused.

"Are you OK, Mom?"

"Just a little nausea, trembling, sweating, dry mouth, dizziness. Everyday side effects of prescription drugs." I laughed tensely.

"You'll be fine. Give me a nice, toothy grin."

I took a breath and dove into my dialogue. "My name is Stephanie Daniels, and I live in Santa Monica with my husband, grandmother, five cats, three birds, and two goldfish," I started. My eyes settled on the goldfish bowl. "Wait, Mark, is that goldfish dead?"

He checked it out. "Yup. Bellied up, eyes bulged. Dead as Dickens's doornail."

"Correction. One goldfish," I said.

Chapter Twenty-Four

"So thanks for holding my hand during my audition tape, Mr. Mars," I said as I got ready for bed.

"Mr. Mars?" Brock asked, confused.

"You figure it out," I replied as he admired his new guitar.

"What do you think of the name Fish out of Water for the band?" he asked.

"Not much. Is there a spiritual significance to it?"

He scratched his head. "Well, maybe not."

I sorta missed his ignoring me from behind his paper. No letters to the editor. No work or sports talk. It was all about making the band.

After thinking a moment, he jumped up. "Better yet, Snapping Turtles."

"If you want to be inducted into the amphibian hall of slime, that might be a good name."

"I was thinking of how the snapping turtle grabs on and won't let go."

"And . . . ," I prompted.

He slumped. "That wouldn't work either, I guess."

"So do you want to see my tape or something?" I asked snottily, as I slipped under the sheets.

"Your tape?"

"The audition tape I made today with my whole family at my side—except you."

There was a pause. "Yeah, sure, I'd like to see it."

"Well, I don't have it," I announced. "Mark has to edit it first."

"So why did you ask, then?"

"Purely for the satisfaction."

He was confused again.

I wasn't being very nice tonight. "You don't think I'll be chosen as the Reality Queen, do you?" I accused.

He hedged. "I don't know."

"You think they'll pick some gorgeous, six-foot blond."

The blank look indicated he wasn't hearing me again. His finger posed in the air confirmed it. "I've got it! Exodus!" he yelled.

"Exodus?"

"For the name of the band."

I rolled my eyes. "That's the name of a band already, Brock. And they've already made their exodus."

"What do you mean?"

"They split up in the nineties."

"Oh. And Genesis is already taken," he said, demoralized.

"What about Lamentations?" I said under my breath.

Since Old Testament times, when the priests blew trumpets of rams' horns and the walls of Jericho came tumbling down, humankind has heeded the call of the trumpeter.

I had no idea who the violator was as I rolled out of bed around nine and put on my old terry robe. I shot out the door and across the wet lawn in my bare feet to the open garage before I was fully awake.

Mystery solved. There stood Simon at the edge of the cement, adjusting the neck strap of his saxophone. I stared at his white Lorenzo Lamas suit. He stared at my rumpled form, then called, "Hey, Nature Girl!" as loudly as though I were a football field away.

"Hey back," I cried weakly.

I noticed the other offenders: Brock on his electric guitar, Jeff on the drums, Jeremy on his keyboards, and Billy on . . . I wasn't completely sure what that instrument was. "What are you making here, guys? Music?"

They all laughed.

"Listen." Brock demonstrated his three-cord musical capabilities.

"You get my vote," I said cutely. "My *sympathy* vote," I muttered under my breath.

Nana showed up with a plate of freshly baked muffins, and I dragged my body back in the house.

A few hours later I had my head stuck in the jam-packed fridge and was deciding on a snack when Mark tapped me on the shoulder. He was trying to tell me something over the band's racket that never quit.

"What?" I asked.

"I won't have your tape until tomorrow," he yelled in my ear. "The editing equipment is giving me fits."

"And they're taking the tapes to Studio City by courier tomorrow," I yelled back.

We jogged down the street so we could hear one another and set up a plan. Mark would meet me in the morning, and I would take the tape.

I suppose it wasn't all that much of a plan.

The next morning, outside the Tenth Street guard gate, Mark passed the tape off as though we were involved in some covert operation. "I'm sorry you didn't get a chance to see it."

"Seeing myself on film is like chewing on shoe leather, as Nana would say."

"Well, you better get used to it, Mom."

I called Shelby on my cell. "I'm down at the gate."

"I'll be right there," she said.

"Here you go!" I turned my audition tape over to her and exhaled.

Despair was written all over her pretty face.

"You said eleven," I said, guessing there was a problem.

She put her hand on my shoulder. "The courier came early. I'm sorry."

I knew it was the van I had seen leaving.

"That is so sad!" she said, feeling my pain.

Until now I hadn't realized how badly I wanted at least a shot at being a producer.

"Why give up so easy? Didn't you say you believe in prayer?" Shelby asked.

"Yes, I believe in prayer." As I said the words aloud to Shelby, I was convicted. Lately I hadn't done much praying. I'd been stuck too far into the whine zone.

"Well then, pray."

I prayed my little heart out.

A second later Shelby's phone rang.

"That was Plum at the front desk. You won't believe it! The courier called. He's heading back because he forgot the directions to the casting company on my desk. That means I can get your tape in with the rest!"

I was waiting on pins and needles—literally.

"Ouch!" I pulled out a pin obviously left behind by Nana in

one of her sewing frenzies. She was sitting next to me, happily reading her cat mystery, a kitten at her feet, another clawing my couch.

I almost didn't care. The waiting was what was getting to me. I absolutely hated waiting. And this was only the first day of waiting. *In a week I'll be a basket case,* I thought. *Waiting, waiting, waiting, waiting, waiting. I am so impatient.*

Katie poked her head in my face. She said she'd been knocking for several minutes and finally had let herself in.

"Sorry. I didn't hear you."

"Pack your overnight bag," she ordered.

"Where are we going?"

"To my house for a pajama party."

"Your house?"

"My other house."

Beyond the iron gates on a scenic hillside, I was standing in Katie's other house, a palatial mansion. *Just like the Taj Mahal in India*, I thought. At least the black and white chessboard marble reminded me of it . . .

When I was nine, I had visited the Taj Mahal. At least that's what I'd told my friend Laura Lane. The truth was, I had been to an Indian restaurant in LA. The lie was borrowed from my father's description of one of the Seven Wonders of the World.

I had impressed Laura. When she asked what my father did for a living, I claimed he was the architect who designed half of Disneyland and impressed her even more.

A couple of weeks passed, and I was invited to Laura's sleepover in a big house in the Hollywood Hills. After we girls were nestled in our sleeping bags and the typical girlish stories had been exhausted, I once again described my Taj Mahal experience.

The next morning my father came to pick me up earlier than expected.

"The Taj Mahal." He laughed as I walked into the front hallway. "I think my daughter's imagination is a flying carpet."

When I saw Laura the following Monday, she tore in to me with the truth. "You've never been to the Taj Mahal, you liar. Your father is a dirty janitor."

"Can we still be friends?" I asked.

"Are you kidding?"

Her sarcastic words rang in my memory . . .

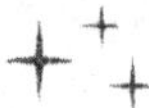

"I'm sorry, Laura, I didn't hear what you said."

"Laura? Who's Laura?" Katie asked.

I blinked. I was back in the present. "I mean, Katie."

She cocked her head toward me. "I was just asking if you wanted to see the grounds or have dinner first."

"Anything else, Madame?"

"No thank you, Alexander," Katie said, as the family's former butler and now trusted property caretaker filled our Evian glasses and left.

"If you're wondering why all the formality, it's for Alexander's sake, not mine. He's comfortable with it."

"When were you here last?" I asked Katie.

"I had a dinner party here a couple of months ago. Remember, I invited you."

"I know. I wasn't hinting or anything." I smiled.

The truth was, some of the company Katie kept intimidated me, and that's why I was conveniently busy when she held her formal dinner parties.

I examined the chandelier, a replica of the one in *Gone with the Wind*, and the formal, antique furniture that darkened the already pompous dining room.

"I'm trying to picture you growing up in this house."

"I can hardly picture it myself anymore." She looked down at the blackened salmon on her plate.

"So it's been nearly twenty years since you lived in this house?"

"That's right. I took an apartment after my parents were carjacked."

"Carjacked? I thought it was a car accident."

Her eyes shone with tears, and she gazed in the opposite direction. "I led you to believe it was a car accident, because my parents' murder was all my fault."

"Of course it wasn't," I said as the news penetrated my consciousness.

"My father made a huge donation to get me in the journalism program at Stanford University because my grades weren't good enough. At the last minute I took a job as a flight attendant for Pan Am instead. My parents died while I was 'gallivanting around the world,' as Daddy put it."

"You don't have to go into it."

"I don't intend to." She sipped her Evian. "Every inch of this place reminds me of that horrible night. That's why I only come here when other people are around."

"If it brings you so much pain, why don't you sell it?"

She didn't speak for a minute. "It's simple. My father set up a fund that takes care of the maintenance of the house and grounds, and I want to honor his wishes."

"I see."

"And at his age Alexander would have trouble finding employment," she rationalized.

"It seems a shame that this beautiful place just sits here looking good."

I waited until she found her voice again. "Maybe I'm not ready to let it go."

"Can I ask you something completely off the subject?"

She leaned forward. "Sure."

"You say your father was a Pulitzer Prize–winning author. Do *you* really want to be a writer?"

Katie looked absolutely terrified by the question, as though she'd never considered it. "It's what my father always wanted for me," she whispered.

I eyed her intensely. "That's not what I asked you, Katie. I asked if it was what *you* wanted."

She squeezed her eyes tight, then opened them slowly. "I'd hate to think that I've given up years of my life for nothing."

"It wouldn't be for nothing. Everything counts for something with God in the picture." I wanted to preach, but Katie did not like to be pushed into anything.

We said nothing for an uncomfortably long time.

"I guess I'll find out on the cruise," she said.

The rest of the evening we enjoyed lighthearted fun.

We spent the night in Katie's old bedroom, talking until around midnight, when, without fair warning, we both dozed off on our white satin pillowcases.

The next morning, after a light breakfast, Katie showed me her idyllic childhood playroom that seemed untouched by time.

"This was my imagination room, where I lived in a castle in a magical forest . . . and dreamed about having brothers and sisters to play with," she recounted sadly.

I understood the loneliness. But for me it had more to do with the loss of my mother, and later my father, than with being an only child.

We stood there and wiggled our toes in the thick shag carpet that looked new. Me in black-and-white-striped toe socks and Katie in her psychedelic, flowered ones.

"I have an idea that is going to blow your socks off!" I said as we were staring down.

She gave me a long, studying look.

"How would you like to play dress up?" I asked, and she winced.

Chapter Twenty-Five

"I feel completely ridiculous," Katie said as she smoothed the layers of her yellow chiffon dress.

"I know, but it's the only way I can think of."

We were standing on the sidewalk outside Raymond's apartment, ready to put my plan into action.

"Wait—why am I dressed up?" It occurred to Katie. "Raymond doesn't even know me."

"Because I don't want to be incognito alone." I smiled and her face pinched.

"Raymond is going to recognize you anyway, Steph."

"In this flowing purple skirt and hat getup?"

"Yes!"

I supposed she was right.

"You better let me do this. I'm feeling brave today," she insisted.

I craned my neck, careful I couldn't be seen as Raymond answered the door.

Consumed with thoughts of vengeance I was casting off to Jesus, I heard Katie's direct opening sentence. "I understand you have a rare Chocolate Point Siamese."

"Where did you hear that?" Raymond's morning voice was craggy. I expected his appearance was the same.

Katie didn't answer his question but proceeded with her own planned script. "I'm willing to pay you one hundred dollars for that cat."

"Are you kidding? The cat is worth five times that much!" Raymond glowered.

I crept a few steps closer, low to the ground and feeling my age.

"I'll pay two hundred," Katie bargained.

"I'm not selling the cat. She's a breeder."

He started to close the door, but Katie's quick foot action muscled her way into his apartment. I fought for a closer look and almost knocked over the neighbor's plant as half a head of a little boy peered out the window.

"I know how you got that cat," she accused.

"It was a stray," he lied. "And I don't know you."

I was appalled at his bogus explanation.

"You got it from the little old lady who lived in this house," Katie stated.

You go girl!

His sentence was inaudible.

I couldn't take it anymore. I wobbled over in my high heels and glared at Raymond in his soiled sweats.

"Who are you—my fairy godmother?" He raised his thick eyebrows.

"Raymond, you stole Nana's cat and you know it!"

"Stephanie?" He blanched.

"Yes, Stephanie, you despicable cat burglar." I glared at him with all the venom I could muster. It wasn't hard.

He groped for an excuse.

"I won't prosecute if you write a formal apology to Nana," I said boldly.

Katie nodded nonstop in agreement.

Muffy ran out of the house and made her home on my feet as Raymond stood stiff and expressionless.

"Write out the apology to Nana!" I ordered.

"Fat chance," he scowled.

I turned to Katie. "I wonder if Raymond here had anything to do with Nana getting kicked out of her apartment."

Within three minutes he was scribbling his admission of guilt.

"And I'll take those kittens as well," I demanded.

Nana was elated to be reunited with her baby.

I was happy for her but still in shock over the addition to my furball collection.

"Muffy, Muffy, Muffy" was all Nana could say for about ten minutes as she gazed at her beloved feline and snuggled her.

When the love fest was over, I showed her Raymond's confession.

She looked more contemplative than sad. "I suppose deep down I always knew there was something wrong with a thirty-two-year-old man who eats Frosted Flakes, plays with a Slinky, and shoots cockroaches with a BB gun."

The phone call came ten long, tired days after the tapes had been couriered to Studio City.

Nearly every waking minute of that time had been spent tending to the kittens and finding them homes (homes that Nana would approve of). In the end my efforts had paid off. Muffy was an only cat.

Nana whispered, "This call is for you, but I can't understand a word this man is saying."

A salesman, I suspected.

"Hello."

"Stephanie. Stephanie Daniels. I hope we didn't catch you too early."

"That depends."

"This is Cody, and I'm representing *Reality Queen*, the television show you applied for. You have been chosen as a prospective candidate."

I wanted to jump out of my skin. "What exactly does that mean?"

"It means that out of twelve hundred audition tapes, you are among thirty semifinalists that we'll be interviewing next week so we can get to know you better."

I took a deep breath.

"The letter coming in the mail will give the details, along with a six-page application for you to complete."

"Six pages?"

"Have you ever been convicted of a crime and such." He laughed.

"And employment history?"

"Hmm," he said, thumbing through the pages. "I don't see it on here."

He ended our conversation saying that I should tell no one but close family members.

"And my best friend?"

"Well, OK. Your best friend."

After I hung up, I fantasized about what to wear. And then I sprinted for the garage where Brock was living these days and calmly asked him to meet me in the house.

"I may be the next Reality Queen!" I said in the entryway as we held hands.

Brock looked like he might faint.

Then I felt suddenly sick to my stomach. What had I gotten myself into?

"A roller-coaster ride" would be the best way to describe my experience from the time I received the call to the time I was escorted to the cozy, private room in the back of the waterside hotel seven days later.

It was a good thing that Shelby was on vacation, or I might have been tempted to blab my good news (I had already used my best-friend token on Katie).

The finalist letter had arrived the day after the phone call and contained not only an application, but a slew of paperwork, including an Interview Confidentiality Agreement, Authorization for Release of Medical Information, Background Investigation Questionnaire, and other paperwork—all very intimidating and nosy.

Too late for second thoughts now, I thought as I reached the room for my interview.

"Stephanie, you're right on time," a smiling blond announced.

She and I shook hands as I tried to maintain the proper amount of eye contact. I told her she could call me Stephy.

I noticed a man I didn't know and sighed in relief. In the back of my mind I had expected Trent to pop out from behind the door, yelling, "BOO!"

"It's nice to meet you," I said and sat down daintily.

"I'm Annie, the casting director with Reality TV Casting. We are assisting the Home Living Channel in their casting, obviously. And this gentleman is one of the sponsors interested in the show. He'll be listening in on our conversation." She didn't give his name or his affiliation.

"Nice to meet you," I said.

He nodded from across the table.

"Can I get you something?" Annie asked.

I noted the half-eaten appetizers. "No, thank you."

"As you can tell, you are not our first interview today," Annie added.

I smiled nervously.

"Stephy, I want to let you know I will be taping our conversation, strictly for the record."

"That's fine," I managed.

"May I have your application packet?"

I pulled it from my big purse and handed it to her.

"Thank you."

"You're welcome."

"Normally the audition process would take weeks, but we're going to hurry it along. Today we are narrowing the group to five finalists. Do you mind if I get right to it?"

"Not at all." I liked this straightforward blond.

"Can you tell me about yourself?"

I hedged. "Such as?"

"Let's start with your marriage."

Her silent partner put at least five packets of sugar in his coffee during our interview. But when it was over, I felt good about the questions and my answers.

"Stephy, I like you," Annie said kindly. "You have a refreshing quality about you that I think the producer is going to appreciate."

"Thank you."

"You should be receiving a phone call anytime. It will either be the end of the road, or hopefully, you'll come in for a final interview at the Home Living Channel."

I swallowed hard. "There is one thing I'd like to mention."

"I'm sure whatever it is, it can be handled. If I were you, I'd hold on to it for now."

"OK," I replied hesitantly.

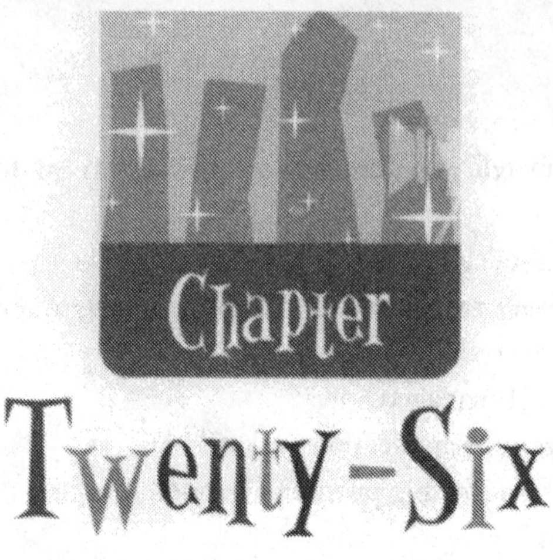

Chapter Twenty-Six

On occasion, when I'm under an enormous amount of stress, I like to have a Yum Yum donut. This was one such occasion.

I rushed out the door with my hair stuffed in a high ponytail, caught my breath at the counter, and ordered a jelly donut. To my disappointment, it ended up being a plain cake donut.

I was seated in the driver's seat with my window down when I discovered the mistake. The officer getting out of his car greeted me.

"They messed up my order," I whined.

He nodded in sympathy, then gave me a ticket for my expired registration tag before he patronized the establishment.

That's when the call came. It was Annie. "The producer wants to see you in an hour. Can you make it?"

A bee buzzed in through the open window, and I frantically ushered it out as I spoke. "Of course."

"Do you know where the Home Living Channel is located?"

"Yes, but I wanted to talk to you about a couple of things."

"Save it for Dane Brodie, the executive producer. From here on out, he's taking over. How does that sound?"

"Scary."

"It won't be."

"Will you be there, Annie?"

"I'm afraid not. But it was nice meeting you, Stephy."

"You too."

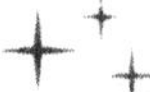

I was waved into the studio grounds by the busy guard, who recognized me.

I called the office on my cell and asked—in a slightly disguised voice, since I wasn't sure if it was Plum I was talking to—if Shelby was back from vacation.

One minute after I told Shelby what was going on, she whisked out the door and joined me in the parking lot. We sat in the front seat of my Volvo.

"I have so much to tell you," she said, out of breath.

"This all seems so deceptive. I'm going to march in there and disqualify myself!" I cried.

"It's too late. They're meeting with finalist number three now." Shelby filled me in on the details. "I don't think Dane is impressed with any of them so far. They are . . . amateurish."

"I should leave right now. There is no way they're choosing me. The fact that I was fired alone is—"

"That's what I wanted to tell you, Steph. Trent is in the doghouse because of it."

She put her hand on my arm.

"You said something to Dane?"

"I didn't have to. Even without knowing the circumstances, he blamed Trent. He told him that ultimately he was accountable and should have taken responsibility. He has him working on a boring documentary, and he's going to lose his office to the Reality Queen." She laughed.

I shook my head in apprehension.

"And not only that," she whispered.

My head was spinning. "What?"

"Matt Cirillo not only fired you. The very next day he fired an old guy in accounting over something insignificant. Well, the old guy happens to be a friend of the Brodie family. Dane rehired him the next day and sent Matt packing."

"This does put a different perspective on things." I shook my head in wonder.

"I'm going back in to listen since the door is wide open." Shelby tore away.

Fifteen nerve-racking minutes later she was in my car again. "Number three walked out the side door bawling. They're meeting with number four now. They just finished watching the tape, and it's not that great."

"Like, how not that great?"

"She shot it at a firehouse with laundry drying on the clothesline and sang 'Rescue Me.' That's not what Dane is looking for."

"So should I come in now?"

"Yeah, come in. I have to go back to my office. If I can, I'll give you an update. Some girl I don't know is attending the front desk."

Shelby never made it back. I sat in the lobby with my knees knocking wildly, regretting my casual outfit and going through all sorts of scenarios in my brain.

Finally, Susie, the casting director, appeared in the same dress she had worn the day of the open auditions. "My, you've been busy," she said in her crisp, British accent. "Honestly, I was gobsmacked when I saw your face on that screen."

"Is gobsmacked a bad thing, Susie?"

"Not a bit," she reassured me. She held my hand and pulled me into the conference area. "Take a couple of deep breaths."

I stood there, consciously maintaining my equilibrium as I was being stared at by a room full of unfamiliar faces, except Dane and Susie.

It was at least three long seconds before Dane stood up and joined me. "Congratulations, Stephy. You have been selected as the Reality Queen!"

I felt my knees wanting to bend.

"And by the way, I never would have fired you," he whispered. "Even if my bagel hadn't been toasted to perfection."

I was so relieved it was over . . . or beginning . . . that all I could do was laugh.

"You'll meet with the press at two o'clock tomorrow," he informed me.

I hardly remember the rest. Mostly I met a lot of people whose names and titles I will never remember and smiled so much it hurt.

After sharing a Twix bar with Shelby and Plum in celebration, I was anxious to get home and share the good news with my loved ones in person.

Unable to fight the strong temptation, I stepped into Trent's office as I was leaving. He was staring into space.

"Not what you expected, eh," I said, pleased.

"Do you mind a suggestion?" He turned toward me.

"I'm not sure," I answered, suspiciously.

"Some beauty sleep."

I refused to allow him to ruin my Cinderella moment.

The sidewalk outside my home was full of neighbors I had never had the occasion to meet, except when our mail ended up in the wrong box. They followed me into my garage, where balloons and streamers had been taped on the walls and rafters.

A sea of familiar faces was gathered. "Surprise!" they yelled in union.

I caught on that a party was being held in my honor. "What, no parade?"

That joke flopped.

"I better talk to my writers about that one," I tried.

That one flopped too.

"Have a good time!" I yelled, and that set the party in full swing.

Brock was the one I wanted to see.

He hugged me. "Congratulations, baby. I'm proud of you!"

I was incredibly happy to hear it, though I hadn't known how he had found out about it.

We kissed.

"Stay there," he ordered.

What—diamonds, pearls, a piece of licorice?

"I composed a song for you."

"A song," I said warily, managing a half smile.

He galloped off to the far corner of the garage, where the band was waiting. "This is a song I wrote for my wife," he said over the mike and started screeching, "Baby, baby, you're the best in the world!"

I smiled for his benefit as Katie hugged me long and sweet. "Hey, who's the guy in the ball cap?" I asked over my supposed love song.

"Titus, the butcher at Safeway."

"Oh sure, I know him. He's cute, Katie." I wiggled my eyebrows.

"It would never work," she said.

"Why, is he married?"

"No, his last name is Tzitzilis."

I looked at her. "What? Not delicate sounding enough for you?"

"I'd never be able to spell it," she said.

"Neither would I."

"Now, if you meet a cute actor with the last name Bob, let me know." Katie grinned.

"There are lots of Billy Bobs in the business. But somehow I picture hideous teeth and a rusty shotgun."

"I have no aspirations to be married, really."

"Neither did Simon. But look at him over there looking smitten . . ." I peered more closely. "And scratching away."

"He is scratching, isn't he?" Katie observed.

"He's allergic to cats," I confided. "But he hasn't let that keep him away from Nana."

Chapter Twenty-Seven

I was wondering where my children were, until Hannah came up and touched my face. "Hey, what happened to my beautiful makeup job?"

Mark came up from behind and kissed my cheek before I could answer. "The way you had her fixed up, she belonged in a horror movie," he told Hannah in his sweet, brotherly way.

"Well, you would know." Hannah stomped away.

I touched Mark's face. "Thank you for all the work you did on my audition tape. They were obviously impressed with it. I think the goldfish sequence helped."

"Ah, go on."

We listened to the band for a moment.

"So do you think they've improved any?" I ventured.

"They've moved from a meteor dropping in a snowstorm to Wal Mart taking over Saks Fifth Avenue." Mark laughed.

We smiled.

"Anyway, Mom, I have to get home to work on my school project. While there's some peace and quiet in my apartment."

"What do you mean?"

"I mean your baby boy is driving me crazy with his twenty-four-seven drumming. I may move back home."

I hoped he didn't mean it.

A tall man interrupted us to shake my hand. "Hi, I'm your attorney neighbor, Gerald Long. I have this great idea for a Reality TV show."

Go figure. I made my best attempt at withering body language.

"You take twelve attorneys, a judge . . . ," he yelled above the music.

And put them in a padded room, I joked to myself.

After innumerable verses of "Baby, baby, you're the best in the world!" the band took a break, but the lawyer wouldn't leave . . . until I asked him what he knew about landlord-tenant law.

Soon there was a line gathered to speak with me. Mostly everyone had this great idea they hoped I would pass off to Reality TV icon Mark Burnett, if I happened to run into him in the halls where he didn't work. This began to irritate me, particularly when my friends who had only loved me for my children became suddenly interested in me again.

I had Hannah put out a suggestion box for Reality TV ideas, and when they started in, I pointed to the box.

After that, some people left, and only my true friends stayed: all two of them. And then Katie left, and there was only Simon and my family.

"Things are going to change, Hollywood Girl," he said.

I was sure he was right.

They say everyone has her fifteen minutes of fame. As Dane showed me to the podium where the press conference would take place, I wondered if this was mine.

We were in the same room at the hotel where we had held the open auditions. Microphones were attached to the podium; journalists were standing at attention.

"Just be yourself," Dane said, reassuring me.

The whole thing was surreal.

"Good afternoon, ladies and gentlemen. I would like to welcome you to our press conference and introduce you to the Home Living Channel's new star of *Reality Queen*, Stephanie Daniels, who wishes to be addressed as Stephy."

A woman quickly powdered my face, and Dane moved to the side.

"Thank you for coming," I said, nervous but determined.

"Could you please give us your definition of a housewife?" The first question came from a pint-sized journalist.

Dane was smiling at me, and I felt somewhat Bill Gatesish.

"Superwoman in an apron," I teased.

"What makes you think that a housewife can produce a Reality TV show?"

At first I wanted to say something dramatic—like if a woman can fly to the moon, why not produce a Reality TV show? Instead, I asked, "What makes you think she can't?" Dane looked satisfied.

"Mrs. Daniels, two questions."

What if I forget the second one?

"With respect to Reality TV, what do you think of some of these edgy shows that are gaining popularity?"

"Not much. We're aiming for respectable Reality TV, and I think our executive producer would agree."

Dane stepped up to the podium and confirmed my position.

The reporter was the one to forget the second question.

There were a few more tame questions, like: "What are you thinking of this very moment?"

"That I wore the wrong shoes," I joked and laughed.

Everyone laughed.

"What are you going to do next?" This guy's hair was slicked back in a ponytail.

"Head to Disneyland." I chuckled.

"Really?" he asked.

"Absolutely, not really. I love you, Mickey Mouse, but I'm afraid with three children finally grown, I'd opt for the opera."

Dane stood up to the podium. "Thank you all for coming."

And that was the end of my fifteen minutes of fame.

We sat down in our cushy velvet seats and I opened the program.

BIOLA OPERA THEATRE

presents

Hansel and Gretel

It was fantastically amusing. Little did I know that when I said I preferred the opera to Disneyland, I'd be attending the festivity with my opera-hating husband a few hours later, courtesy of the journalist who had posed the question.

Even though my daughter attended this university, I didn't even know they had an opera department.

"It's too bad Hannah couldn't come," I commented.

"I'd rather her than me," Brock said under his breath, but I heard him.

"I think it will be nice to have some culture for a change."

His eyes opened wide. "*Hansel and Gretel* is culture?"

"So it's not the Sydney Opera House."

"Couldn't you have said you wanted to see a hockey game or the Los Angeles Lakers?" Brock whined.

We sat silent for a minute, watching the seats fill up. I waited for him to notice how beautiful I looked in my black velvet dress . . . he didn't.

Pouting was useless. I ought to know after twenty-two years

of marriage. So I gave up and examined my surroundings with my binoculars. At least I finally had an occasion for which I could wear the black dress.

"So there aren't going to be sugarplum fairies dancing on the stage and all that, right?" Brock pleaded.

"You're joking, I hope," I said as I watched a couple of Hannah's friends getting ready to play in the orchestra pit.

"You ever notice that a lot of opera houses catch fire?" Brock noted.

I turned to him and thought how handsome he looked. "You know, you're right about that. There was the Vienna Opera House and the New York City Metropolitan . . ." Suddenly I wondered why.

"You ever notice how fires rarely happen at sporting events?" He slowly raised his eyebrows.

This was unbelievable. I was moving into Trent's office. There went the back of his curly head, a box in his arms.

"Stephy, I want you to meet Dora Michaels, our legal counsel," Dane said.

Because I had baby-sat our three-year-old neighbor on occasion, I couldn't help but sing the *Dora the Explorer* theme song in my head.

"Nice to meet you," I replied, inwardly telling myself to behave.

After I was happily sipping on my cappuccino, Dora informed me there were a few documents to sign.

I straightened up in my comfortable, upholstered chair at the side table.

"Article one of your contract . . . ," she began.

We were ten minutes into her explanation, and she was losing me.

The letters were reversing on the page. I couldn't even read the smaller print with my bad eyes. For the first time I had an idea what Katie went through on a daily basis.

Dora skipped over something about the camera crew inside my

home. When I asked her about it, she said, "Oh, it's nothing."

I didn't believe her, but I wanted all the paperwork over with.

As time went on, I wondered if I should have Johnny Peacock review the contract.

I could be signing for lobotomy surgery for all I know.

"Now sign here," she said, handing me a shiny pen. "And keep the pen."

Is this what they call under duress?

I signed anyway.

Later that afternoon I was trying to figure out what to do next when Dane popped his head in and introduced my personal assistant, Veronica Strange. She was about twenty-nine, suave, sleek, and not smiling.

"Veronica is the brains of this operation," Dane said casually. "She'll go over the rest with you."

"I won't disappoint you, Dane," I heard myself say as he walked out the door. I glanced at the time. "Five o'clock already." I grabbed my purse.

"Are you leaving?" my new personal assistant asked.

She seemed surprised, but I left anyway, convincing myself that my family was still my top priority.

"Thanks for giving us all that attention today," Plum told me in the parking lot.

"I couldn't help it!" I protested. "They whisked me away as soon as I walked in the door."

Shelby walked up, swinging her purse around. "Yeah, thanks a lot. I love sharing my hole in the wall with that moron."

"Wait, Shelby! Yesterday you were enthralled with the idea of me being chosen for *Reality Queen*."

"And you were going to pick us for your staff!" she said, her voice like a dagger with eyes to match.

"We haven't gotten that far yet," I tried to explain.

"I get it." Shelby jumped all over me. "We're, like, your last priority," she added, adjusting her glasses.

She and Plum started walking away.

"You guys," I pleaded, "don't walk away from me when I'm talking to you."

"She's already ordering us around," Plum said, flinging her long, blond hair in the air.

"We're going out," Shelby stated.

"Can I come with?" I begged.

"What's this 'come with'?" Shelby asked, annoyed.

She was right. It did sound young. I tried again. "Do you prefer King James language from an old lady like me? 'Come hither' or something?"

I got eye rolls from both, and they walked away.

I looked down at the abandoned expanse of asphalt. It was like being on my own planet. When I was little, I always wanted my own planet. But now it felt really, really lonely.

Chapter Twenty-Eight

The phone call had come at seven the previous night.

As Dora plainly put it, Article Seven of my five-inch contract called for public appearances on demand . . . all in my best interest, of course.

My fear of public speaking escalated on hearing that Charlie Deanna was going to be interviewing me on her show, *Which Way Is Up?*

Charlie Deanna was a chew-you-up and spit-you-out kinda talk-show host, not like those nice people Dane handpicked for the press conference who thought I was so cute and perky and didn't mind ten-second pauses.

Rumor had it that it was not unusual for Charlie's guests to run out of the studio crying, "I want my mommy!"

She was a feminist with harsh political views. A direct quote of hers was: "Bush should be taken out and shot." (Or maybe that was Al Franken's quote?) Either way, I knew for sure she had this thing against housewives. Phrases like "male oppression" and "gender antagonism" peppered her interviews.

So, needless to say, I was shaking as I sat in the studio green room (it was actually blue) at nine the next morning.

The limo ride had been fun. The last time I'd ridden in a limo had been the night of my junior prom with Todd Raven, a nerdy senior who wore running shoes with his father's borrowed tux. The limo ride had been fun then too. It had started out as a magical evening. I was part of the 1978 Homecoming Court and was floating down the beautiful, winding staircase at the Crown Plaza Hotel when I tripped and pushed the sophomore princess in front of me. She fell and then—you guessed it—the domino effect took over.

The production coordinator peered in and said I'd be on in fifteen minutes.

A guy the size of John Wayne, wearing a broad hat and cowboy boots, looked fleetingly in my direction.

"Aren't you Doug Kozak?" I asked, my voice mouselike.

"That's right," he replied and went on reading his newspaper.

"You're one of my husband's favorite guitarists."

"That's real nice," he said and smiled, maintaining eye contact with his paper.

"He's a musician too," I ventured.

He nodded. I'll bet he heard that all the time.

"I love the way you put Christian words to Beatles tunes. I'll bet you reach a bigger audience that way."

"Uh huh." He took a sip of his coffee.

"And the work you do with the Literacy Volunteers of America is awesome."

"Yeah, it's a great charity."

Another nod from Doug.

"I hope they don't expect me to ask to take my picture with Charlie." I was talking to myself.

Later as we waited in the nondescript hallway, Doug was about as talkative.

"Where are the rest of the guests?" I asked the production coordinator, hoping they would help carry the show.

"You two are it," she replied as she sped away.

I looked at Doug. "Two Christians on one show?"

"It must be providence," he said.

The human nervous system consists of billions of nerve cells. All of mine were jumping.

The next thing I knew I was a rigid column on an uncomfortable couch, trying to listen to a woman dressed in a red turtleneck and blazer, with a Snidely Whiplash grin.

This was no carpool mom. I began to tremble. I hardly heard her introduction.

"Putting together a Reality TV show in a time crunch doesn't sound like an easy task," she began.

"No," I said, only now realizing we were on the air.

She stared at me, anticipating more.

"No, it's not," I elaborated.

"Don't you think it's a rather ambitious project for a housewife?"

"Uh, yes." *Is that all you can say?* I asked myself.

"Yes, what?"

"I don't agree."

She pursed her lips. "Don't agree with what?"

Frankly, I had no idea. "Mm-mm" was all I could manage. *Oh, boy, this is going real well.*

She plastered a fake smile at the camera. "Let's take a short commercial break, then continue our stimulating talk with Stephanie Daniels, housewife extraordinaire. Later in the show we have musician Doug Kozak." The light went red, and she flung me a look as thick as mud. "I'll be right back," she told the production assistant.

I gave a humongous sigh and closed my eyes, trying to picture wildflowers. When I opened them, Doug was sitting next to me, taking up half the stiff-leather couch.

"So you don't do this very often, do you?" he asked kindly.

"Often? Try never." I wiped a tiny tear.

"She doesn't seem to like you."

"Funny, I got that impression too." I exhaled.

"Mind if I pray for you?" he asked gently.

I shook my head in agreement.

His calloused fingers touched my hand, and he began to pray. An amazing feeling of calm assurance came over me as he finished.

"You gonna be OK?" He squeezed my hand.

I blinked, overcome with thankfulness. Doug was really a humble guy. Not nearly as scary as he'd looked to me as we'd waited together.

"I'll be fine." I took a deep breath.

"I'm sorry if I ignored you earlier, but I'm a nocturnal kind of guy," he explained. "I need some major coffee just to get up in the morning." He grinned.

"It's OK," I assured him.

He told me an Adam and Eve joke that made me laugh so loud I snorted. I had only a moment to collect myself before Charlie rushed to her seat. Then the green light went on again.

"So, Stephy, you're an average housewife producing a show. Isn't that a bit like Hilary Duff taking over Oprah's job?"

I had sudden, unshakable confidence. "The Home Living Channel has faith in me."

"The Home Living Channel is not exactly CBS," Charlie said snottily.

I wanted to say, "and you're not Oprah," but I didn't.

"So are you hoping for some national interest?" she prodded.

"I'm hoping to do a good show."

She turned up the heat. "What is it like to get out of your cage?"

"Define cage?"

"Your humble abode." She smirked for the camera.

What does she do with all that nasty energy when she goes home at night?

"Women need more than laundry and love, don't you agree?" Charlie threw in.

"Being a housewife is more—," I began to respond.

She cut me off. "Drudgery can get old, don't you agree?"

"Drudgery?"

"The ol' housewife routine obviously got old for you, or you wouldn't have applied for the show," she said bluntly.

"Housewives are not scullery maids, Charlie," I insisted. "We are flesh-and-blood human beings who desire to have a part in the lives of the people we cherish."

And on the debate went.

When I stepped off the stage, I felt as though I'd been in a wrestling match.

Doug was strapping on his guitar. He handed me a guitar pick. "You done good, Stephy. If you ever need anything, you let me know."

Right now what I needed was an hour of prayer to calm down and find my focus again. I had to settle for a few minutes on my limo ride to the office.

Once I got there, I received another cold greeting from my coworkers, Plum and Shelby, which was so unfair.

After going through some messages and papers on my desk, I glanced at the time. It was already after five o'clock. As I got up to leave, Veronica made that same, "You're not leaving, are you?" comment.

"Actually, I was," I said.

"Stephy, you don't seem to realize you have a show to put together on a very tight schedule."

She was right, you know.

Maybe Charlie was right too. Would I be better as a scullery maid?

"Since you'll be working late, can I order you something in? A salad perhaps?" Veronica recommended.

"I was thinking more like a Tommy's burger and fries. Some high-calorie comfort food to help me deal with the stress." I rubbed my tired eyes.

She tried to pacify me. "We'll add some croutons. How's that?"

Chapter Twenty-Nine

Can a person get chronic fatigue syndrome overnight? I was sure I had it. The physical exhaustion was bad, but the emotional exhaustion was indescribably more draining than anything I had known.

"Honey, will you get me the newspaper since you're already up?" Brock asked, still flat in bed.

I was happy to. Maybe Brock had given up his bad idea of being an aged music idol.

"There's an article in the *Times* on WGS," he added.

"What is WGS?"

"Worldwide Guitar Seminars."

That figured.

Stepping into the kitchen, I gave the disorderly counter a dirty look and plugged in the coffee maker. I stood there until I heard that reassuring percolating sound: *blurp, blurp, blurp.*

Mechanically, I turned on the radio.

"Today we will be discussing fungal infection of the toenail."

Who wants to hear about fungus at six in the morning—or six at night, for that matter? Obviously, Nana's station.

I turned off the radio and said hello to the birds.

"I'm a chicken," Herbert the conure said.

"So am I," I told the bird.

"Honey, the newspaper!" Brock yelled from the bedroom.

"I know. Hold on to your guitar," I called back as I stepped into the front hallway and stood in front of the mirror. "You look like a bag lady," I told my reflection.

After adjusting my old robe, I opened the door and stood, bewildered, on my front porch steps.

People ran toward me. Cameras and microphones were thrust my way.

"So how do you feel about being the new Reality Queen?" a blurry form asked.

Would this be reporters swarming me, or do I need glasses?

"Stephy, what does your husband think about all this?" another voice asked.

"Brock, Brock," I called inside, but to no avail. All those badges and phony smiles weren't going anywhere. "Why all the attention?" I uttered.

"This is a national story, Stephy," a reporter said.

"What's a national story?" I blurted.

"You!" he said, shoving his mike in my face.

Cameras clicked away.

I pictured my unflattering photograph on the front page of all of Brock's newspapers. Why couldn't I look like Katie Couric in the morning?

"Honestly, I just came out to get the newspaper," I said, shaken.

"So, is this how you really are in the morning, or is this a put-on?" another voice shouted.

That's when I slammed the door, bolted the lock, and had a minimeltdown.

I'm guessing it was at least five minutes later that Brock trotted down the hallway as my iPod hummed a tune.

He stared annoyingly. "Where's my newspaper?"

I stared, annoyed. "Take that thing off!" I ripped the tiny head off his ear.

"What did I do?" he complained

He honestly had no idea.

"Brock, a few minutes ago at least nine reporters accosted me on our front yard. We're probably going to have to resod the lawn. They were trampling all over it."

"You were dreaming," he said, eyeing me carefully. "You've been through a great deal of stress."

"Look for yourself!" I pointed toward the window.

He peered out toward the front yard.

"Are the news vans still out there?" I asked.

"No, just my newspaper."

I exhaled in frustration. It took my showing Brock the footprints and his trampled newspaper before he actually believed my true story.

"Well, you wanted celebrity status," he stated.

"I never said I wanted celebrity status," I said assuredly.

A few minutes later Brock was in the shower and I was still in my robe, trying to regroup, when there was another knock on the door.

I opened it, reluctantly, to find a woman standing there. I didn't give her a chance to say a word before I ordered her away.

"*No comprendo*," she said.

It was then it occurred to me that most reporters don't go around wearing black-and-white uniforms.

"Who are you with?" I demanded.

She looked at her card and smiled insecurely. "The Good Help Agency," she said carefully.

The maid, I deduced. (I had forgotten a live-in maid was one of the perks of the show.)

"You Reality Queen?" She continued to smile.

I nodded yes.

"I Lupe."

"Hi, Lupe. Come in." I directed her to the kitchen and told her I'd be with her "*un momento.*"

On my way to the bedroom, Nana appeared in sponge curlers. "Who was that at the door?"

My cell rang.

"Yes."

"Stephy. They're looking for you," Veronica said.

"I'm on my way," I replied, suspecting the "they" was really her.

I sat at my new, shiny, mahogany desk, disbelieving my circumstance once again.

Trent was evidently disbelieving his circumstance also. He stood in my doorway, looking less like the villain and more like a little boy longing to play in a neighbor's sandbox.

"Trent, if you're going to stand there staring, why don't you get our Stephy a coffee drink?"

It was Veronica's request, but he glared at me.

In my mind I ordered a triple-shot, high-foam, extra-hot, sugar-free, vanilla-caramel macchiato . . . in the name of sweet revenge.

That was in my mind. I couldn't do it. Not even to Trent Powers.

"A single, no-flavor latte, please," I told Trent as he eyed me suspiciously.

Veronica and I were discussing the budget when a woman strolled into my office, asked me to stand up, and started taking my measurements, as though it were a perfectly normal part of executive life.

"Did you call Ann Taylor, or did I?" I asked Veronica.

"This is Corrine, your image consultant."

The pale redhead stepped back and appraised me. "I'm here to make you look good. You can ignore me."

She looked pretty good herself. Flawless, like a porcelain doll.

It was a little hard to ignore, what with being maneuvered like a mannequin. And when Jack, the cameraman, stepped in and started filming me, Veronica said to ignore him too.

As I tried to appear natural, it was hard to stay focused on Veronica's complex explanations of TV production.

"Are you catching all this?" she asked.

"Go on, go on." I smiled at the camera.

When Jack left with his camera, I took a deep breath and realized I hadn't absorbed any knowledge whatsoever.

Veronica continued on anyway as I rapped my fingers on the desk. "Can I ask you something, Veronica?"

"What?"

"What have you been saying the last hour?"

"That's cute," she said.

"Can we take a little break?" I begged.

There was a gap in time as I sat, entirely dysfunctional.

"This may be a good time for your massage," Veronica suggested.

My acquaintance with massage up to this point was the shiatsu chair at my local department store.

"Dane has arranged for you to have thirty minutes a day with his masseuse," Veronica explained.

Poor King Nebuchadnezzar had to eat grass for seven years to regain his sanity. For me, it only took five minutes of Ajaye's massage.

I was immersed in another world when Veronica shook me. "We need to get back to work."

"I'll be right there," I told her, hoping to manage a few more minutes of bliss.

"I think we should go NOW!" she said authoritatively.

"Veronica, I think I'm the boss here."

She smiled. "Yeah, but you have no clue what you're doing." She gave me a long, scrutinizing look.

That was true. How could I argue?

"I'll be there in a minute," I said from the table as Ajaye ignored our conversation.

As I stepped out of the trailer, I felt marvelously refreshed to face the rest of the day.

At that precise moment I noted a familiar but unanticipated sight—Raymond's Grinch-like form on the other side of the studio gate. He was at the catering truck, talking to the owner in an animated, cartoon-character-like fashion.

Brimming with curiosity, I passed through the gate and edged toward the truck, where I heard Raymond going on about the refuse containers. I had this stabbing hunch that something was up.

Raymond was so involved in his conversation he wouldn't have noticed a siren. I hid on the other side of the trailer, eavesdropping.

"Improper refrigeration and rusted canned goods as well," he claimed.

"I can take care of those easily enough," the owner said.

"Let's see. Cockroaches, flies, rats . . . ," Raymond began.

"What are you talking about?" The owner's voice got louder.

"You know what I'm talking about. And I think I can come up with a few more dirty little secrets."

"You mean *make up*," the owner emphasized.

I couldn't believe what I was hearing. What Raymond had done to Nana was unconscionable. But this was even lower than I expected of the snake.

"So, are we still operating under the same arrangement?" Raymond asked.

"Blackmail, you mean?" the owner said angrily.

"It doesn't take much for people to lose their appetite, you know."

I inched closer.

Raymond pulled a plastic bag out of his pocket and waved it

around. "A few rat droppings would cause quite a stir with your lunch crowd over there."

Yuk!

I walked to the front of the catering truck and stood in line. When I got up to the window, I tried to tell the busy woman I needed to talk to her about something important. But since she didn't speak English fluently, and a long line of people was waiting impatiently, I left.

Not knowing what else to do, I barged into Shelby's office (after ensuring Trent wasn't around) and began sharing my shocking discovery.

"So what do you want from me?" Shelby snipped. "I don't eat off the roach coach."

"I don't know why you're mad at me." I meant it. "You're going to be part of my team, I promise."

She looked away.

"I can't handle you being mad at me!" I cried.

She looked at me, softened. "You mean that, don't you?"

"Yes, I do."

"I'm sorry, Steph. Trent said you'd turned into a diva, and I guess I believed him."

"You believed Trent?"

She hung her head. "Sorry. Forgive me?"

"Forgiven. And will you please tell Plum I'm still the same?"

"I will, but she's pretty mad at you for demanding she make your coffee drink."

"Trent!" I bellowed.

The sound of the name lingered, like fingernails on chalkboard.

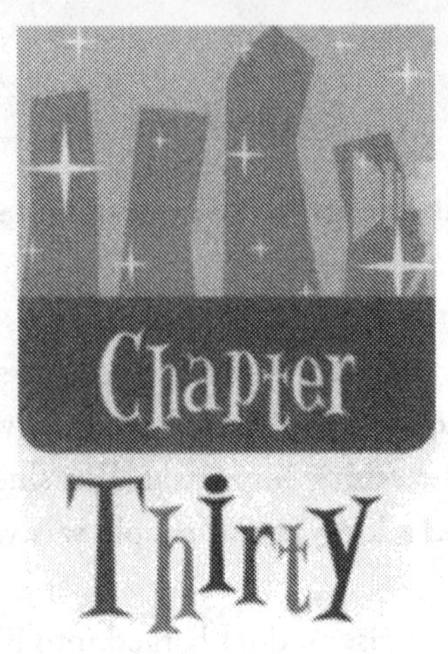

Chapter Thirty

It was three o'clock. I was famished and slightly cranky when the girl with the bad bangs delivered our takeout orders to my office.

Veronica set a salad in front of me.

"I didn't order that"—I pointed—"I ordered a roast beef sandwich, extra mayo."

"Weight control," Veronica said, tossing me a package of whole-wheat crackers.

"Weight control?" I gasped.

"Strictly for image," she said and bit into her appetizing sandwich.

"Is size six considered overweight?" I asked, stunned.

She swallowed and gave me a funny look.

"OK, size eight," I admitted.

"Corrine had a few suggestions," Veronica said.

"Corrine, my image consultant?"

She nodded. "She's a graduate of the London Image Institute, you know."

I was impressed.

"In Atlanta," she added.

The London Image Institute in Atlanta? An oxymoron, to be sure.

"I didn't realize we were filming the *Swan* here," I said.

"It's in your contract." She took a massive bite of her sandwich.

I erupted. "I gave you guys permission to put me on a diet?"

"We need to keep up with current trends," she said, "and the current trend continues to be 'thin is in.'"

"Foot-binding was the current trend in China in the thirteenth century. That doesn't mean it was a good thing."

"Tenth century," she corrected and took a sip of soda.

Resigned, I bit into my salad.

Veronica was staring at my hair. "What kind of shampoo do you use?"

"Suave. Why?"

"Suave?" She looked shocked.

"What's wrong with Suave?"

"If you don't know, then I'm not going to tell you."

She was the nosiest personal assistant I'd ever had. Of course, she was also the first.

"Veronica, out of curiosity, where did you go to school?" I gave her the eye. *The London Personal Assistant Institute in Bakersfield? Heh! Heh!*

"My graduate program was at Columbia University School of the Arts in New York City."

That was thoroughly intimidating.

At the end of the day, I hadn't accomplished much of anything. I remembered the days I ran around like a mad housewife and at bedtime had nothing to show for it.

Maybe everybody has these days, I comforted myself.

"Ah, I feel like I've accomplished so much today," Veronica said, stretching her thin, beautiful body.

Then again, maybe not.

I arrived home to find Lupe and Nana fighting in the kitchen.

I confiscated a butter knife from Lupe and a flour sifter from Nana.

Lupe was trying to explain something in rapid Spanish, but I wasn't catching it. "*Uno momento,* Lupe. Me go for *el neighboro.*"

The minute I reached his front lawn, I screamed, "Simon!" (The intellectual spoke three languages.) Simon's silver-haired head popped out his front door immediately. "Hey, Hollywood Girl."

"I need you for an interpreter," I begged.

Back in my kitchen, Lupe was making a fruit salad, and Nana was making a yummy white sauce for her Swedish meatballs.

Simon translated, "Lupe says she has strict instructions to serve you a special diet."

"Oh," I said, understanding all too well.

"I don't like it. I don't like it. This woman is taking over *my* house!" Nana wailed.

Whose house?

"Why, she even took the toilet paper out of the dishwasher," Nana continued.

"It could get wet in there," Simon astutely observed.

"You two are going to have to work it out," I said.

There was a knock on my door. Jack, the cameraman, was here to record our precious Kodak moments.

"Mind if I do a little filming? It will only be for a few minutes."

"Splendid."

Since I was about to pull my Suaved hair out by the roots, I pointed Jack to the action in the kitchen.

Jack was getting some great shots of Lupe and Nana arguing and Simon starting unfinished sentences when I spotted one of Nana's delicious homemade biscotti on the counter. I grabbed it and headed for the bedroom.

Just as I was biting into the delicacy, the paparazzi showed up. "Hi Jack." I waved to the camera.

"May I have that?" he asked, unfettering my fingers.

So even the cameraman was in on the plot.

That next morning Mexican music played on the radio.

Lupe had waved a newspaper in my face, so I'd supposed my bad picture was in there.

My breakfast had consisted of a boiled egg and applesauce.

Nana had winked. "Not to worry, honey. You'll get your nourishment."

I hadn't been clear on what she meant until I found the bacon smashed in a napkin in my purse later that morning. Or shall I say Veronica found it while searching for a sewing kit to stitch her skirt hem (every housewife carries one, you know).

"Oh wow, how did that get in there?" I asked, surprised.

"We have to talk," Veronica said, acting the dominant blond.

"Honestly, I didn't know it was in there. Do you think I want my purse saturated in grease?" I hate being accused of things I didn't do, so I changed the subject. "So why hasn't Dane dropped by?"

"He's on location all week, but he did call and ask how things were going."

"And how are they going?" I asked.

"Badly," she said frankly.

Veronica had confirmed my suspicions.

"Did you tell him that?" I braced myself for the answer.

"Of course not. I used a much milder word. If I give you a bad grade, I get a bad grade." She leaned back in her chair.

"I'll take any suggestions you have."

"My suggestion is very simple, actually."

I was listening.

"Get a creative team together pronto and come up with a fantastic show idea."

Why hadn't I thought of that?

Twenty minutes later I called my first brainstorming session with Shelby and Plum. "So let's have some brilliant ideas," I urged.

Plum started. "I think a show about fashion would be good."

"That's a little too predictable," I said gently, hoping not to offend her.

"I've got it!" Shelby announced. "A cooking show."

This time Plum said, "That is too predictable."

"You're right," Shelby agreed. "I know—maybe we could renovate a strip mall."

"Do you have experience in construction?" I inquired.

"I dated a guy whose father owned a construction company once," Plum said dreamily.

Jack and the permanent fixture attached to his shoulder hustled into the conference room.

"We're doing some free thinking here," I explained.

"Why don't you run over some of your better ideas for the camera?" he said after he was arranged. So we did. But after a minute he asked if I wouldn't mind saying something intelligent. "For the record."

At this point, failure was making me daffy. "Ah yes, Gaius Octavius, grandnephew of Julius Caesar." My cell rang. "Cut!" I yelled.

"What was all that?" Jack asked the girls.

I was hoping it was Brock. He'd gotten in around midnight after band practice at Jeff's apartment, and I had been real mean about it.

It was Nana. She said Lupe had thrown her empty Kleenex box away.

"So?" I said curtly.

"I keep my upside-down lotion bottle in an empty Kleenex box," she explained. "That way I don't have to whack the thing to death to get a speck of lotion."

"Nana, I'll buy you a new bottle of lotion."

Next thing I knew, Lupe was on the line, railing in Spanish.

I held the phone to the air. "*El habla espanol* anyone?"

"I do." Plum took the phone. "I dated a bullfighter from Mexico City," she teased. After a minute she explained. "Lupe is kinda like upset because the old woman hid all the spices or something."

"Lovely," I wailed.

"You know, Stephy, we might get more usable footage if we filmed your grandmother and the maid," Jack said.

He was probably right.

Chapter Thirty-One

"You do realize you have a meeting with the director after your facial?" Veronica informed me.

"I do?"

"I told you yesterday while they were taking your 'before' pictures, but I don't think you were listening."

"A meeting about what?"

"You'll be going over the ideas you have so far."

That will be a quick meeting.

"Is it the same director from *Dog Wars*?"

"No, it's Ron Howard." Veronica's face looked serious.

"Ron Howard!"

"Not really. I think Ronny has Hollywood conquered. Your guy is slightly less well known. Craig Barnes."

I squirmed nervously.

"Would you mind sitting still?" my traveling cosmetologist asked, impatiently, as she softened my skin with smelly lotion.

Craig Barnes was sitting across from me wearing a baseball cap backward. "So tell me what you have so far."

I gulped. "Sort of a cooking, fashion, adventure kind of a thing," I said, hoping to get by.

It wasn't working.

"Look, Stephy, I'm the director, not the cameraman. You can tell me your ideas and not worry about me leaking it to the uninterested press. I'm the guy." He pounded his chest.

Guys did that a lot.

I went on. "My idea is to move away from the stereotypical housewife, can't-read-a-corporate-graph-if-her-life-depended-on-it kind of thing."

"We don't use many graphs around here," Craig stated and cradled his black head.

He raised his head.

"I'm trying to catch your vision."

"You see, I plan to examine the inner depths of the soul, yet preserve the dignity."

He crossed his arms. "Stephy, Stephy, are we running for office here?"

"No, why?"

"All this political sidestepping." Craig crossed one leg over the other and sighed. "I need specifics!"

"Specifics are good. Sure, I believe in specifics."

"You weaseled your way out of that one," Veronica said after Craig had left.

"Did he say anything to you about it?"

"He said you were either brilliant or idiotic, and he can't figure out which."

"At least Jack didn't get it on film. Where is he?" I asked.

"Ah," Jack said, walking in the door and stretching.

"I told him he could take your massage appointment today because you were busy," Veronica told me.

"Wah!" I cried in regret.

"Hey, that camera can get awfully heavy," Jack said smiling, stretching his long arms some more and releasing another lingering "ah."

I parked on the street, and the Home Living Channel van hit the curb right behind me.

Even with the car window closed, I could hear the Flying Eagles were out of tune. (The Flying Eagles was the name Brock settled on, because the band name Eagles was already taken).

"Oh, man, that music should be censored," Jack said as he filmed.

After a minute he followed me into the house. I tried to be bouncy and cheery. "It's good to be home!"

Nana was on Lupe's tail.

Lupe had cotton stuffed in her ears. I wasn't sure if it was because of the music or because of Nana.

Another van parked in front of the house.

"Oh, lookie, a visitor," I said to the camera.

A guy in a Sears uniform walked in the open front door and yelled, "We have a delivery here!"

The deliveryman dropped a big box in the only available corner and left. The lettering said it contained a treadmill.

"I hope that's an incredible shrinking machine," I said to the camera. "The Home Living Channel has me on a diet. There is no way I'll be exercising on my free time." I stared at the size of it. "It will make a good coat rack, I suppose."

"None of the sound is going to come out with that noise coming from the garage." Jack turned off the camera.

"Pity," I said.

"Do you mind if I give some tips to the band? I'm a guitarist myself," Jack added.

"Go ahead. I'm sure they could use it . . . Uh, do you mind if I take a bath?" (Here I was, reduced to asking the cameraman for permission to take a bath.)

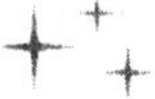

Reality TV News was sitting on my desk late the next morning (I had no intention of reading what they might say about me), along with a mug of herbal tea and a bowl of goat-milk yogurt that Corrine intended to be my lunch.

"Do you have any ideas for a show, Veronica?" I asked when it was clear that my brain was drained of all inspiration.

"I have tons of magnificently brilliant ideas," she said, smiling. "But I'm not allowed to help. Sorry."

"It's in the contract, right?"

"Yup."

"Can you give hints?"

"No." Veronica leaned against my desk. "Look, Stephy, you're not giving yourself enough credit. After all, you thought of a Reality TV show doing a Reality TV show."

"I think this low-calorie diet is depriving my brain of oxygen. I didn't think it was going to be so hard!"

Up until then I hadn't noticed Jack in the corner, catching all of this on film. But by now I didn't care. "Can I at least have heated soy milk with a teaspoon of molasses and a cinnamon stick like I made for the Chihuahua?" I begged.

"Corrine thought herbal tea would be better," Veronica said.

"Just one itty-bitty slice of pizza."

"I can't undermine Corrine," Veronica said firmly.

"One of your Girl Scout cookies? I'd be contributing to a good cause."

"You are sounding desperate," she noted.

"I am desperate! You try eating this granola menu for ten years."

"It's been one day," she said.

Jack moved in with his camera.

"Listen, all you attorneys out there hungry for a lawsuit. They're depriving me of carbs and caffeine!" I yelled.

"They're going to edit that out, you know," Veronica stated.

"I'm in charge of this project, and I'll keep it in."

"You're in charge of *your* project, but the Home Living Channel has creative control."

"It's in the contract, right?" I nearly cried.

"I can't advise you on that, Stephy. If you want, you can make an appointment with Dora."

"She's probably off exploring." I put my head down on my desk. I knew I was being a crybaby, but I simply couldn't help it.

Jack tapped me on the shoulder. "Since you're in no shape for your massage, can I have Ajaye again?"

I raised my head. "I'll trade you the massage if you smuggle me in a grande latte."

"Sure," Jack said. "But I think you mean a venti. Venti is bigger than a grande."

"You won't even get her a tall, Jack," Veronica said. "Unless you want to be standing in line at the cameraman's union."

He frowned.

"Take the massage anyway, Jack," I offered.

He grinned. "Thank you!"

"You're welcome."

He left smiling.

"I am such a nice person," I commended myself.

"Oh come on. You just wanted the camera out of your face," Veronica accused.

"Hmm." *How come I wasn't devious enough to think of it myself?*

"You know, when we start filming the show, there will be several cameramen following you around."

I hadn't thought of that either. I took a deep breath.

"Do you think if I leave you alone for a while, you might think better?" Veronica asked.

"That's probably it," I said aloud.

Fifteen minutes later I doubted that was it.

There's something about knowing you can't have something. All I could think of was high-carb, high-caloric food. I was on the Adkins diet for two whole days once. After getting sick of pork rinds, I went out and had the highest carb meal I'd ever eaten in my life.

I stared at my goat-milk yogurt and rebelled. *You can keep your cultured dairy products, I want pizza!*

I sneaked out the back door.

Brock had recently rented *The Great Escape* with Steve McQueen. If POWs could escape from a German camp with barbed wire, I figured I could drive out the gate without Veronica spotting me . . . but not without my keys I left on my desk.

Drat! The back door was locked, and the front-desk receptionist was Veronica's pawn. I was outside Avril's window, but I couldn't get her attention.

Trent stopped in his tin can of a car, exhaust fumes choking me. "Need a ride?" he asked, one big, round, smiley face.

From anybody else that would have been a reasonable question.

"Not from you," I said, definite about it.

"Suit yourself." He shrugged.

"Wait. Where are you going?"

"To Johnnie's New York Pizzeria."

"You're joking."

"I'm not."

"Clarify something for me, Trent. Why would you offer me a ride?"

"Because I'm a nice guy."

"Give me a better reason."

He scratched his stubby chin. "If you must know, I have an agenda."

That was honest. I gave in. The thought of pizza was just too alluring.

"Well, OK. But we eat at separate tables."

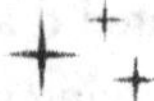

I've never enjoyed pizza more in my life. As I gobbled at the next table, Trent asked me why I hadn't chosen him to work with me.

He was completely serious.

"You had a moronic idea for a Noah's Ark Survivor, stole my show idea, and got me fired. And you want to know why?"

You have to be blunt with guys like Trent.

"OK," he hedged. "So I had bad judgment that one time."

"*Three* times."

"Believe me—I'm a better man than that."

Any man is a better man than that.

"Look, Stephy, I've paid for my mistakes. Ever since you were fired, Dane's got me on unbelievably boring work. I've been working in Reality TV since its inception, and I know a lot about it."

"Tell me the real reason you want to work with me."

"To get back in Dane's good graces." He stretched and patted his belly.

"And make my good friends Shelby and Plum furious?" I inhaled another huge bite.

"I'll apologize to them. Even though I'm not sure what I'd be apologizing for."

"Would you be willing to bring me coffee on demand?"

"I'd be willing to fly to Colombia to personally pick the coffee beans off the bush."

Tree, I thought. "That might make up for half of the rotten things you've done," I said.

Chapter Thirty-Two

My conscience was burning a hole in my stomach, or was it the three slices of pizza?

"Is something wrong? You look pale." Veronica raised her perfectly arched eyebrows.

"OK, OK," I confessed. "I tossed the yogurt and had pizza for lunch."

"I know," she said.

"How?"

"It's written all over your breath." She laughed.

"It was garlic chicken." I deposited a Listerine strip in my mouth.

"The dumped yogurt in the trash was another huge clue. And the fact that you were gone for well over an hour."

I winced. "So I'm not the most clever criminal."

"Cleverest," she corrected.

"Any other dead giveaways?"

"The camera."

I turned nervously. "What camera? Where?"

"There." She pointed to a corner near the ceiling.

"A camera in my office?" I frowned.

"It was installed when you were gone. It's standard video-surveillance technology and not meant to invade your privacy."

"I know, I know. It's in the contract, right?" I waved to the camera. "Hello out there in TV land!"

The surveillance continued at my home.

Jack's camera was three inches from my face as Brock and I sat on the bench in our backyard holding hands.

"How romantic," I said sarcastically.

Brock pulled his hand away to retrieve a cookie from Nana's ever-present cookie plate.

"Jack, you sure keep long hours," I muttered.

"Yeah, why don't you take a break?" Brock suggested.

"I could use one all right." Jack put his camera down and pulled some Black Jack chewing gum out of his back pocket.

The next thing I knew, he was sitting with us, and he and Brock were discussing music.

That ought to keep them busy for a few hours.

That was fine with me. Nana was over at Simon's, giving him an earful of her domestic troubles, and Lupe was shopping.

A moment of peace. It was hard to believe I had worked so hard to get away from it. I shook my head. *What was I thinking, God?*

I was headed toward the bookcase in the guest room for some therapeutic reading (the only room besides our bedroom not overtaken by Nana) when I remembered that it was Lupe's room now.

It didn't matter. Two seconds later Hannah showed up with a smile and purple highlights in her hair.

I reasoned it would be nice to spend some quality time with my daughter. However, my wide smile dissolved when she said, "My class is here to observe you."

"Observe. Like a specimen?" I asked.

"Seriously, Mom, they're waiting outside. I wanted to let you know first, in case you had a clay mask on your face or something."

She must have taken my blank stare as permission. A minute later, six strangers—all with purple highlights in their hair—walked into my living room.

"Hi group. You'll have to excuse me, but I've just been through the worst day of my life."

They all smiled excessively but said nothing.

I looked down at my feet. "Is it my shoes?"

They started laughing—explosively.

I looked at my daughter. "I guess I exceeded my own comedic expectations, Hannah, because apparently I'm hilarious."

"Mom, they don't speak English very well."

"Isn't this your psychology class?"

"No. These are foreign-exchange students from my Bible study."

Well, that explained half of it.

"This is Luca from Chile, Armand from France, Jan from the Czech Republic . . ."

That was where she lost me.

"Nice to meet you," I said to the entire group.

Each regarded me politely.

"I told them you were a TV star," Hannah prompted.

I tried to look happy.

"We dyed hair today. Do you think their host families will mind?"

"I dunno." (I did but wasn't saying.)

"It comes out in three washes," she explained.

"Honey, I would love to stand here and chat, but . . ." My nerves were starting to fray. I wiggled my toes, fretfully.

Jan elbowed Hannah.

"Oh yeah," Hannah blurted. "Mom, one of the other reasons I'm here . . ." She gave Jan a sideways glance.

This was going to be good.

"Jan really does not like her host family. The father snores and the little brother puts squishy things in her shoes."

"And . . . ," I urged.

"Can she flop here?" Hannah asked.

"Flop . . . here?" I asked, thinking *No way*.

"On the couch."

"For how long?"

Hannah played with her purple-tinted hair. "About a year."

I straightened from my slump. "I'm a fervent believer in foreign-exchange programs, but . . . absolutely not."

Brock and Jack came in from outside.

Hannah introduced the group again.

"Hold those smiles," Jack said and started filming.

The students giggled and waved to the camera, particularly the girls.

"Mom, can you fix us some Rice Krispy treats? These guys can't believe that cereal and marshmallows taste good together."

"That sounds great!" Jack agreed.

Trent had his feet on the table when I walked into the conference room the following morning with my skinny, decaf latte. (Corrine and I had agreed to a compromise.)

"Excuse me, Trent, but that is not a footstool."

He took his feet off the table without confrontation. Surprise, surprise.

I was determined to give the man a chance, because bad ideas are better than no ideas. "Remember, you agreed to apologize to the girls."

"I know," he said, appearing resigned to his fate.

When Shelby and Plum walked in, I prompted him with a nod.

"Hey, I wanted to tell you guys I'm sorry," he said as he straightened his Looney Tunes silk necktie.

I pushed him along. "Sorry for what, Trent?"

"Yeah, for what?" He turned to me, looking puzzled.

"For being a jerk." I said.

"Oh yeah, for being . . . a jerk."

"A supreme jerk," Plum added. She was looking chic as always, in a fringed blouse and lime green pants.

"Do you promise to quit belching, cracking your knuckles, and changing the screen saver on my computer to Dr. Spock?" Shelby asked.

"I promise," Trent said.

"Now that the touching apology is out of the way, let's get down to business." I felt a wave of power as I leaned back in my big chair.

Jack strode into the room and took his place on the wall. The camera that never ran out of film rolled happily along.

"Have you girls had any more ideas since our last meeting?" I asked, sounding professional.

No one said anything.

"Shelby, what about you and your Johns Hopkins degree? Anything in your vault?" I wanted Trent to know he wasn't the only one around with a college degree.

"I don't think a political Reality TV show would be much fun," she said, and I had to agree with that.

"Plum, what about you?"

"Nothing. I'm sorry." She tilted her head.

"Trent then."

"I have a couple of brave ideas."

"Go ahead."

"A show named *Homesick*. You take rich kids going off to boarding school, put them in adverse situations so they get homesick, and film it."

Shelby and Plum rolled her eyes in unison.

"That sounds mean," I said, holding back.

"It does?" Trent seemed honestly shocked.

"What else do you have?"

Without hesitation he plunged in. "How about a show called *Combat Housewives*? The housewives dress in fatigues and have a cleaning competition. The cleanest house in the neighborhood wins something totally anti-suburbia, like a trip to the rain forest."

"I'm thinking most housewives won't be into cleaning. Am I right, ladies?"

"Definitely," Plum said.

"And I'm not sure the rain forest would be much of a vacation either," Shelby added.

Behind the lens, Jack was thriving on all this bad TV with gratuitous interest.

"Have some Girl Scout cookies," I offered my brainstormers, moving the tempting tray within reach. "Jack, can you meet me in the hallway with the camera turned off?"

"Sure." He grabbed a Samoa on his way out.

"How would you like *my* massage again today?" I whispered once we were in the hallway.

His gray eyes lit up. "Sure! When?"

"Now!" I smiled slyly.

Chapter Thirty-Three

"Did you hear me?"

"What?" I asked.

It was Sunday evening, and Brock was seeking my attention as I was reading one of his Sunday papers. Talk about role reversal.

"Our open audition for 'Song of the Lamb' is coming up soon," Brock said.

"Where?"

"At the TV station in Costa Mesa. Doug Kozak is one of the judges." Brock wore a silly smile.

"That's nice." I turned a page.

"Can you put in a good word for me?" he pleaded.

I gritted my teeth. "Not without having some major humiliation issues." *And it's a sin to tell a lie*, I thought as I went back to reading.

"I know. I'll have Nana bake Doug some cookies!" He jumped out of his chair toward the kitchen.

"You can't do that," I called after him. "It would be unethical."

But it might work.

The morning was mostly used up with Veronica's being frustrated with me while I drew happy faces in the inedible low-fat dip with carrot sticks. Where is brilliance when you need it?

"I can't believe you don't know what your show is yet!" She was wearing out the carpet with her pacing again.

"You've said that five hundred times already, Veronica."

Katie phoned from the cruise ship later that afternoon. She'd left two days before. However, in my predicament, I had nearly forgotten.

"I had my first editor appointment today," she shared.

"What did your friendly editor say?"

"He asked me if I had ever considered becoming a barista."

"You're making that up!" I said.

"I am not," she asserted.

"That sounds cold."

"Or hot, depending on how you order it." She laughed.

"You're in awfully good humor."

"Astounding, isn't it? I feel like dancing. In fact, I think I will. There's this guy Roger I met playing shuffleboard . . ."

Meanwhile, back at the ranch, Nana and Lupe continued their cooking competition as Simon quoted lines from first-century philosophers. (Don't ask me why.)

When I returned to the kitchen, there was a red taped line dividing the counter. "Oh," I teased, "we're having a track meet on the counter with the Borrowers."

"Now that would be silly," Simon said.

"Well, what then?" I tapped my toe, waiting.

"Lupe's side, Amanda's side," he announced proudly, as though he had used Solomon's brains to come up with the solution.

I didn't ask how the dishwasher was divided.

Veronica was sick; Mattie was sick; half the office was sick.

I was sick of the office, and the questions from employees who begged me to tell them what my show was (which I didn't know anyway), so I could chance their leaking it.

But mostly I was sick of the camera in my face 24/7. Jack was a decent guy, but who wanted to think about every syllable that came out of her mouth? Especially when some of those syllables added up to sentences that were hugely embarrassing.

Basically I needed a break from my too-public life.

I called Mattie, and she gave me permission to use her office. And so when Jack visited the bathroom (after an enormous coffee drink I'd personally delivered to him), Shelby, Plum, Trent, and I sneaked out the back door to her trailer.

In the first hour we filled a big wastebasket with bad Reality TV show ideas. In the next hour my creative team munched on junk food while I ate sunflower seeds.

In the middle of a bad sunflower seed, my cell rang.

"Stephy, Stephy, Stephy," the voice proclaimed.

"Katie, Katie, Katie." I was so happy for the diversion. "So tell me about today's appointment."

"This editor said my protagonist was obscure."

I grimaced. "Whatever that means."

"I don't think it means anything good."

"Did it upset you?"

"Upset me? I'm deliriously happy. My shipmate's having dreams about her baby being carved up like a Christmas goose, and I'm deliriously happy."

"Gross! Is your roommate a cannibal?" My stomach revolted against the sunflower seeds.

"Oh, no, the baby is her book. Don't you see?"

"Not really."

Jack managed to find us in Mattie's trailer the following day.

"Do you know what I did all day yesterday?" he sneered.

"I'm sorry. You can have my massage today," I said, feeling the weight of self-imposed guilt.

"Cool," he replied. "Actually, I played Minesweeper on your computer."

"I hope you didn't mess with my scores," Trent growled, never looking up from his cell-phone video game.

After he positioned himself, Jack said, "So go ahead and look natural."

Ten minutes later he was yawning as I tossed another half-baked idea in the mounting trash. "This is what you missed yesterday, Jack. And this is *all* you missed yesterday."

Trent was now playing with his laptop.

Shelby was doodling.

Plum was designing a dress out of a napkin.

Mattie's phone rang and we all jumped.

"I hope that's somebody interesting," Jack said.

"Hi, Stephanie."

"Hi, Corrine," I answered unenthusiastically. "I thought you were sick today."

"I am but wanted to be sure you don't miss your exercise two days in a row." Her tone was resolute.

"Corrine, we're using Mattie's office, and there's no exercise equipment in here."

"Yes there is. In the bottom drawer you'll find a Thighmaster."

I opened the drawer, thinking this must be the last one in the entire world.

That did it. "There is absolutely no way I'm demonstrating a Thighmaster on camera!"

Veronica was over being sick the next day, and she wanted answers. "Be straight with me, Stephy. Do you even know yet? Have you come up with your show?"

"I plead the Fifth." I folded my arms.

"That may work with me, but not Dane."

I sighed. "I am fully aware of that."

"Being aware and being prepared are two different things," she said, increasing her volume.

"I'm aware of that too."

"I hate to be the spoiler . . ."

Do you really, Veronica. Do you really?

"You have a meeting tomorrow to pitch your show."

Gulp.

That afternoon I was so happy to see Katie and her five hundred pounds of luggage at the San Pedro pier that I cried.

"You didn't have to meet me," she said, but she looked grateful.

"I wanted to."

We hugged.

"How was the weather the rest of the cruise?" I asked.

"Foggy." She frowned and lowered her Gucci sunglasses. "And let's hear about you."

I stared at her pile of luggage. "Foggy is a good way to describe my week too."

"Why?"

"I'm going to be in breach of contract. They're going to take the family farm." I tried to make a desperate face.

Katie looked confused. "You have a family farm?"

"Of course not, silly. But I'll be in big trouble if I don't come up with something before my meeting tomorrow. Any ideas?"

"Nope," Katie shrugged.

"I could dress up in sackcloth and fast and pray," I thought aloud.

"The way you make it sound, you *are* fasting," Katie pointed out.

I sighed. "And sackcloth doesn't do anything for me. I think I'll stick with prayer."

"Where's your faithful cameraman?" Katie realized I was alone for once.

"I lost him on West Sixth in front of a music store he happened to mention he loves."

"You know, those bags are very popular these days," I commented as Katie and I stood in her living room.

It wasn't her designer handbag I was referring to. It was the garbage bag she hauled out of her empty suitcase, like the one Shelby had brought to the pier.

Katie paused for a second, as if waiting for me to say something.

"OK, so what's in the bag?" I asked.

"Guess," she said.

"Let's see. Shredded paper."

"That's right," she verified.

"It is?"

"Put your hand in and pull out a handful," she urged.

"A handful of what?"

"Confetti."

The shredder at the office doesn't make confetti, only long strips.

"I'm missing something . . . ," I began as Katie threw handfuls of tiny pieces all over her manicured carpet. "What are you doing? Reenacting your cruise departure?"

"No, this is my book. I borrowed the captain's paper shredder."

"Your book? Oh, Katie, not your blood, sweat, and tears. I can't believe it." I put my hand on her shoulder.

She tossed some more confetti onto the carpet. "Stephy, you were right. This was never my dream. It was my father's dream. I hate writing. I absolutely hate everything about it."

"And you couldn't figure it out before?"

"I may have known it deep down, but the pieces didn't come together until after my talk with the ship's chaplain." She sighed.

"Is he married?" I asked quickly.

"I don't know." She gave me that "leave-it-alone" look. "Anyway," she continued, "he said my father wouldn't have wanted me to sacrifice my life doing what I hate to do."

"It's true, Katie. But what is *your* dream?"

She had a faraway look in her eyes. "I don't know for sure," she replied. "But I do know it isn't staring at a blank screen all day, throwing my speller at the wall."

"I can see how that would be less than fulfilling," I empathized.

"So, help me out here!"

I helped in the only way I knew how. I reached in the bag and threw a fistful of confetti in her hair. She threw some in mine. We giggled like schoolgirls.

"Hey, what was this book about?" I finally asked. "Since you never would tell me when it was all in one piece . . ."

She cleared her throat. "It's about a woman who works in a Laundromat."

I left it at that.

After all the fun, I stared at the floor. "Goodie. Now we get to clean it all up."

"Maybe I should have burned it," Katie concurred.

We stood there staring for another moment until Katie yelled excitedly, "By George, I've got it!"

"Got what?"

"The idea for your show."

"What, what?" I stood on the balls of my feet.

"A Reality TV show about a housewife trying to come up with a Reality TV show, but then she comes up with nothing."

My face went blank. "I hope your novel was better than that."

"It wasn't. But don't you get it? It would have the Geraldo twist to it. Remember the Al Capone safe? All that hype and then the thing was empty?"

"I remember it too well. I don't think it was Geraldo's best career move, Katie."

"Really?"

"I don't think people would want to waste ten weeks watching the show to find out the lady was a complete idiot." I chuckled. "Even if it's true."

Chapter Thirty-Four

I bit into a 150-calorie Balance bar as I sat down with the twelve people too busy stuffing their faces to even notice me.

Normally I would have been taken aback to find the United Nations seated at my breakfast table, especially on a Friday morning. But not today. My thoughts were occupied with my own personal Doomsday approaching. My meeting was in a few hours, and the best idea for a Reality TV show so far was in my dreams (or nightmares).

Lupe's side of the table, which included Hannah and her foreign-exchange students, was digging into their *huevos rancheros*, and Nana's side, graced by Brock, Mark, Jeff, and Simon, was eating eggs and bratwurst.

Nobody said anything for a while. I sat dazed until it dawned on me. "Didn't I see Jack's van out there?"

Hannah pointed to the head under the sombrero.

Jack smiled and waved. "*Hola,* Stephy. Just a couple more bites, and I'll get to your exciting TV life."

"Take all the time you want."

"*Hola* is hello in Spanish. *Buenos dias* is good morning," someone clarified.

"How do you say it in Japanese?" Hannah asked her friend.

"*Ohayo-gozaimasu*," the friend responded.

"*Jambo* in Swahili," our African visitor said.

"*Kali Mera* in Greek."

"*Bonjour*."

"*Guten Morgen*."

"This is a very cool international club," Jack said, his mouth still full of huevos rancheros.

"It is pretty cool, isn't it?" I looked around at the group. An idea sparked. "Hey, maybe *you all* can be my Reality TV show."

I sat across from Dane at the conference table, trying not to show my nervousness. It was somewhat like telling a chihuahua not to tremble when he's paw to paw with a German Shepherd.

"Go, ahead, Stephy," Dane urged.

"I'd like Susie's assistance in casting for the show," I said.

"Can you start with the show?" Dane asked.

"Yes, please start with the show," Craig entreated.

Veronica, who was there for "moral support," looked doubtful. And Trent, who had sneaked into the room at the last minute, was going to be trouble, no doubt.

"The show is called *Culture Link*."

"*Culture Link*?" Dane furrowed his brows.

"But I'm not married to the title," I said quickly.

"Good," he said.

"Let's get into the show, please." Craig tapped his fingers on the table. He had been more than patient with me, so I didn't blame him.

"You take ten people and put them under one roof . . . ," I began.

Oh no! I thought, startled. *That sounded just like my obnoxious lawyer neighbor.*

Dane and Craig looked at each other, confounded.

"It's not a completely original idea to put ten people under one roof. In fact, it's been done rather often, and badly," Dane said, looking disappointed.

"But this would be different."

"How? By staging a terrestrial abduction?" Trent offered.

What was it with Trent? He got around Dane and reverted to being a complete jerk.

"Ten episodes, Stephy. We have ten episodes to make interesting," Dane reminded me.

"I know. The people in the house would be from different countries and would be sharing their culture. A melting pot." I put my finger up. "*Melting Pot* . . . that's the title!"

"And that's the show?" Dane asked.

"That's the general idea of the show." My palms started to sweat. I thought only men got sweaty palms.

"But there would be competitions, of course." Veronica helped me along.

"Yes, of course," I said, though I hadn't thought of them yet.

"Slinging escargot and rice balls would be a blast."

That does it, Trent. You're not working with me anymore!

I maintained a placid look, despite my irritation. "Yes, competitions, but dignified competitions."

"I don't know." Dane was skeptical. He slouched and crossed his arms.

"It's kind of 'out there,'" Craig said, unconvinced.

I defended my idea. "I disagree. 'Out there' is eating a pizza made with rancid cheese and blood paste for the *possibility* of winning fifty thousand dollars."

"Oh yuk." Veronica's face went white.

"I'm not opposed to the show in theory, Stephy," Dane explained. "We simply aren't catching your vision."

"Vision" is a highly overused word around here.

"Have you picked a filming location?" Craig asked.

"What about the Malibu mansion we used for *Dog Wars*?"

"It's being renovated."

"That's fine. I have other ideas."

Katie, can I borrow your mansion for a couple of months?

"I thought somehow you'd be making more of a statement, Stephy." Dane took a sip of coffee.

I sat up straighter. "This is a statement. I want to show that Reality TV can be about something besides watching people fail and be miserable."

"Failure and humiliation are what America wants to see," Trent interjected.

I wanted so badly to kick him in the shins under the table, but I couldn't reach him.

"I've put an enormous amount of faith in you," Dane said. "We can't afford a Reality TV train wreck."

"I know Dane. It won't be," I promised, reassuring myself in my head.

"OK." Dane nodded. "I'll agree to this, unless our sponsor shoots it down." He addressed Craig. "Your thoughts on this?"

The corner of Craig's mouth twitched. "It will be a challenge, but then so was that messy medical-school reality show."

Hmm.

"So now we need to get you a production team, Stephy. Do you have any preferences?" Dane asked.

I looked away from Trent so I could pretend he wasn't there. "Can I use whoever I want?"

"Whomever," Veronica whispered.

"As long as they can do the job," Dane said.

"Great. I'd like to use Shelby and Plum." I tapped my forehead in thought. "I haven't worked with Avril much in the office, but she was great on location. I'd like to use her in some capacity." I took a deep breath. "Other than that, anyone you choose will be fine."

Trent stretched before making his bold suggestion. "Dane, I'd like to be the associate producer."

Dane stiffened. "What are *you* doing in here?"

Thank you for finally noticing him, Dane. Now kick him out!

"I've been working with Stephy," Trent proclaimed. "She asked me to be on her team."

"Is this true, Stephy?" Dane turned to me, awe on his face. "After he got you fired?"

"Yes, but . . . but—," I stuttered.

"Giving the guy another chance, huh? That may be a noble gesture."

Court jester.

I wanted to explain my blaring apprehension without putting my foot in my mouth.

But Trent interrupted, as usual. "*Montgomery Street* is in the cutting room. And I have produced before."

Dane smirked. "Are you referring to your short stint as the consulting producer for *Reality Queen*?"

Trent sat up straight for once. "Not just that."

"Let me guess. You produced a play in college," Dane added sarcastically.

"Yes, sir."

Dane laughed. "I'd be willing to *try* you out as *assistant* producer. Since Stephy is willing to be so generous, I won't object."

"Thank you, sir," Trent said cockily.

Mrs. Give-the-Man-One-More-Chance shoots herself in the foot. I was lost in my bad thoughts.

"Stephy." Dane turned suddenly serious. "Here is where the hours get longer and the demands on you intensify."

"I realize that."

"Have you ever fired somebody?"

"My paperboy." And then I added, "Well, actually my husband fired him."

"Before this is over, you will have." He dropped a quarter-inch document on the table. "Here's the budget. I want you to give it a closer look. In the meantime I'll put together a group of talented, driven people for your production team."

I was hoping to be alone to clear my head when Shelby skipped over to me.

"So what am I?" she asked first thing.

"What do you want to be?" My voice echoed in the empty studio.

"A production manager."

"I hereby dub you production manager." I knighted her lightly on the shoulder with my pen.

"And what about me?" Plum appeared out of nowhere.

"What were you thinking?"

She looked wistful. "I want to be the set designer."

"You're good at decorating, right?"

"I'm da bomb," she said, using Mark's favorite slang.

"Then I dub you set designer." I repeated the ceremony with as much enthusiasm as I could muster, given the fact that my arch enemy was my new right-hand man.

Plum danced around, reminding me of a young Katie.

"And you can make Trent the trash boy," Plum suggested.

Both girls laughed.

"Try assistant producer." I choked on the words.

"What?" they cried in unison.

"I know, I know, but hold the rocks until I explain."

Thirty-Five

After a Dorothy-in-Kansas whirlwind afternoon, I sat at the table with my family. They looked incredulous, but they were supportive.

"So, Mom, if you're in any kind of a jam, you say, 'We'll worry about the money and logistics later,'" Mark said.

"We'll worry about the money and logistics later." I practiced a couple of times.

"And don't wear pink," Hannah advised.

"No pink," I echoed.

There was an extended silence.

I turned to my younger son. "And you, Jeff. No advice for your mother?"

"No advice," he said flatly. Then he smiled. "But if you see any cute girls, send them my way."

"Only after a grueling interview." I laughed, glad to see his sense of humor was returning post-Kelly.

"You're awfully quiet, Brock." *Probably thinking about the band.*

He rubbed his unshaven chin. "I'm proud of my housewife-turned-producer," he said slowly. "I always knew you were beautiful, but I didn't know you were so brilliant."

I beamed. How nice of him to finally notice!

"I don't know if I'd call it brilliant," I replied. "I didn't even know what a gapper was a month ago."

"A gaffer," Mark corrected me.

"A gaffer," I said embarrassed.

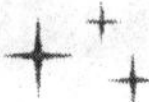

"This is so unbelievably good," I said to Susie at Spago Beverly Hills the following evening.

"Only Wolfgang Puck could make chicken a dream," Susie agreed.

"Everything in here is exquisite. Absolutely exquisite," I swooned. "And since Corrine has officially announced me as a size six, I'm having dessert."

"Order anything you want. Dane gave me his credit card."

"Chocolate Truffle Cake." I eyed the dessert menu and sighed.

"So is it all getting to you?" Susie examined me.

"Is what getting to me?"

"You're wearing the same gown Kate Winslet wore to the Oscars."

"It's rented."

"And a five-thousand-dollar necklace," Susie added.

I clutched at my throat, caressing the "girl's best friends" with new respect. "It belongs to Dane's wife."

"It got the attention of the photographers."

"One photographer," I clarified. "And it was arranged by the publicist." I laughed in a ladylike fashion. "This is nothing new to you, Susie. You're a casting director."

"One of many. And a casting director is not a producer. I can't yell, 'Clear the room, people!' and watch everyone disappear. That's what I call power!"

"If I yelled that at home, my family wouldn't clear the room. They wouldn't even clean the room."

She gave a brief smile before her expression turned serious. "I don't think you realize the fame you're in for, Stephy."

"Everything is still liquid Jell-O in my mind. I didn't get anything done today."

"I'll be happy to handle the casting completely. It's what I usually do anyway."

"That will help."

I said good-bye to Susie, slid into the limo, sank into the leather seat, and called Katie.

"Hey, you. Guess where I am!"

There was a long pause. "Steph, do you know what time it is?"

"Late. OK, so you won't guess. I'm calling from my chauffeur-driven limo on Sunset Boulevard."

"It's nearly midnight, and for your information, I was asleep."

"I'm sorry, Katie. I knew Brock wouldn't want me to wake him, but I didn't think you'd mind."

She didn't say anything.

"I just had dinner at Spago's, and the time got away from me—what with a movie star walking by every five minutes."

"Every five minutes, huh."

"I'm talking Spago's, Katie!"

"So, I'm very impressed."

But her voice didn't sound like it.

"Or jealous," I guessed.

"Jealous?" she snapped. "Of what? I used to eat at Spago's at least once a month!"

I sighed. "Oh, right. I forgot all this glamour is no big deal to you."

She sighed. "I'm sorry. You know I'm cranky when I'm awakened out of a dead sleep."

"I'm sorry too."

"Anything you do is a big deal to me," Katie assured me. "And since I'm half awake now, anything else you want to tell me?"

"They're willing to update your house if you let them use it."

"I may take them up on that. I'm thinking about selling anyway."

"That's a big step, Katie."

"Just trying to keep up with my best friend."

"*My best friend.*" I like the sound of that.

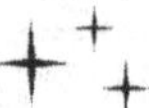

Veronica put up a big whiteboard and handed me a marker. I smiled at my new staff congregated around the conference table. It was so smart of me to get rid of Trent by sending him to scout a location when I already had one. Or was that devious?

I was feeling tired and grouchy from being out so late the night before (I was understanding Katie's bad mood) and would have been apt to wring his pencil neck if he said anything out of line, which he'd be apt to do.

I tried to look like I knew what I was doing. "So, we'll get started." I drew ten stick figures on the board.

"What's that?" someone asked.

"Our contestants." I drew triangle dresses on half of them, and then I drew a big box. "And this is the mansion."

Then the panic set in.

"We'll worry about the money and logistics later," I said authoritatively.

All the perplexed faces were a blur. My mind was a blur.

"Can I see you in my office for a moment, Veronica?" I grabbed her hand. "In the meantime, why don't you . . . do what you guys do? I'll be right back."

"What is with you?" Veronica asked as we reached my office.

"I don't know what I'm doing!"

"You do know what you're doing," she assured me. "We've been over it several times."

"Well, then, I forgot what I'm doing."

"You are crafting the scenes, remember? We need some sort of guide so we know how to stage the show and where you want to go with it."

"Oh yeah."

"Just remember the five points."

"The premise, the people, the tone, the product, the structure, and then . . . hand out lollipops."

"Close enough. Now go in there and look like you know what you're doing!" Her eyes sparkled with warmth.

I smiled. "Aw, you do care about me, don't you, Veronica?"

"I sure do, Blondie."

"Blondie?"

"Corrine has determined that you should be a blond. You have an appointment with a colorist after this and then a fitting and a promo to shoot."

"Will I ever get to see my husband again?"

"If you're a good girl, we can squeeze in a late lunch with him in the studio later. Now get back in that conference room and show them what a producer does."

"Can we run over that one more time?" I asked sheepishly.

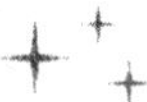

A few hours later Brock was staring at me as we sat on the risers in the studio before my promotional video shoot.

"You don't like it, do you?" I ventured.

"I don't know. I never thought of you as a blond."

"Me neither." I crossed and recrossed my legs, feeling antsy.

"And the makeup is pretty heavy," he added.

"It has to be for the camera to hide these dark circles under my eyes. Can you tell I'm beat?"

He didn't answer, which meant yes.

"Hey, where's the espresso I asked for twenty minutes ago?" I yelled suddenly.

Brock stiffened. "Stephy, aren't you being a little . . . demanding?"

"What do you think a producer does anyway, Brock? It's expected. If I walk around being nice, no one will take me seriously when I order them around the set."

He shrugged. "Speaking of ordering around, make sure you have that diva of yours put my audition for 'Song of the Lamb' on your schedule for next week."

"If it weren't for that diva, I'd be making a complete fool of myself. She's basically the producer in personal-assistant's clothing, so I don't make a complete fool of the station and myself." I squeezed his hand. "And, as for your audition, I wouldn't miss my favorite husband's big day."

A complete stranger handed me my espresso. "Five more minutes."

"Are you having dinner at home tonight? Nana is making grilled halibut, and the kids are coming over."

I felt my heart squeeze over not spending time with my family. "I can't. I'll probably be here until at least ten, then out the door at five again."

"At least I'll see your picture in the paper."

"Do you know any reporters who get up at four?"

"Hannah is keeping a scrapbook."

"That's nice."

Veronica tapped me on the shoulder. "Three minutes, Stephy."

"Thanks. I'll be right there." I put my espresso down and tried not to look frazzled.

"I feel like we're changing." Brock's voice was sad.

"We are changing. But it's a good thing. I'm accomplishing something important here."

"And me?" He sounded like a lost little boy.

"You too."

He looked down.

"You know, baby, I'm making a tremendous amount of money," I said, smiling.

He shuffled his feet. "Is that a shot?"

"You know me better than that. I was just thinking you should go out and buy yourself a Mazda Miata."

"Is that a bribe then?" he asked.

"A bribe sounds deceitful. Let's call it something else."

"Guilt," he said matter-of-factly.

Veronica interrupted. "Come on, Steph. You have to go!" she said firmly.

"I'm sorry, honey. I have to go." I wobbled away on my heels. When I was a yard away, I turned back and called, "Make it an RX-8."

Brock looked pleased.

"And it's not guilt!" I yelled.

But, of course, it was.

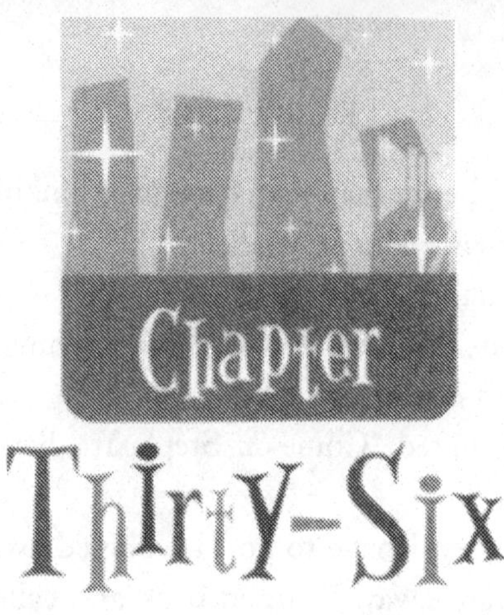

Chapter Thirty-Six

The next morning I was accosted by seven people on the way to my office and followed by two cameramen.

"May I ask why it is necessary for more than one camera to trail me?"

"We need to get your best angles," the new cameraman said.

"I thought all my angles were my best angles." I laughed facetiously.

The crowd followed my failing sense of humor into my office.

"Someone get me a latte so I can function here!" I called out. I was becoming keenly aware why caffeine was the beverage of choice.

After tugging on my sleeve like one of my children, Trent won the attention contest. "I need bios on the contestants."

"Go talk to Susie. I've given her complete control over the casting."

One down. I took a deep breath. "Veronica, help me out here. I'm getting overwhelmed."

"I'll take care of things. You take your call."

I picked up. "Hello."

"Stephy? Where were you? On an African safari?"

"Katie, just the person I wanted to talk to," I said loudly over the noise in the background.

"Your cell's message box is full. I wanted to confirm lunch," she said pleasantly.

"Oh, lunch. I forgot. I'm headed to your place in a few minutes. Can we meet there? We need to walk through with the set designer and—"

She interrupted. "When I told Alexander a Reality TV show would be filmed in the house, he took off for England. I'm so upset about it."

"Well, that may work out for the better," I said, hoping it didn't sound callous. But I was sure it did.

My wardrobe gal got past the mob and waved an outfit in front of me. "Is this OK?"

"I don't care. You guys are going to do what you want anyway," I told her.

She stared at me for an instant, then walked away.

Was it me who said that? I wondered. *I really need to get back to my Bible study.*

"What?" Katie said.

"Not you, Katie. Some girl from the wardrobe department. Don't you think I look wretched in Prada stripes?"

"I've never seen you in Prada stripes." Katie said.

"They're trying to demonstrate how I've gone from frumpy housewife to glamour girl or something."

"Look, Steph, I'll catch you later when I can get a word in edgewise."

"My grandmother can do better than this." I tossed the appetizer back on the plate the young woman was holding in front of me. "In fact, call my grandmother and get her recipe." I dictated the number.

"Done," she said and walked away as Katie walked up.

"Where is my stuff?" Katie asked, appearing slightly annoyed.

"Hello to you too." I forced a smile. "Your things are safe in the garage. I told them to be very careful with your personal belongings."

"And who are all these people?"

"I have no idea what half their titles are, but they seem to know their jobs."

Katie's eyes grew large as she looked around the room. "I don't believe it."

"I know, like an executive producer really dresses in silk cargo pants like this." I rolled my eyes.

"Not you, Steph. I can't believe they're painting my living-room walls emerald green."

Plum liked it; I liked it.

"You can still change your mind."

"No, I can't. I signed a contract."

I tried to look sympathetic before going on, but I was also relieved. "Katie, since Alexander is gone, can I camp out in your guesthouse? I'll be going to bed near midnight and getting up around five. I don't see the point in driving back and forth."

"Sure. I'll stay with you." She gave me a hug.

Craig came up with a headset on. "I think we need to sit down and go over your outline."

"I'm aware of that, but I can't right now," I told him. "I have an interview with a Reality TV magazine in about three minutes."

"Katie, will you please be me and do my interview? Ever since my mauling on *Which Way Is Up?* I'm scared to death to do any interviews."

"You'll be fine," she assured me.

I took a deep breath.

"Your eye is stuck shut," she observed.

"These stupid false eyelashes," I said, aggravated. "Will somebody pull these miserable spiders off before I scream?"

"All my bags are packed. I'm ready to go, Brock." I kissed him on the cheek.

He moaned and sat up in bed.

"I hate to wake you up. It's only five o'clock."

"In the morning?" He groaned.

"Yes, in the morning."

There went Billy Newcastle's first *Kee-ya!* to confirm it.

"How long will you be gone?"

"At least two weeks," I reminded him. "Are you sure you can get along without me?"

Brock paused. "Positive. It will give me some jamming time."

He could pretend to miss me more.

"I'm taking Lupe with me so she and Nana won't kill each other."

"Good." He exhaled in relief. "I feel like a fatted calf every time I set foot in the kitchen, what with their culinary competition."

I smiled. "Brock, you will come by the set often, won't you?"

He sat up in bed. "No offense, honey, but I got claustrophobic in the driveway last night when I visited the location. I can't imagine what it will be like from here on out. Don't be hurt if I don't come by," he said softly.

Weekend women's retreats and two-day business trips were the only times we'd been apart. Now it was becoming easier than it should be to part. I had my work; he had his music.

He held me tight and I missed our less-complicated life for the minute before I had to leave.

Preproduction was a madhouse, as expected.

Crew members were hauling equipment around. Lots of tape was going down, and signs were going up. Deliveries were being made.

Still, it was organized chaos. I watched it all, amazed.

Production manager Shelby said everything was going well, except . . .

"What?" I asked.

"I need to talk to you, Steph."

"Go ahead."

"We need to do some shaving."

Yikes. I looked down at my covered legs and wondered how she knew.

She caught my glance. "The budget, silly."

"I'd like to shave Trent out of the budget altogether." I watched him ordering people around for fun. He was wearing a T-shirt that said, "Deny Everything!" It seemed so typical to me.

Veronica put her arm on my shoulder. "I can ease your distress by shaving a chunk off your budget right away."

"How?"

"You can do without a personal assistant at this point. My job here is done. I've already told Dane."

"No, I can't," I said desperately.

"I wasn't intending on cheating on you, Stephy, but I got an offer to work on *Surf Island*. So aloha."

"Just like that?" I felt numb.

"Just like that." She bit into a bagel.

"No, wait, Veronica. I need you!"

"It's nothing personal, Stephy. I was slightly doubtful about you at first, but you've convinced me. Now all you have to do is convince your viewing audience."

We hugged, and her bagel landed on the floor.

"One thing, though. When you get off the island, I'd go back to the hair you had."

"Tell me something I don't know," I said, catching her reference to *Survivor*, even though I never watched the show.

"And don't let them play up the frumpy housewife-turned-smart person."

"Thanks for the advice."

"Before I go, I have something for you." She dropped a bottle in my hand. "Take my Vitamin C. You're going to need it."

And then she was gone.

There was peace for about an hour, as I reflected on how things seemed to be running on their own. *Producing is like a raft,* I began to think. *You push it into water, and it floats in the right direction.*

Wrong!

Katie was at the same point of frustration where I used to get when my children were out of control. "My neighbors are furious because our quiet street that never even gets pedestrians has vans and trucks parked all over the place. The production crew is overtaking the sidewalk. It's like a tailgate party!"

"So let's order in some pizza and tell them to join us," I suggested calmly.

"No offense, Stephy, but my neighbors eat beluga caviar at a hundred dollars an ounce, not pizza," she said in a sharper voice.

"None taken." I scratched my blond head. "Then we'll invite them over for the first night of shooting. That ought to appease them."

"I'll deal with it myself," she said, understandably upset, and she walked away.

A girl in shorts came up to me. "Are they supposed to be knocking down walls and taking down the chandelier?"

"Absolutely not!"

The wardrobe lady was on my heels again. "Can you come upstairs to be measured?"

"In an hour," I replied.

"I'll hold you to that," she said menacingly.

"The electricity just blew!" someone yelled in my ear.

"Well, go flip those flippy things," I directed.

"The flippy things?" the sandy-blond crewmember asked.

"Better yet, go get Trent!" I insisted.

The crewmember wrinkled his forehead.

"Trent, the assistant producer," I clarified.

"What does he look like?"

"Greg Brady, with bigger ears."

"Oh, that guy. I thought he was joking when he told me who he was."

The blond crewmember vanished, and Trent appeared.

"Did you rub the genie lamp?" Trent said playfully.

"Can you go get the electrician person to fix the outage?" I asked.

"The key grip?" he clarified.

"Yeah, whatever, Trent. Just get it taken care of with the least amount of drama possible."

Things were heating up fast on the stress thermometer.

Chapter Thirty-Seven

A thousand production details were running through my mind as I flopped into a chair around 4:00 p.m.

And then more bad news. A health inspector was harassing the workers in the kitchen.

I gasped when I spotted my adversary. "Tell me you are Raymond's nicer twin brother."

"Why, Stephanie Daniels. Could you ever have predicted this *chance* reunion?"

I could feel my eyes narrowing. "Why are you here? We already have all the necessary permits and approvals."

"One of the friendly neighbors suspected that your operation may not be up to code, and this just happens to be my territory."

"I'll bet."

"I saw that guy milling around yesterday," Jack informed me as he rolled the film.

"I suspect, Raymond, that it was you who approached the friendly neighbor, if the friendly neighbor even exists."

"I'll just have a look around," he said and proceeded to stick his pointy nose in the cupboards.

"You will see everything is in order," I insisted.

"This kitchen is antiquated."

"It meets all the requirements. You won't find a thing."

"Don't worry," he warned, "I will."

"Maybe you're right." I recalled the incident with the catering truck owner. "Check his pockets!" I ordered one of the crew members.

"Don't touch me!" Raymond screamed girlishly as a plastic bag was found in his pocket. He tried to knock the camera down.

"Jack, keep that camera rolling! Just keep it rolling."

Raymond was in shock.

"Would that be vermin droppings?" I cried. "Can you say 'jail time'?"

After all that excitement (and the great feeling of satisfaction I had after finally catching crafty Raymond in the act), I had a good night's sleep, in between Katie's delicate snores.

"Go easy on the powder," I told the makeup artist the next morning, but she didn't listen.

"So, Craig, what were you thinking here?"

"A tour of the place before the contestants arrive."

"Like Jackie O's famous White House tour?"

"I wouldn't know. I wasn't born yet."

"OK, Mr. Smart Aleck. Laura Bush, then."

"And here's where Lincoln slept." I chuckled.

"You're wasting film," Jack said.

"This is weird talking to a camera when no one is talking back."

"Then say 'cut,'" Jack prompted.

"Cut!" I yelled. "You know what the problem is here?"

"What?" Jack asked.

I yanked at my pantsuit. “I am so completely uncomfortable in this Donna Karan wardrobe.”

“Versace,” the production assistant said.

“Penny Marshall wears a baseball cap when she produces.”

“She’s a director,” Jack pointed out.

“I wish I had some jeans with me.” I looked at the P.A.

She caught the look. “You’re not getting my jeans.”

“Sophie, is it?”

“Sonia.”

“Sonia, do you like to shop?”

“Duh!” She tilted her head and looked at me quizzically.

“I’ll give you two hours off tomorrow if you go get me a couple of normal outfits.”

“Three hours,” she negotiated.

“OK, deal. Go see Maria in wardrobe for my sizes and some cash.”

Susie beamed. “I want you to meet our host, Seth Greene,” she said quickly.

“Bye, Susie,” I said, then addressed the tall, dark, and handsome actor. “It’s nice to meet you, Mr. Greene.”

“Yes, I know.”

He *must* be kidding.

“You probably want to do some type of run-through, I’ll bet.”

“I wouldn’t have it any other way.” He smiled, and his teeth gleamed.

“Have you taken a look at the script?”

“I will. Five minutes before I have to.” He laughed dryly.

The P.A. standing nearby was wildly excited. “You’re that doctor who got killed off on that soap opera, aren’t you?”

He turned and scowled. “That is a sore subject.”

Trent boldly overtook the conversation. “I’m the assistant producer.”

“Charmed,” Seth said condescendingly.

"I'm sure you have some more important details to attend to, so go ahead, Stephy. I can take it from here," Trent said.

You can have him, I thought.

"So, Seth, haven't I met you before?" Trent started. "On the set of *My Mother Married a Vampire*?"

"I don't think so," Seth growled as Trent pulled him away.

And there came Sonia, carrying three big shopping bags—my new wardrobe.

I had this feeling there was something important about today, besides it being the first day of production.

Oh well. Must be the jitters.

The production coordinator gave her report. "I just got a call from the bus driver. He's leaving the lot with the contestants now. They should be here in about twenty minutes."

"Thanks," I said. "Oh, wait a second." I read her name tag. "Piper. Have you seen my family?"

"No," she replied.

That hurts. Not one of my family members shows up for my big day. I showed up for all their big days.

"Wait. Your grandmother was in the kitchen earlier," she said.

"She was?"

"You were busy."

"From now on, Piper, when a family member of mine shows up, I'm not busy."

Piper shrugged. "I'm sorry."

"It's OK."

I moved to the kitchen. "Did anyone see my grandmother a bit ago?"

"See her?" George bellowed. "She rearranged the whole kitchen."

"She left a note for you on the fridge," a dark-haired woman said as she chopped onions.

"The fridge?" I pulled off the scribbled note.

DON'T FORGET BROCK'S BIG DAY!

Brock's big day. She must have meant my big day.

Then it hit me. "Have you seen Katie today?" I asked the kitchen workers.

"She left with your grandmother," one of them said.

"May twenty-third, at 11:00 a.m. That's today. Oh, no! Veronica had it on the calendar she took with her!" I looked at my watch. "Get Trent in here," I yelled.

He showed up a minute later in baggy pants and the same T-shirt he'd worn the day before. "You rang?"

"Trent, I have to go to my husband's audition. Can you handle things while I'm gone?"

"Can I handle things? Why, I'm the assistant producer."

I met his gaze. "Where's Craig?"

"He's on the phone with Dane. I can handle it. Trust me."

Like I trust a cockroach.

"It would mean meeting the contestants and going over the rules. Oh, and making sure the contestants are interviewed."

"A precap. Yes, I know."

"And making sure Seth knows what to do."

"Let me take the world off your fragile shoulders, Stephy. You go to your little party. Now scoot!"

A taxi dropped me off at the studio where the "Song of the Lamb" auditions were being held.

I said hi to Nana, waved to Hannah, and settled in next to Katie on the risers in my so-called normal outfit, which was still way more color than I was used to.

A young hip band was exiting the stage, and the Flying Eagles were taking the stage.

I squinted. "Who is missing up there, Katie?"

"Jeremy. I saw him running by, looking pale a couple of minutes ago. I guess they're going on without him."

And he's the only one with talent.

Brock was wearing Tommy Hilfiger cargo pants and a yellow T-shirt that accentuated the small inner tube he'd recently gained. His hair was overly sprayed to the point of hurricane resistance.

But, then, so was mine.

Simon was sporting his white Lorenzo Lamas suit.

Billy Newcastle was wearing his karate top over his tan slacks.

Jeff was wearing a white shirt and jeans.

They were like something you would pull out of a grab bag.

As soon as the group started to play, it was obvious that Billy's maracas were the only things in tune. When the bad vocals rose to a screech, the faces in the audience contorted.

"Are there a lot of disillusioned people in this world, or what?" a voice behind me critiqued.

The judges were struggling to maintain their poker faces.

I noticed Doug Kozak smiling in my direction.

If this were *The Gong Show*, you would have heard a big boom at this point.

When the song was over, the band exited the stage, but I couldn't see their expressions. I took some comfort in the fact that this was a TV station dedicated to spiritual growth and not making a mockery of other people's dreams.

"Weren't they something?" Nana commented.

"They were something all right."

"Stephy," Katie said softly, "I know you want to stay for the outcome, but I think we can guess."

I stared at the ground.

"I want to make sure my house isn't burned down."

I had a hard time leaving. Brock's dream was about to be deflated, and my dreams were coming true. I felt bad about it.

Chapter Thirty-Eight

"As you can see, everything is running smoothly. Nobody even noticed you were gone."

Trent's words made me suspicious.

"You know what I would suggest, Steph."

"What?"

"Relaxing under the sunlamp for a few."

He looked like he meant it.

I wished I had a mirror. "Do I look that bad?"

He coughed a couple of times. "Ten minutes will do you wonders. You don't want to go meeting the contestants while you're falling apart."

"Falling apart?" I hoped I didn't look that bad. "I'm just a little upset about my husband, that's all."

"Tsk, tsk. Trouble in paradise?"

"No, nothing like that." I scrunched my forehead. "But maybe you're right."

"Hey, it works for me."

Nothing works for you.

A few minutes later the music soothed me and the heated lights warmed me. Outside of one of Ajaye's massages, I'd never felt so relaxed.

I drifted, and drifted, until I drifted off to sleep . . .

The timer went off.

It took me a minute to realize something was wrong—the front of my body was scorched.

"Help!" I screamed, and Plum appeared with a paintbrush.

"Stephy. You're burned." She helped me sit up in Katie's borrowed shorts and top. "On one side, anyway."

I moaned.

"It wasn't very smart falling asleep under a sunlamp, Steph!"

Comforting words of wisdom.

I ambled down the steps in pain, my anger burning as hot as my skin.

"Now, now, don't be too hard on yourself," Trent said as I got in his face at the bottom of the winding staircase. "It's not your fault that old machine has a faulty timer. You can't blame yourself."

I was speechless in my fury.

"Hey, I averted a bomb threat while you were napping."

"You cannot joke your way out of this one, Trent."

He held up a Perrier. "Going once, going twice . . . sold to the lady in the lobster suit."

My makeup artist was able to lessen the reddening, at least on my face, but the pain was still throbbing.

"Maybe it *was* the timer," Katie reasoned, as she cooled my skin with aloe-vera gel. "That machine hasn't been used in years."

"Just like Trent to leave me doubting his motives."

"When in doubt, forgive," she reminded me. "That's what you always say, right?"

I'd better practice what I preach.

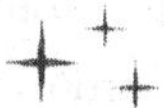

Craig advised me to have an individual chat with *my* contestants. "Trent has already gotten to know them . . . while you were out partying."

"Craig, it wasn't a party. It was more of a concert."

"Obviously an outdoor concert." He walked away, shaking his head.

Why do I even try to explain?

The first of our ten contestants sat in front of me. A casually dressed blond with a cute figure.

I started off by clarifying that I was the producer. "Trent Powers is the assistant producer," I added.

She seemed disinterested.

"So both your parents are from Sweden?"

"Yes, but only my father was born there."

"So you speak Swedish."

"Ya. Ya."

I brightened.

"Not really," she said.

"But you do adhere to your ancestry and customs?" I asked her.

"Is that like traditions and all that?"

"Yes. Traditions and all that."

"I eat Swedish fish." She laughed.

"You want to get in touch with your roots, though."

"Why, are they showing?" She touched her hair. "My roommate told me to get a touch-up. Do you have a hairdresser on the set?"

As I sat down with my fourth contestant, Siva, representing Malaysia, I was getting this feeling that the only thing international about our group was the names.

"Can I ask the primary reason you applied for *Melting Pot*?"

"You mean, besides the trip around the world?"

"Yes, besides the trip."

"I tried out for *The Apprentice*, but they didn't choose me."

"Well, literally hundreds of thousands of people apply for that show."

"Of course, I've never had a real job, so maybe that's why."

"About our show, Siva. Do you have any questions?"

"Is the trip around the world first-class?"

I changed the subject since I didn't know. "I imagine you're anxious to meet some of your relatives."

"Not really. Do you think if I win, they'll let me trade the ticket in? A first-class ticket around the world has got to be worth a lot."

"Is there someplace you'd rather be than Milan, Zurich, Beijing, and Rio de Janeiro?"

"Surfing Newport without having to work for six months would be pretty cool."

As soon as I sat down with Enrique, he thrust his head forward like a turtle and said, "I'll bet you can't stuff five hot chili peppers in your mouth at a time."

"I haven't tried it lately," I admitted.

"Once I made seven . . . and a half."

"That's impressive."

"With my toes."

"I guess you're not likely to get paper cuts on your toes."

"What?"

"You know, a paper cut with chili juice. Ouch!"

"Sure," he said blankly.

This was . . . scary.

"So, do you have any questions about your accommodations?"

"Yeah, are those flowers floating in the glass bowl in the bathroom edible?"

"I'll check into that." I was pressed for conversation. "So how's the political situation in Colombia, Enrique?"

He thought for a minute. "Is there one?"

When I finally sat down with my last contestant, I was exhausted.

"So how are you feeling, Shannon?"

"I can't believe this whole experience. I am so, like, in awe that I got chosen from, like, fifty billion people."

I looked at her bio. "What is your ancestry again?"

"Actually, I'm Irish. I was born in Dublin and came here when I was nine."

"That's what I thought," I said, puzzled.

"What? Oh, I get it. 'Cause I don't sound like it. Well, that's because I went to school in the San Fernando Valley. But my mother totally sounds like Roma Downey."

"Roma Downey?" My brain cells weren't connecting.

"You know, on *Touched by an Angel*? And Roma can, like, talk totally American too. I saw her, like, do it in a Christmas movie once."

"Really?"

"Seriously, if it would, like, make for better TV or something, I could talk like that."

"Your normal speaking voice is very nice."

"Wow, I feel special."

This is nuts.

As soon as Shannon left, I pulled Shelby into a corner. "Where is Susie?"

"She's probably, *like*, casting for another show already," Shelby said, being cute. And then she grew more serious. "Why, what do you want with her?"

"I trusted her to do the casting completely on her own, and she's gotten me a college fraternity club."

"It's not her fault. I'm sure she did the best with what she had. She did it in, *like*, a week."

Chapter Thirty-Nine

"So tell me you are kidding about the karaoke," our obnoxious host said bitterly as he reviewed the script with our director in the living room.

"Seth, I am not in the habit of playing games with my actors." Craig looked insulted.

I joined the discussion. "Every night we're going to have a country theme, and we're starting off with 'Honor America Night.' You know, hot dogs, s'mores, and karaoke. It all goes together."

"Like potato chips and sushi. Karaoke isn't even American," Seth complained.

"Maybe I should have done that on Japanese night." I tapped my forehead in thought, forgetting my sunburn until my skin tingled.

"This is the lamest show I've ever been on," Seth continued. "Your contestants are over there throwing gummi bears at one another, and your teenage producer is encouraging it."

"They're bonding," I said. "And it's Swedish fish, not gummi bears."

"Oh, what's the difference? You should have called this show *Kindergarten Playground.* It was misrepresented to me."

He threw his hands up and started walking away.

"Where are you going, Mr. Greene?" I tried to sound forceful, but honestly, I wasn't all that upset.

He turned around and snarled, "Talk to my agent!"

"I think you just lost your charming host," Avril said as Craig ran after him.

"What do you think about the karaoke, Avril? My daughter and her friends love it."

She paused and ran her fingers through her short, blond hair. "It was really cool in the seventh grade."

"That bad?" I sighed.

"Maybe if they were singing with someone famous."

"Then let's get someone famous!"

"You call Britney. I'll call Jessica." She laughed, but she was giving me an idea.

I called Katie over. She looked more beautiful than ever in her designer clothes. I grinned and took her arm. "Who are your famous neighbors?"

"Neighbors, like how far away?"

"Say, in a seven-mile radius."

"Halle Berry, Nicholas Cage, Jackie Chan, Sylvester Stallone, and if you're looking for scary, Ozzy Osborne."

"No kidding?"

"But then, Beverly Hills is only six square miles."

"Funny girl," I said.

"No, I'm not sure where she lives," Katie said. "She donated her Malibu mansion to a conservancy after the fires."

"What about your street? Do you have any movie stars on your street?" I was getting nervous about our situation.

"There's a movie star next door."

"Who?"

"A silent film star, but she's bedridden."

"You went to Beverly Hills High School with all those famous people? What was that like?" Normally reserved Avril seemed genuinely impressed.

"Grass, students, lockers, homework."

"And the police respond in about two seconds," Trent said as he walked by.

"Wait," Katie added. "I met Randy Travis yesterday as I was smoothing things over with one of my new neighbors."

"Randy Travis lives on your street?"

"No, but his publicist does, and he's staying with him for a couple of days."

"Well, let's go pay a visit."

"It doesn't work like that, Stephy. You don't go knocking on the door and say, 'Randy, will you perform for my TV show for nothing?'"

"But if the show raises some money for his charity, he might. I hear he's a very generous man."

Simon grabbed Nana's generous waist and spun her around as Randy Travis sang in sync to his own karaoke tunes.

Our young contestants, in cowboy hats rented from a Hollywood costume store, were doing a country-western line dance they had learned twenty minutes before from a choreographer one of the crew members knew.

Katie's neighbors were looking entertained, sitting on folding chairs, relaxed and unstuffy. My family was all in a row, and Brock had a massive smile on his face I was happy to see. He hadn't said much about his audition, only that he was taking his new guitar back.

Dane showed up and reminded my brain we were taping a show here. He grabbed a brownie from a plate bulging with desserts and looked around, impressed.

I grabbed Katie for moral support and headed over. "Can we speak outside, Dane?"

It felt good to be in the fresh air. The mansion was hot and airless with all the lights.

"It appears to be going very well. And Randy Travis. I didn't know you had connections." Dane pulled off his ball cap and scratched his bald head.

"This is my connection." I introduced him to Katie, and she said how pleased she was with the renovations to the house. (I knew Plum's chic decorating style would grow on her.)

I confessed right off that our host had walked off the set.

Dane shrugged it off. He said he'd received a message to that effect, but not to worry. He never could stand the guy anyway. Then he looked at Katie in this long, strange way and asked, "What about her as a host?"

"What do you think, Katie?"

"Who, me?" Katie flushed redder than my sunburned face.

Seeing her all the time, I didn't think much about the appeal she had, but she did have it.

"You have an easy presence about you." He stared some more. "Stephy, go get the script."

And that was that.

After all the excitement of the night before, I expected a buzz at the breakfast table, but none of the houseguests were saying a word.

Trent was the only one talking, and he was supposed to be working. "So did you like my Elvis impression last night? Thank you very much!"

Plum had been right about the karaoke. She giggled as she situated some props nearby.

I laughed for her benefit but was bothered by the obvious tension. I called Kristin, my Swedish contestant, over. "Do you know why no one is talking?"

She looked around. "Because one of us is a mole, and everyone's afraid they'll say something wrong."

"Thanks, Kristin. I'll clear that up." I walked over to the long table. "I would like to squelch the rumor that there is a mole among us. There is no mole."

Everyone looked at everyone relieved.

"Are there any other rumors to dispel?"

And the questions came:

"Is it true the music piped into the bedrooms has subliminal messages?"

"Of course not, Matthew."

I guessed he was reading Reality TV Web sites.

"Are the patterns on the wallpaper really miniature microphones?"

"No, Shannon, they're candy," I said sarcastically.

"Candy, really?" she asked, wide-eyed.

"No, not really."

"What about the truth serum sprayed in the air?" That came from our Malaysian jokester.

"I don't think the technology exists, or I might use it on a certain assistant producer."

They murmured.

"This is a simple game. So don't worry, be happy." I faked a smile. "You'll be getting your first assignment in a few minutes."

"I heard it's coming in on the back of a tap-dancing camel?" Trent wisecracked.

I suspected he was the instigator of the mole rumor. I tried not to glare.

"A maid in a black-and-white uniform will be presenting it on a silver platter under a dome," I informed the group.

The contestants started chatting.

"That is all!" I announced.

"Hey, maybe this is a reenactment of *Clue*, and the maid is going to poison us," I heard as I left.

We stood on Randy Travis's star on the Hollywood Walk of Fame three hours later for our first challenge. A huge crowd was gathered behind the tape, and the sheriff's department was assisting with the diverse-looking crowd.

Back in the late nineties, I had watched *Inspector Gadget* being filmed here, and now I was the producer? It seemed entirely impossible.

More impossible was where the time had gone. My father and I had often frequented this sidewalk, and I missed him tremendously. Maybe now, more than ever, since he loved the film industry.

Katie, our new host, looked calm.

Craig had everything under control.

Trent the Trekkie was down the street, intent on finding Leonard Nimoy's star. I hoped, selfishly, that it was the furthest star so he would stay out of the way. In fact, I wished it were in outer space.

Katie started in with her dialogue, and I read with her on the script that I had proudly penned with the script editor after some quick research.

"This challenge is going to test your independence, resourcefulness, and resolve. Are you ready to hear what you'll be doing today?"

"Yes!" our casually dressed participants erupted.

"There are over twenty-five hundred stars on the Hollywood Walk of Fame and over twenty-one hundred are already taken. The twenty stars you are going to visit today belong to either first- or second-generation immigrants, like all of you. That group includes such notables as Alex Trebek, Sophia Loren, Ingrid Bergman, Audrey Hepburn, and Charlie Chaplin. Each from a different country."

The explanation went on.

"But first, you must find a recent citizen of the United States. We have twenty of them milling up and down Hollywood Boulevard wearing Sony digital cameras. If you see a tourist-looking type, say, "Do you love America?" If the person begins to recite the Preamble to the *Constitution*, enlist the person to help you find all twenty stars on the list that your new citizen will provide. The proof will be the picture your companion takes of you standing beside each star."

I saw my children standing behind the yellow tape. Instructing the cameraman to get some closeups of them, I waved proudly.

Katie presented the last of the challenge, which involved taking the same quiz required to become a citizen of the United States. "Since I don't believe in luck, I'll say, 'try hard.'"

She winked at me.

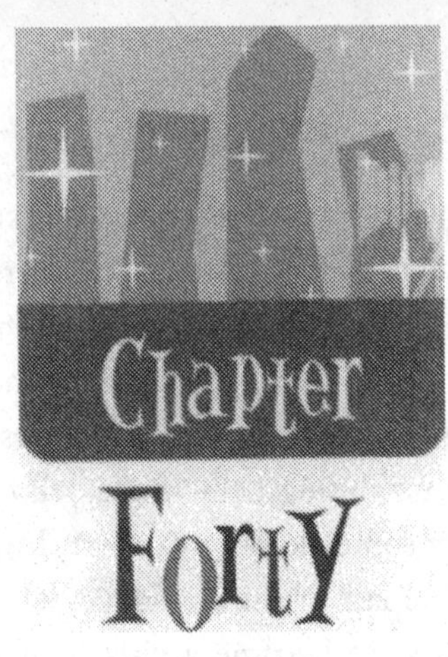

Melana from Yugoslavia was eliminated before I'd perfected the pronunciation of her last name. That meant a dinner was held in honor of her country. The fish skewers with tomato relish received rave reviews.

I wanted it to be a celebration, not a humiliating experience, and it was. The festivities included folk music and poetry readings. A digital slide show documenting Sarajevo under siege ended in twenty-first-century hope. Some of Melana's personal pictures were included.

I had no clue when and where all this media had been put together. It was as though hidden elves had worked through the night.

In her exit interview, Melana gave her thoughts on what her country meant to her. Since her own family had been through a great deal of hardship and she had relatives in Sarajevo, she seemed to be the most in tune with her heritage.

Her country's flag was lowered on one of the miniature make-shift poles. She was interviewed and whisked away by limo to a hotel unknown to the media.

While the remaining houseguests played board games in the

living room, we watched some clips in Katie's home theater that evening.

"They're getting along so well," I said happily.

"And that is exactly the problem," Trent protested.

"Why is that a problem?"

"B-O-R-I-N-G." Trent broadcast his subjective opinion.

"Craig, what's your take?"

"It's a bit 'documentary,' but I'm sure the script editors can weave it into a tale."

A fight erupted in the living room the next morning after breakfast.

"You stole my grandmother's locket," Shannon accused Maya as she waved it in her face.

"I did not," Maya stated adamantly. "Why would I want your stupid locket?"

"How can you say you didn't take it when it was in your bag?"

"That thing is sterling silver. Why would I want it?" Maya was seething.

"Because it's a family heirloom!"

"Well, it's not *my* family heirloom. My family isn't into cheap."

Contestants started taking sides. More accusations broke out.

"Enrique accused Siva of a racial slur."

"What? 'Cause I said you like to laze around? You're hypersensitive." Enrique looked like he wanted to fight.

"Wait, Enrique. *You* should talk. You called me cheap," Matthew exploded. He'd barely said a word before now.

"You are. You admitted you don't tip fifteen percent," Enrique fired back.

"I said I tip depending on the service." Matthew got in Enrique's face.

Some of the others who were watching tried to calm their friends down.

The cameramen were getting the action on film, and Trent was yelling, "Milk it for all it's worth!"

That's when I grabbed the megaphone. "Everyone stop!"

They began to settle down.

"I'm ashamed of you guys. When we picked you, it wasn't based on how much contention you could cause." I took a breath. "Look, the conditions here aren't exactly stressful. We're feeding you well; you get plenty of rest." I eyed each one of them. "Now please go back to being your charming, sweet selves."

Five minutes later the contestants were chatting happily as they waited for breakfast to be served.

"Something smells strange," I noted. "And it's not the food."

"It smells like burning rubber," Shannon said as she filed her nails.

"No, it's more like my sons' room when they hid their dirty clothes under their beds," I mused.

I nosed around. Finding a bag hidden in the corner, I sniffed. "These T-shirts are from yesterday."

The odor was almost nauseating.

"What are these sweaty T-shirts doing here?" I said, trying to hold my temper in check.

"I guess I put them there," Trent finally admitted, trying to grab the bag before I handed it off to Piper and instructed her to give them to Lupe to launder. "But—"

"But what, Trent?" I asked, hands on my hips in disgust.

"I was going to auction them on eBay for a bundle."

"Sweat and all?" I shook my head.

"You get paid more for the sweaty ones, especially for the popular contestants," he claimed as he slithered away.

I tell you, it's like baby-sitting.

So now what? Keiko was sobbing, and Kristin was comforting her.

"Tokyo had a nine-point-five," Kristin whispered. "And she has relatives there."

Maya seemed equally upset.

I touched her shoulder. "What's wrong?"

"India is under water," she said in desperation.

"The coast?"

"The whole country!" she wailed.

"The world is falling apart, and here we are, cut off," cried Nicky, dramatically.

"That sounds like an extreme amount of worldwide tragedy for one day. Where did this report come from?" I asked.

"The Internet," Matthew replied.

"The Internet, where? You're not supposed to be using electronic devices."

"We didn't. The laptop was sitting over there on the coffee table," Siva explained.

I read the headlines.

KILLER VIRUS SWEEPS THROUGH EUROPE

HONG KONG REAL-ESTATE PRICES PLUNGE

Shelby stood next to me. "This is a hoax. One of those fake Web sites where you put in your own headlines." She directed me to what she said was the URL. "Free Web pages—see?"

"Who is responsible for this teenage prank?" I demanded.

No one answered.

"Well, whose laptop is this?"

"One guess," Shelby said.

We were meeting in the blue room because tomato juice had been spilled on the carpet in the living room and it was being cleaned.

The paint in the blue room was still fresh, and I was getting a headache.

Craig, who had been having breakfast with Dane, touched my still-tender shoulder. "What happened to you?"

He was referring, I knew, to my frayed appearance.

"It's a long story you don't want to hear." I half-laughed, half-cried.

Katie announced the challenge. "In five minutes a call will be dispatched to one of your relatives abroad. You will write down the ingredients of their favorite pre-approved recipe, using your designated interpreters, if required. Then take one of the cabs waiting in the driveway and head out to buy your rare ingredients with the amount of money you are given. We'll see how well you know your ethnic stores, how well you can get around the city, and if bargaining is your thing."

"Trent, stay!" I called as he walked away.

"What—am I a dog?"

"I should fire you right now," I said heatedly. "I know you are responsible for ninety-nine percent of everything that has gone wrong today."

"But you won't, because I'll be quietly working on my computer, not saying another word the rest of the day."

Unbelievably, I agreed to the arrangement. I was, once again, trying to be the forgiving Christian.

Nicky from Trinidad was eliminated. The Caribbean-themed party was a blast, and the calypso was engaging.

It was getting harder to think of this as a game. There were real emotions involved, and I was having as much trouble as anyone.

I kept a notebook with adjectives to describe each contestant so I could remember them better and pray for them. Here were the remaining ones:

Name	Country	Notes
Azi	Nigeria	easygoing, would make a good talk-show host
Keiko	Japan	dainty, only Christian in bunch, just plain fun
Matthew	Israel	off the wall, witty, looks like actor in *Napoleon Dynamite*
Shannon	Ireland	personable, considerate, overuses slang phrases
Siva	Malaysia	loner, surfer, jokester
Maya	India	feminist, intellectual, reserved, good dresser
Enrique	Columbia	likes the spotlight, laugh-out-loud funny, curious
Kristin	Sweden	hyper, always primping, easily con-fused

I was growing weary the next day when the houseguests left for their challenge. Avril assured me she could handle things.

Trent was furious he had to stay behind again, but I didn't trust him. I set him up to work in Katie's old playroom to keep him out of trouble.

It was a good thing I didn't go. I had forgotten I had invited my family to the set. Mark's dark eyes grew big, like when he'd been given his first camera. "Go upstairs and Plum will show you around Disneyland," I told him.

He bounded up the stairs.

Hannah smiled at me. "I didn't know Aunt Katie was this rich!"

I ignored the comment and asked, "Where's Jeff?"

"You won't believe this one, Mom. He's checking out colleges!"

"Yes!"

Jeff had always wanted to go to college, until Kelly had convinced him otherwise. Now I knew my boy was back.

"And your father?" I continued.

We spoke on the phone every night, but Brock wasn't saying much.

"He's working hard at the office," Hannah assured me.

I hoped that was a good thing. That he wasn't just drowning himself in his work because he had failed as a musician. I wanted to be there with him in case he needed my consolation, but I couldn't be in two places at once.

"Simon took Nana to a museum," Hannah added.

I missed Nana, too, and Sam, my goldfish, and Muffy. The list went on.

I gave Hannah a meaningful look.

A few months ago I had no life (as my children pointed out), and now I had too much of a life. Everything was changing so fast. Would my feet land firmly on the ground when this roller-coaster ride ended?

Hannah scanned the room as the crew members went about their business. Then she said out of the blue, "So, I was the brat who inspired all this?"

She was almost reading my thoughts.

"All this?" I asked.

"When I told you to get a life." She looked at me seriously. "I'm sorry. I didn't know I still needed my mommy. I thought I was grown up and wanted to do things all on my own. I'm happy, in a way, that you're famous, but . . . in another way, I'm sad."

"Famous." I fought tears. And then I smiled and used one of her favorite phrases. "Get out of here." I brushed away the tear that was starting to drip down my cheek and said, "How about a tour?" I started up the stairs.

"And this is Katie's old playroom." I waved my arm like a game-show hostess as I opened the door. "It's the only room left untouched . . . for sentimental reasons."

Trent startled Hannah by clearing his throat.

I gestured toward him. "And that's Trent in the corner with his laptop."

Hannah, who characterized herself as a great judge of character, gave him a tentative look.

"Hi," he said.

"He's being a good boy, aren't you, Trent?"

He puffed up for a minute. "I resent that deflamatory comment."

"Defamatory, and I'm almost positive you're using it wrong." I closed the door, and Hannah and I made it down the hall before we burst out laughing.

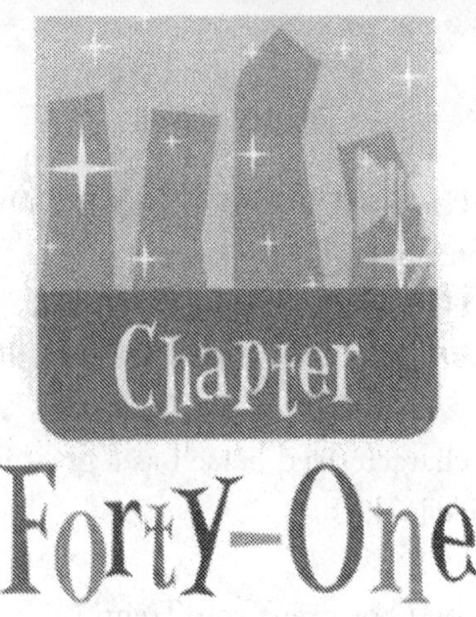

Chapter Forty-One

Hannah and I sat on Katie's couch for a quiet moment.

I was falling asleep when she bumped me awake.

"So what's with the hidden cameras?"

"Where?"

She pointed. "In that plant."

A closer look revealed a tiny, suspicious instrument.

The heavyset cameraman was the only one in sight. I called him over. "Malcolm, what is that in this plant? It looks like a camera."

"Because it is," he said nonchalantly. "Trent had me put it there." He cleared his throat.

"Has it been running the whole time?"

"Until the film ran out."

"Why would Trent do that?"

"For a staged scene, maybe."

"From now on, I want all this surveillance to quit. When someone is being filmed, they should know it," I said pointedly.

"It's standard on every show I've ever worked on. Sometimes we put them in the fish tanks and one-way mirrors." He smiled unrepentantly.

"Well, this is my show, and it's not going to be standard. Can we take a look at the footage?"

"Sure. From what point?"

"Five minutes before the fight started over the locket."

I had a hunch.

"I'll get it up and running," he said apathetically.

"There it is. See that," I said excitedly a few minutes later as we viewed the film.

"Rewind it, Malcolm."

The frames streaked backward.

"Did you see that? Trent took Shannon's locket and put it in Maya's beach bag as clear as the nose on your face."

Hannah's mouth gaped open.

"Thanks, Malcolm. I've seen enough. We'll be having a meeting when the crew gets back."

Malcolm didn't say a word.

"Caught on his own hidden camera," I remarked.

"Like Spy TV reversed." Hannah held on to my arm like a child, as though there was some intrigue involved.

For at least ten minutes I walked in circles. Now that I knew without a doubt how shameful Trent was, I had to take action. I had given him chance after chance, but now it was time to send the man packing.

"Mom, I've seen you this mad maybe one time in my life," Hannah said.

I waited for her to say something philosophical. When she didn't, I simply said, "Pray for me" and trudged up the stairs.

When I opened the door of the playroom, Trent looked at me

expectantly. "Save your breath, Stephy. I quit."

I wasn't expecting that. Instantly my anger melted. "You know why I'm here, then."

"I heard from a little bird."

"Why did you do it, Trent?" I asked softly.

"For ratings, why else?" He stretched back in the chair.

"More likely you're trying to sabotage me." I braced myself for a harsh response.

"You can think that if you want, but I'm a nice guy, Steph."

Nice guy? I doubted it.

He closed his laptop and stood up. We stood toe to toe.

"At the end of the day, you have to live with yourself. It's about integrity, Trent."

"Integrity, smegrity," he said under his breath.

I felt awkward, slightly fearful, and small. I had never noticed how tall Trent was.

"Oh, by the way, I've just finished publishing the *Reality Queen* Web site." His tone was too friendly.

I stared at his round face, trying to figure him out. "How could you work on a Web site from here?"

"Technology, Stephy. It's a brave new world we live in. HTML, JavaScript."

"Don't we have a Webmaster in the office who handles that?"

"Tony handles the Home Living Channel Web site. But he's on vacation. So I set you up your very own special one. RealityQueen .com. Registered the name for you and everything."

I didn't speak; I couldn't.

"You're welcome," he said and turned around and stuffed his belongings into his briefcase.

Tears were welling in my eyes; the stress was almost too much.

"Aw! Are you worried about me? Don't be. There are plenty of people who don't give a hoot about integrity."

"I don't believe that," I said resolutely.

"And one more thing," he said before he made his exit. "Good luck figuring out the password."

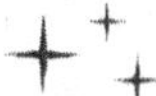

Trent wasn't lying. The Webmaster was on vacation on a dude ranch somewhere in Wyoming.

Since it was Saturday, the office was closed.

Dane was away for the weekend.

Plum tried to comfort me.

Hannah urged me to survey the damage. "You better check it out, Mom."

"Would you please, honey?" I begged.

Hannah opened the laptop and called up RealityQueen.com. "Oh no, Mom."

"Tell me straight out." I sat on Katie's tiny fairy chair, wishing I were in her magical forest.

"Where did he get all this?" Hannah asked.

"He has access to all the film," Plum said. Her tone was resigned.

How naive I had been.

I covered my eyes. "I can't look. Tell me."

"The captions on these video clips are outrageous!" Hannah shrieked.

Plum gasped.

Hannah read out loud:

I THOUGHT ALL MY ANGLES WERE MY BEST ANGLES.

THE MAID AND THE GRANDMOTHER WAR OVER CALORIE INTAKE.

ONE WOMAN'S DREAM GOES TO HER HEAD.

Plum read the next caption:

DON'T I LOOK WRETCHED IN PRADA STRIPES?

Then she commented, "I mean, stripes would look wretched on anybody."

"But, realistically, Mom, who's going to see this?" Hannah asked.

"Anybody who types in the keywords *Reality Queen*," Plum confirmed. "And people tend to use a search instead of going directly to the channel Web site."

"That's comforting," I said.

"Sorry, but it's true."

Then Plum smacked herself in the head. "Hey, maybe Shelby can fix it when she gets back. She's a techno-geek!"

By the time our houseguests returned from their challenge, I'd calmed down and knew what I had to do.

As the contestants dragged their tired bodies into Katie's mansion, I picked up the megaphone. "I have an announcement to make. And not only to the crew. I want everyone to hear this."

Everyone congregated around me.

"Trent quit!"

There was silence.

I gazed at Avril, and she looked at me incredulously.

"Avril, you're our new assistant producer."

Her chin dropped, and the place erupted in cheers.

Then all the unbelievable stories—ones I didn't particularly want to hear—poured out about Trent's antics.

My assessment? It would have taken an elephant tranquilizer to have tamed the man.

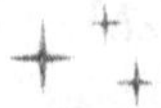

Siva was eliminated that evening.

I missed the Malaysian celebration. I was there, but I missed it. I kept running back upstairs to see if Shelby had fixed my Web site.

She said she couldn't open the application without the password. She had tried every one of Trent's catch phrases she could think of before going on to free thinking.

"Moron, imbecile, dude, dawg," she said.

The room was excruciatingly hot, and she dabbed her face with a Kleenex.

"Did you try Slinky or Frosted Flakes?" I suggested.

She squinted.

"Just a thought. Keep trying," I exhorted. "And Shelby"—I patted her shoulder—"I *really* appreciate it."

In an interview with the families of the remaining contestants, it was discovered their parents shared one thing in common: they all had menial jobs back in their countries of origin.

The competition with our seven remaining contestants today was going to be our biggest challenge yet. Or maybe that was what we said every day.

"You are going to do your parents' jobs today." Katie went on with the explanation.

Kristin was working on a dairy farm.

Enrique was picking fruit.

Keiko was working in a sushi bar.

Azi was a street vendor in the jewelry district.

And so on and so forth with the other remaining three.

"This is not *The Simple Life* with Paris Hilton. We expect a real performance, not cute little lines. You will get dirty, you will get sweaty, and you will be rated by your employers on the job you do."

Excellent job, Katie!

Who would have known she had it in her?

One by one the contestants came back, exhausted and dirty, with few words.

They barely made it through the prose of the celebrated Nigerian poet, or even more amazingly, through the African dance that rocked the house. They could have cared less about the food.

Azi was fine with being eliminated.

His exit interview was short. "Hey, man, I'm pooped. All I can say is that I want to thank my parents for providing me an education." Other contestants nodded and said similar things. All of them were quiet and seemed thoughtful.

As the crew was wrapping things up and the editor was shutting down his computer, Craig walked over. I was sure he was going to say something about how I needed to play a more active role. Instead, his smile indicated he was pleased. "I've got to hand it to you, Stephy. I think what you're doing here is unheard of."

"What's that?"

"Making Reality TV noble. You're making me proud. Keep up the good work."

That was the point when everything changed with the remaining six contestants. You remember the Grinch and how his heart grew really big, really fast? It was like that.

What the "it" was, I couldn't exactly pinpoint. Maybe it was understanding for the first time the sacrifice, opportunity, and privilege of being a citizen of a country founded on godly principles.

This was the heart I couldn't express in words that day in the conference room when I'd pitched the show. My fears went into remission.

I'd seen the light from the guesthouse and knew Shelby had been up into the wee hours of the night. And here she was at 7:00 a.m., up and at it again.

"I know, you need me down there," she said, her eyes glued to the monitor.

"Things are running fine downstairs. It's you I'm worried about. Go get some sleep," I told her.

She was silent for a moment as she concentrated. I stared at her, amazed and humbled by her determination. *I really like this kid*, I thought. Who would have imagined I could become friends with someone close to my children's ages. What was more amazing is that *she liked me*.

"Not until I crack this password! There's no way I'm going to let Trent win." Her eyes narrowed at the keyboard, as if it were the enemy.

"Maybe Trent will be back for his laptop," I said hopefully.

She harrumphed. "Even he knows that wouldn't be smart. We could press charges, you know."

That would be extreme, I thought.

"Did you try pizza?" I asked.

"Yes."

"Minesweeper."

"Yup."

"Excuse me," a familiar male voice said from the doorway.

Jeff was a welcomed sight. I watched him, noticing features he shared with Brock. He had his perfect nose, his lips, his coloring, and *my* personality. We hugged and chatted for the first time since the "Song of the Lamb" audition. He admitted he knew their band was lousy, but he had done it for his dad. What a man I raised! He verified the college report was true, and I was thrilled.

I introduced him to Shelby, then shared our dilemma.

"Have you tried gopher?" he said right off.

"Gopher?" I repeated.

"Gopher. No, I haven't," Shelby exclaimed.

Three seconds later Shelby and I were dancing around.

Shelby's smile showed her dimples. "Now I can close it down.

And we'll deal with the rest when the Webmaster gets back next week."

I was sure that some people had already seen it (we had gotten a lot of publicity), and there would be some damage control we'd have to do. But at least it had only been out there for less than twenty-four hours.

"Shelby, go to bed," I ordered.

"I can't. I'm on an adrenaline rush."

"Go take a couple of hours somewhere and have breakfast then," I urged, trying to push her out the door.

"That sounds good. I haven't eaten since yesterday afternoon," she replied, glassy-eyed like she needed to eat. "But don't you need me?"

"No, go." I gave her another shove toward the door.

"But I don't have my car."

I turned to Jeff.

He was staring at Shelby.

"Jeff," I prompted, "why don't you go with her? I'd take you out myself, Shelby, but I'm running a show here."

When they left together, I was pretty sure I'd seen a goofy expression on Jeff's face. The kind of look I hadn't seen for a long time . . . since Kelly, that is.

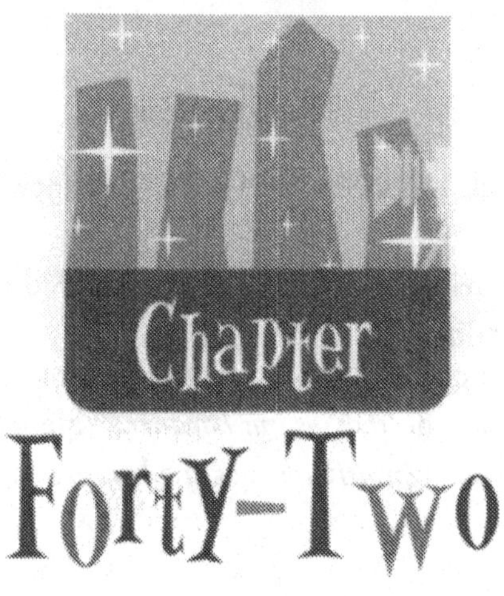

On Day Five of the competition, seamstresses were sitting anxiously at their sewing machines, waiting for our "designer" contestants to create the designs and select the fabrics they would sew into Miss Universe–type gowns that in some way paid tribute to their countries of origin.

Since it could be a clear disadvantage to be a male in a fashion competition, each candidate was assigned the help of a designer/consultant, whom they could ignore or use to their advantage.

Maya's design won. It was a floor-length gown of red silk, with fake red rubies.

Enrique's gown was also red, with little red-hot chili peppers along the velvet sleeves. Needless to say, it was all his idea. His designer, a celebrated marketer of bridal wear, couldn't stop bobbing her head up and down in astonishment.

At the end of the day, Enrique left the show good-naturedly. After all, he'd easily won the red-hot chili-pepper contest we'd staged earlier that day just for fun (and yes, he used his toes).

Off-camera, Jack challenged him to a duel. "Hey, try one of these hot banana peppers. These are homegrown babies."

I grinned. Jack had been waiting for this showdown since Day One.

Jack couldn't handle one bite. Enrique chewed it and swallowed it like it was nothing.

As his eye twitched, he made a promise to the group. "One day I'm going to down the red *savina habanero.*" He gained an accent. "It's in the *Guinness World Records* as the hottest chili pepper in the world."

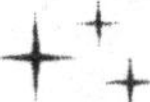

Our five remaining contestants—Keiko, Kristin, Matthew, Maya, and Shannon—were still drinking gallons of water as Katie announced the Day Six challenge.

Frankly, I was tired, and tired of the game. Even with all the breakthroughs and Kodak moments and epiphanies.

"Go away." I told the cameraman aloud what I had been thinking in my head for the past ten minutes—and didn't even feel bad about it. If this challenge hadn't been for a good cause—which Katie was about to reveal—I'd be tempted to bail. I was spent.

At least the exhaustion I was feeling wasn't all attributable to age, I consoled myself. I could see the weariness on the faces of our young contestants as well. The way they no longer wiped the perspiration off their foreheads in the 80-degree heat; the way they didn't care whether the camera was there or not.

Only the production team was thriving on the two-hundred-hour workweek.

"We are celebrating *human excellence,*" Katie said passionately.

She woke me up as Jack's camera panned the room.

"We have a room set up with costumes of every kind you can imagine, courtesy of Moorehead Costumes, and we're going to the international fair in Santa Barbara to raise money for a noble charity: Literacy Volunteers of North America. There will be no eliminations today. So grab a costume."

Katie had found her niche. Oh no! Maybe she'd become a host of a show after this and be too busy for little ol' me.

"Hit the streets!" she yelled.

I wanted to hit the mattress.

But my own words resounded in my head: *You are the captain. A captain cannot bail.*

When I called my new friend Doug Kozak late that afternoon to tell him how much money our group had raised for Literacy Volunteers of North America, he said two words: "hold on."

I did, as the door to my temporary office kept opening and closing.

Craig said we needed to work out tomorrow's shooting schedule.

Avril wanted to arrange a voice-over.

"OK, whoever you are, you're the last one I'm going to talk to today!" I yelled as someone else knocked on the door.

It was the guy with the cropped hair I had been seeing all week. I had no idea what his name was or what he did.

"I'm on hold. What do you need?"

"Have you selected an opening song for the show?"

"I like the song from *Chariots of Fire*. It's cute." I positioned the phone on my other ear.

"Cute and copyrighted," he said.

"Come up with some ideas and run them past me later."

"OK," he agreed.

"And please lock the door when you leave!"

There was still no Doug on the other end of the line. I got cocky for a nanosecond and thought, *Hey, I'm a producer. What am I doing on hold for ten minutes?*

Finally a voice came over the line. "Stephy, are you there?"

"Yes, I am, Doug," I said as patiently as I could.

"Not Doug. This is Gordon Keyes of Joy-Love Christian Radio Network."

"Hey, I listen to you all the time. But I'm confused. I thought I was talking to Doug."

"We're on a conference call, Stephy," Doug said.

"Stephy, we're going live in three minutes. I'm going to interview you," Gordon said.

"You're going to interview *me*?"

"I want to do you a favor. After all, you raised all that money for my favorite charity," Doug piped in.

"Favor? This is a favor? I'm hopelessly inarticulate at impromptu interviews." My pulse began to race. "Can you send me the questions first?"

"We're on in thirty seconds," Gordon interrupted and began the countdown. Then he announced suddenly, "We're on the air talking to Stephy Daniels, producer of the upcoming daytime Reality TV series, the *Melting Pot,* on the Home Living Channel. Steph, how did you get started in producing?"

Can I be excused? I have to go to the bathroom.

"Uh, when my grown children told me to get a life." I winced. "Did I say that?"

"Yes, you did, Stephy, but that's OK," he assured me. "Was being a housewife and mother stressful?"

"Only when my kids grew up. Before that we had so much fun."

"And how did you deal with that stress?"

"A one-dollar fly swatter works wonders. My pastor recommends it."

That was supposed to be funny. But it was so not funny.

"Your pastor recommends fly swatters?"

"Well no, actually, he prefers flower and candy."

"Sounds like a cult to me. I think we're on a rabbit trail here, folks," Gordon observed.

"Well, then, how about if I hop off that trail and you can go to a commercial break, Gordon?" I pleaded.

"Perhaps it was your witty sense of humor that has taken you so far. But, honestly, Stephy, you must have a message for all those housewives out there listening."

"I do. I do have something to say."

"You are live on the air, so go ahead," he prompted.

"This is for all you women out there who are dealing with the empty nest you thought would never come. The time when your little birds go flying off and you're left all alone within your four walls and don't know how to faux paint. But I want to encourage you not to give up—you can do it."

"Who can do what?" Gordon interjected, sounding confused.

"You housewives can do whatever you want to do. You can find new dreams and follow them. Your ability to dream doesn't need to end just because your children are no longer home. So listen, ladies, I have no idea what that 'it' is for you, but for me it was proving I could do something new, something different from just selling Tupperware."

Gordon broke in. "Hey, my mother sold Tupperware. What's wrong with Tupperware?"

"Nothing at all," I replied. "But that's not the kind of dream I wanted to pursue. God had something else in mind for me . . . and he has something in mind for you too."

"I may not be able to understand half of what you said, Stephy, but I'm sure my wife—and all the other housewives out there—will."

"I hope so."

"Thank you for being with us. Your show will be great. For more information go to the *Reality Queen* Web site."

"No, don't!" I said quickly. "It's a pack of lies!"

Gordon chuckled. "Well, you heard it from the horse's mouth."

"But when my Webmaster gets off his horse and back to his computer, it will all be better," I said confidently.

"I'm sure it will, Stephy. Thank you for being with us."

A few minutes later, as I was still wondering how I get into these situations and mourning how stupid I must have sounded, Doug called me back.

"So can I do you *another* favor?"

I gulped. "I botched that one, didn't I?"

"Nah. I'm just asking 'cause I like you."

"Liar."

He boomed in laughter.

"Actually," I said, my tone serious, "you can go by and see my husband, Brock Daniels, in Santa Monica."

There was a pause. "The name is familiar."

"Does a band named the Flying Eagles ring a bell?"

He exhaled. "A big one. It's all coming back to me now . . . sorta painfully."

"Doug, you don't have to pretend he has talent or anything. Just go over and jam with him. Make him love music again."

"Are you sure that's what you want, Stephy?"

"A week ago, no way. Today, yes."

Doug cleared his throat. "Before you go getting poetic on me, I'll do it."

"Thank you."

"One question, though."

"What?"

"Have you got any earmuffs in the house?" he teased.

I laughed. "Cotton works just as well. Ask Lupe."

"Tell me something, Stephy. Does anybody ever understand a word you say?"

A postcard arrived at my office from Trent Powers. It showed a beautiful, white beach and said *Jamaica*, but the location was highly suspect. What with the card's being postmarked *Hermosa Beach*.

The first words on the card were: *THE PASSWORD IS GOPHER*.

Even the worst of us have a conscience, I thought.

And then I scanned the P.S.:

> *In case you want to sue me, I don't have anything to put a lien on. My car is registered in my mother's name. In case you don't want to sue me, can I use you as a reference for* Big Brother*?*

It was so Trent, right down to the end.

Chapter Forty-Three

Day Seven of the competition sped by. The journalistic task required each contestant to write a story about an international event taking place in LA, complete with digital photos.

After the initial work was done, our reporters were rushed to a computer lab, where they put it all together. The final product was judged by a journalist Katie knew.

"Keiko is going home tonight," Katie informed me as I moaned at the makeup artist annoying me with a powder brush at the end of another long day.

She's joining Hannah's international Bible study," I said, knowing I'd see her around and wondering what my role would be in my daughter's life when all this was over.

"Close your eyes," Gloria, my makeup artist, demanded, and drew a pencil across my eyelid.

I could feel Katie scrutinizing my face, which I guessed meant I was being smothered in too much makeup.

"Enough!" I protested, as more eye shadow went on.

"Let me decide that," Gloria said.

Even when you're the boss, people boss, you around, I thought.

"*Sayonara*," Keiko said at the end of the elimination ceremony, bowing gracefully to the camera, before she glided toward the limo on the other side of the iron gates.

It was a great evening.

There was a rice-ball fight we didn't have, and a premiere sushi buffet we did have. But the highlight was our introduction to the world of Robot Sumo wresting.

I hadn't realized all the men running around the set were still little boys at heart. They couldn't stop talking about making their homebuilt robots. They even made a pact to meet at the Robot Sumo Tournament at the Anaheim Convention Center in July.

Avril and I sat down with Craig near midnight. He said the ideas we had come up with weren't dramatic enough for the final three days of shooting.

"Let's just toilet paper the embassy!" I joked and realized I sounded like Trent. My mind was faltering from lack of sleep, and I wanted my own bed and husband.

"What are you trying to achieve here, Stephy?" Avril asked.

I thought a long time before I answered. "Awareness."

Avril nodded. "That gives me something to work with. I'll take it from here."

I was thankful for that. The glamour of Hollywood was losing its luster, and I was counting down the days.

I wouldn't have called it a restful sleep. All night I felt like I was pulling a horse trailer up a never-ending hill. Katie, a frequent reader of the *Insomniac's Handbook,* said I slept like a groveling warthog.

Brock phoned as I was stumbling out of bed. "Doug came by last night and taught me a few chords on my old guitar, which I decided I prefer." He sounded like a little boy.

Aren't all men little boys? I thought.

"I'm glad," I said. And I really was. I'd liked to have seen it.

He went into a detailed description of every chord he had learned and used terms like *capo,* which I had no idea about. At the end of his long walk through the history of music, he asked, "Does Doug have an ear infection?"

"What?"

"Does Doug have a double ear infection?"

"I don't know," I replied, stumped. "Why?"

"He had cotton stuffed in his ears."

Brock was completely back to my lovable, workaholic, sports-fanatic newsboy.

Men have that bounce-back quality.

Women let go of things slowly.

Take Katie, for example.

The only occasion Katie and I had to chat was in the mornings while she was running through her lines over and over again "for the benefit of my dyslexic brain," she claimed.

With her acting so completely normal—excelling, in fact—how would I know that she was letting go?

The big clue was the Fanta.

Katie didn't normally drink soda pop, but she was draining every drop of every can of Fanta at the craft-services table: orange, strawberry, grape, and pineapple. But particularly orange.

Interestingly, orange Fanta was her father's favorite drink. (I only knew this because I'd come across his Fanta memorabilia from the forties.)

Whatever it takes to come to peace with the past, I thought. But I never said it to Katie. She preferred to heal alone.

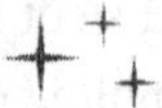

By Day Eight the four remaining contestants—Kristin, Shannon, Maya, and Matthew—had become like my children. And, like my children, they wanted to sleep in.

Avril had other plans. The contestants were jostled out of bed and told to meet in the driveway in ten minutes with an overnight bag.

Matthew, the only male, was, not surprisingly, the first to arrive. The girls showed up a few minutes later with twice the amount of luggage, putting the finishing touches on their makeup.

"We're going on a reward trip," Katie announced, and our sleepy houseguests looked up in the sky, as though a helicopter was going to appear and whisk them away.

Instead, two yellow cabs drove up.

"Two in a cab," she ordered, "and leave room for the cameraman. That's all I'm telling you until we reach our next destination."

Avril filled me in on the details along the way. I had handed the reigns to the right woman—Avril was a natural. I was glad . . . for her and for me.

When we arrived at the designated meeting spot, a grassy promenade dotted with palm trees, our contestants were being interviewed.

Katie was memorizing the script Avril had written on the trip. Five minutes later she looked as confident as Diane Sawyer.

"Over there is the famous Hotel del Coronado, one of the last great resort hotels on the Pacific, since eighteen eighty-eight." She pointed in the opposite direction. "On the other side we have Mexico. You may spend your reward as you wish. You can spend the night at the hotel swimming in luxury, dining in luxury, bathing in luxury, and sleeping in luxury, or"—she took a three-second pause for effect—"you can choose to spend the night in Mexico."

The contestants looked at each other. The cameramen tried to go about their business, even though a strong wind was interfering.

"I suppose you want to hear about Mexico?" Katie asked. Another three-second pause. "You'd be visiting an orphanage and spreading cheer."

Slight disappointment showed on the contestants' faces.

"I'm not going to lie," Katie continued. "The place we're going to is not pretty. The food is not what you're used to. You'll be bringing your own drinking water, even to brush your teeth with."

Matthew interrupted. "And we get a new Ford Mustang if we choose Mexico, right?"

Katie ad-libbed. "There will be no prizes, except the ones you hold in your heart, which will last longer than any car."

I was so proud of her.

The girls eyed one another.

"Your limo is waiting; a van is waiting. You have five minutes to make up your mind before your chauffeur drives away. There is no turning back."

In three minutes they were all in the van with the luggage.

I made my first trip across the border when I was eleven. I shared my old clothes with the orphanage children.

This was a different orphanage, and these were different children, but they had the same big, brown eyes, warm smiles, and enthusiastic hugs awaited us.

Kristin summarized the entire experience for the camera: "This was a life-changing, unforgettable experience. Those children taught me so much about love and happiness."

So let's face it: the pressure of the cameras had aided the right choice along in the first place. However, donating one hundred dollars of shopping money to buy presents for the children was not in the script.

Life is better unscripted.

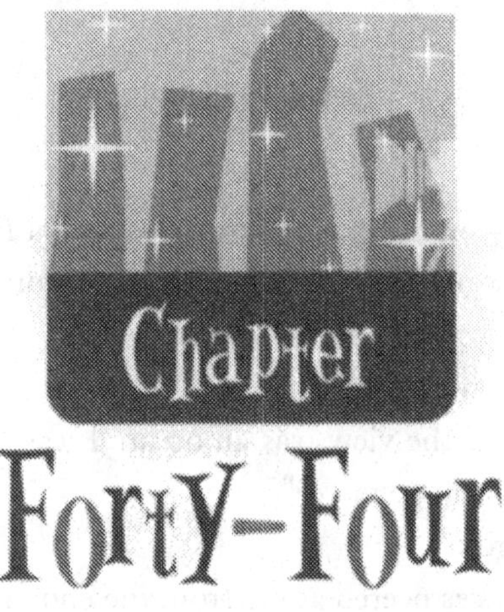

Forty-Four

On Day Nine we were back across the border near San Diego, standing in the sweltering heat in Balboa Park, where our treasure-box challenge would begin.

"We're going on a scavenger hunt." Katie waved the clues in her hand.

I was excited to be back on American soil, but I wasn't feeling right. My stomach was nauseous, my head was throbbing.

Montezuma's revenge, my minimal wits reasoned.

There was this little taco stand I'd kept returning to the day before, even though I knew it was a risky venture.

"Two are going home tonight," Katie announced.

Just then my blood pressure dropped, and I dropped on the sand.

Someone began to slap me in the face, calling, "Wake up! Wake up!"

I remember wanting to slap them back.

And then I don't remember another thing.

"It's me, Steph."

The voice entered my consciousness—faint at first, then louder.

I looked up at my husband. His eyes were worried.

"Brock, what happened?"

"You're in the hospital."

I was in a bed. The view was an ocean. I was trying to put it all together. "The hospital where?"

"In San Diego."

Three more faces peered at me from the end of my bed.

"Hi, Mom," the boys said in unison, touching my feet.

Hannah rushed over to the side of the bed and squeezed my hand. "Mommy!"

I stared down at my hospital gown. "Was I in an accident?"

Brock responded from the opposite side of the bed. "No, nothing like that. Just a bad case of dehydration, and exhaustion besides. They're keeping you for observation."

I noticed the tubes in my arm. "How long have I been here?"

"Since this morning," Brock explained.

"The show!" I cried.

"Avril is handling things. You need to rest." Brock moved in closer. "Is there anything you need?"

I thought and smiled. "For you all to have some fun while you're in San Diego."

"We couldn't have any fun without you, honey," Brock said.

I gazed into his eyes and knew he meant it. "Well, try anyway."

"Anything else?" Hannah asked.

"Yes, there is something else."

Four expectant faces watched me.

"Cold Stone Creamery ice cream. I dreamed I was at the Ice Hotel in Sweden and all they had to eat was cake-batter ice cream with Reese's Pieces. It was wonderful!"

A short while later Hannah smuggled a cup of ice cream into my hospital room, and I giggled excitedly.

After one scrumptious bite of the creamy delight, I asked about the boys (which included Brock).

"They're watching the Padres' batting practice," Hannah said.

That made me happy to know they were happy.

"And how is Nana?" I asked.

"Oh, I forgot. She knitted you something." Hannah pulled a crocheted bookmark out of her purse. "She sent brownies, too, but we ate them on the way—or Jeff did."

A nurse with bright orange hair walked in and frowned. She looked intent on taking the ice cream I was holding like a life preserver to my chest.

"Let's talk dehydration!" she said.

Hannah came to my defense. "Do you know who my mother is?"

"No."

"She's all over the front page of every newspaper."

The nurse studied my face. "I don't recognize her."

Hannah went on bragging.

I couldn't help thinking, *I am not all over the front page of every newspaper. I hope. I hope.*

I had about ten good bites before the nurse apprehended my dessert.

Those ten bites nearly killed me, but it was worth it.

I was returning from the bathroom when Maya and Shannon came to visit me. They had both been eliminated but were still in excellent spirits.

"So, like, do you, like, want me to paint your toenails or something?" Shannon asked.

Nana called.

Katie called.

Nana called.

Avril called.

Nana and Simon called.

And then lots of reporters called, and I turned off the ringer.

When a second bold reporter dressed in scrubs crept in my room to flash another bad picture, a security guard was posted at the door.

"Who do you want me to let in the room?" he asked, after he swallowed a cube of my purple Jell-O.

"Family members and good friends," I said, closing my eyes.

Ten minutes later he called from his post. "Your nephew Trent is here."

"My nephew?"

I was about to say, "I don't have a nephew!"

Next thing I knew Trent Powers was in the room, looking like his usual rumpled self.

"I got you flowers," he said.

I swallowed hard. What do you say when someone you can't stand visits you in the hospital with a bouquet of . . . "Weeds, Trent. You brought me weeds." (Only Simon is allowed to bring me weeds and get away with it.)

"Dandelions."

"Dandelions are weeds."

He laid them on my nightstand.

"So what are you doing all the way down here?" I asked, snippety.

"I was registering to vote."

I rolled my eyes.

"OK, I came to see you. I read about you in the paper."

I didn't ask what the papers said.

"So how was the weather in Jamaica?" I asked. "Similar to here, I'll bet."

He dropped his head. "You're not going to press charges, are you?"

I let him sweat.

"Stephy, I'm sorry. I suffer from low self-esteem."

"I figured that," I said, almost feeling sorry for him again. "We won't press charges, I promise. Now will you go away?"

He hesitated, shuffling his feet. "After you promise you forgive me."

"Why do you care?"

"Because you have connections."

"You mean *Katie* has connections."

He raised his head. "No, I mean the big guy."

"Big guy?" I asked, stumped.

"The one up in the clouds that could make my life miserable."

I took a deep breath. "Trent, I forgive you," I said.

He looked embarrassed and changed the subject.

"I'm joining the army. Camp Pendleton is down the street, and I'm meeting with a recruiter."

"That's the marines."

He ate the roll off my food tray as I watched him, amused.

He smiled wide. "So you forgive me for the billboard too?"

I cringed.

Some things would never change.

The following sunny morning my children waited until I was wheeled out to the hospital parking lot to say good-bye. I waved as they drove off in Hannah's VW Bug.

Brock was pulling the car around when someone yelled, "It's her!"

With a rush of energy, I bounded into the passenger seat of his new Mazda Miata (yes, he took me up on my offer and purchased his dream car) before it came to a complete stop.

"Drive!" I yelled.

Brock drove. I crouched.

Within a few miles I forgot all about the paparazzi. It was just me and Brock, speeding down the 405 in his convertible, the ocean in the distance. We reminisced, and soon the conversation turned to the children and then to Brock's work.

In an unprecedented first, I was really listening as he droned on about real estate.

I understood now, because I wanted to drone on about all the production details I needed to attend to. It was good to see him passionate about something that didn't hurt my ears.

Brock dropped me off at the filming location as though he were dropping me off at the grocery store where I worked. "See you later, honey," he called.

I blew him a kiss.

Just like the old days . . . only better.

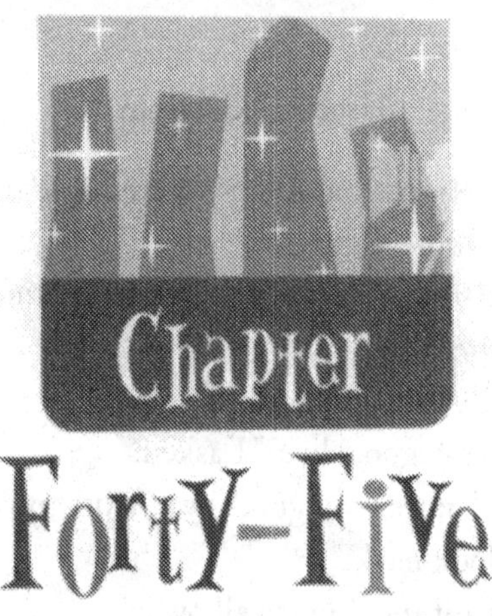

Chapter Forty-Five

Katie kissed me on the cheek, told me she missed me, and handed me some blue Gatorade. "Drink, drink, drink," she said and sped off.

We were standing in front of the downtown LA youth center. It was the last day of the competition.

Avril breathlessly filled me in on the details of the past twenty-four plus hours, as Katie explained the challenge.

All the contestants had returned to be on either Kristin or Matthew's team. They were painting a multicultural mural on the outdoor handball courts as renowned artists Katie knew were judging.

The teams worked feverishly for several hours as I talked to the press, knowing the attention would serve this underprivileged neighborhood.

The final product was no less than amazing.

+ + +

The elimination ceremony for the finale episode was sweet and entertaining.

Kristin won the tour around the world, and I was pleased. All she could talk about was meeting her relatives in Sweden. I remember the day I first met her when all she seemed to care about was her hair.

Her world, in my opinion, had been the smallest, and she had grown the most. Kinda like me, I guess.

When the last flag was lowered, I asked Dane, "So, how many times have you done this?"

"Quite a few," he said and smiled.

"Isn't it hard to say good-bye?" I asked.

"I don't know. I never say good-bye. I just move on to the next project and don't look back."

The realization hit me. "So it's all over?"

"Far from over for me." He exhaled slowly. "I'll be working with the post-production supervisor in the cutting room where hundreds of hours of footage will be condensed into a winning show."

I wasn't sure if I wanted to be invited into the cutting room. I didn't think so. I was beat.

"You can go back to your old life," he added

I can't go back to my old life, I thought. *My old life isn't there anymore.*

He seemed to be reading my expression and made an offer.

"Would you like to produce another show, Stephy?"

"Another show?" I asked hesitantly.

"It's one of our less-prestigious projects called *Furr and Feathers*. I think the subject matter is fairly obvious." He laughed.

I didn't need to hear any more. "Thank you, Dane, for this lovely opportunity, but no."

We shook hands.

"Our publicist will be in touch before the show airs next spring."

I flung my hair in the air. "Can I dye my hair back to brunette in the meantime?"

Say yes, say yes, say yes, I begged in my mind.

He gave me an appraising look. "Sure. It will give those Reality TV Web site chat rooms something to talk about."

The next afternoon, after my hair appointment, I drove to the park.

As I walked along at a leisurely pace, I congratulated myself on a job well done. I had been successful beyond my dreams.

It's out of my hands now, I told myself one last time. And then I looked up and saw the Red Hat Society ladies at the same table where we met that day last fall. I stopped and watched them for a minute.

"Over here, Stephy!" the white-haired Jane cried.

I couldn't believe she remembered me. I sped over to the table and flung my straightened brunette hair.

"I heard you on the radio," she said excitedly.

I cringed, unsure which one of my bad interviews she had heard.

"You really showed them!" she continued.

I wasn't sure who *them* was, but I was glad I had showed them.

"I heard you on Joy-Love Christian Radio Network," she explained.

"Oh." My face fell.

"So are you over your identity crisis?"

I had to stop and think a minute before I could answer. To my surprise, a feeling of warm calm began to come over me.

"Yeah, I'm over it," I said quietly.

She smiled, as though she expected more.

So I gathered my thoughts, and my surprise slowly gave way to understanding as my confidence grew. "Yeah. I've finally figured it out. All this time I was trying to find myself, but I was looking in all the wrong places. I looked *inside* myself and I looked *outside* myself—but I forgot to look *up*. What I've finally figured out is that my true identity is found in God. Strange as this may sound"—my thoughts seemed to clarify themselves as I spoke—"I think the way to me is inside Him."

That about summed it up.

"Not that we are competent in ourselves to claim anything for ourselves, but our competence comes from God," she impressed me by quoting from Second Corinthians.

"That is a reassuring truth, isn't it," I said, satisfied.

She nodded her hat-adorned head in agreement.

I sighed, remembering the loneliness I had felt that day we first met. That horrible, no good, unloved feeling was completely gone.

"I was giving so much and feeling depleted and not understanding why," I told Jane as I reflected. "And it was because I was doing it on my own and choosing the accolades of others over the peace of God."

Jane waved her red linen napkin. "So you won't be needing this anymore."

"Not for now." I shook my head, smiling.

"You look so full of joy," Jane observed. "I can hardly believe you're the same woman."

"I'm not the same woman."

Jane asked me to sit down and have tea.

I listened to the other Red Hats chat like magpies and missed Katie's fun and friendship. She was still struggling, I could tell.

"What's next in your career path?" Jane asked, at the end of our tea.

"We'll see what comes next. For now I want to be with my friends and family . . . and spend time with God."

"And yourself. Do you want to be with yourself?"

That was a good question, and I knew the answer.

"I feel very comfortable with myself. Let's put it that way." I chuckled as Jane took off her red pumps and squeezed her toes.

I noticed her watching my feet and knew what she was thinking.

"How about a free-spirit run," she suggested after a minute of smiling her head off.

I kicked off my Keds, and we went for a short but invigorating barefoot run as the other Red Hats yelled, "Way to go, Girls!"

And, "You don't need to be Britney Spears, baby."

Life was back to a habitual routine.

The evenings were a blast. Most of the time one of my three children visited. Most of the time Brock ate dinner at home. Simon joined us half the time.

Nana was in love and as hyper as a new kitten. She and Simon were relishing their time together, and I was able to get past the clutter in my living room by repeating the phrase I'd heard in a movie: "I can't organize the world."

Brock was now allowed to ignore me behind his newspaper while I read my Jane Austen classic.

I no longer minded picking up his wet towels and dirty socks . . . but his clean, cut toenails were his job.

I called Hannah in the mornings before class when I felt like it. I cooked food and brought it to the boys when I felt like it. I met Brock for lunch when I felt like it. I gave interviews when I felt like it.

You get the point?

I spent a lot of time alone with God, even when I didn't feel like it. But most of the time I did . . . feel like it.

Everything was well with my soul.

I still worried about Katie, though. That girl had disappeared off the face of the earth. She was never home anymore.

But, like Mark said, we have to go through our own stuff.

Several days later I knocked on Katie's door to find she wasn't home—again. I decided it was time to be upfront with my best friend.

I drove to Katie's Beverly Hills house and rushed up the driveway.

"Don't you ever lock your door?" I cried as I burst through her big, ornamental front door.

It was three in the afternoon, and she was sitting on the Oriental rug drinking Fanta.

"What are you doing?" I asked, even though I knew.

"Rotting my teeth."

"You said you were working on your house, but you haven't changed a thing." I looked around. "At least not that I can tell."

"I know," she said, "but there's nothing to improve on. Plum did a fabulous job."

"Katie, tell me what's wrong." I could see she had been crying.

She drained the last of her can. "I'm working some things out."

I sat down next to her on the rug. "So you're going to keep the house?"

"No," she said quickly. "I'm donating it to charity as soon as I can find a charity I'm wild about."

"And then what will you do?" I prodded gently.

"I'm thinking about being a barista on a cruise ship."

I frowned. "Like Mattie was going to operate a bulldozer in Antarctica?"

It's called escape, Katie, I said to myself, not sure if she was ready to hear it.

She teared up. "I have this terrible, gnawing emptiness. While I was writing, I could ignore it, but now—"

"I know how you feel."

"No, you don't know." Her voice sounded so sad. "You have love in your life. I have people who come to my parties because of who my father was."

"Then why don't you go back to caring about the people who love you for who you are, Katie Dillard?" I smiled reassuringly.

She sobbed. I held her while she sobbed.

There was nothing more I could say.

I noted a Bible a few feet away. "Is that a family Bible?" I asked.

"It was my father's Bible."

"You two were close, weren't you?"

"I was Daddy's girl alright."

"You know, Katie, I miss my father too."

"I know you do."

She looked away.

"But God is my father now."

She said nothing.

"He wants a relationship with you, and he's alive and well!"

I took the Bible and set it in her lap and left her with the truth.

Epilogue

Katie and I were hosting a benefit at her mansion for our new international club, a dream we unearthed together.

Reality Queen had aired and gotten rave reviews. I was using that advantage for promotion.

The *Los Angeles Times* reporter who had just left promised a big spread for our organization. To further our publicity, we would let the readers decide the name of our club.

A woman walked up and said she thought it was a fantastic idea to give foreign-exchange children a safe haven to learn about America and other cultures. She left me with a check. My hand trembled when I saw the amount.

Mark put his hand on my back. "Is that John Tesh over there?" he whispered.

"No, that's the consulate general of Sri Lanka."

I looked around. "Where's your father?"

"He's in Aunt Katie's guesthouse, practicing his accordion solo for later this evening." Mark smiled.

"I wore this black velvet dress for him, and he's off making music?" I complained. But I really didn't mind. I would soon be wearing it on our cruise to Tahiti.

"Why did Dad take up the accordion? It's sort of a dorky instrument."

"Simon and Nana wanted him to play the bagpipes at their wedding, but he found all those pipes cumbersome. And the recorder, which he could play, was limited when it came to wedding songs."

"Hmm."

"He actually plays the wedding polka very well. He's been taking lessons from a New Zealander."

"It's for the best, I guess. I can't picture Dad wearing a kilt." Mark snickered.

But Plum would look good in anything. She was in the corner looking fantastic in a bright green dress, giving Mark the eye.

"I think Plum is trying to get your attention," I encouraged.

"Oh, yeah."

"You two have been seeing a lot of each other," I commented and waved.

"Well, um, we're writing a movie script together."

"About?"

"That's the part we haven't agreed on yet." He rushed off, grinning.

Jeff and Shelby were here as a couple. It hadn't taken long for me to get over their four-year age difference. In fact, I hoped she'd be my daughter-in-law when Jeff finished the physical-therapy program. Or was that his major last week?

Doug Kozak was chatting with Randy Travis's publicist. Jane from the Red Hat Society waved from across the room. Hannah's foreign-exchange students were in the corner laughing and chatting in several languages.

Several contestants from the show were having a great time reminiscing. Enrique was in the corner with Jack, reading the ingredients on a jar of red-hot chili peppers.

What a beautiful life!

Katie was the barista tonight and rather enjoying it.

I was happy to see her love her childhood home again. She had let go of all the bad memories and kept the better ones. She was a new woman: in heart and spirit. And particularly in spirit, since she had finally and 100 percent given her life to God.

And she had finally conceded to the idea of marrying . . . someday. But his name had to be Bob, she insisted, so her dyslexic brain could spell it.

Silly girl, I thought.

"And what can I get you?" she smiled, amused, as I approached the counter.

"Make it a triple-shot, high-foam, extra-hot, sugar-free, vanilla-caramel macchiato."

"*No problemo*," she said.

"Just kidding. A single please."

"Flavor?"

"No flavor."

As she was swirling my drink in the machine, she asked me if I knew the guy sitting by himself in the corner.

"Who?"

"That distinguished gentlemen in the pinstriped suit with no wedding ring."

"Oh, you mean Bob over there." I chuckled.

"His name can be Habakkuk for all I care," she said, forgetting her pact with herself.

I winked at her. "I never could spell Habakkuk either." I stood watching the man for a second. He was tall, dark, handsome, and looking very interested. "Hold that latte. I'll go grill the man."

I walked over and introduced myself. "Hello, I'm Stephy Daniels, your hostess tonight. Would you care for a coffee drink?"

"If it would help me meet the barista—absolutely." His smile was charming and genuine.

"It would."

"Is she single, by the way?" the man asked.

He certainly doesn't beat around the bush, I thought. *Just the kind of guy Katie would like.*

I caught his eye. "She's never been married."

"Neither have I." He smiled at Katie from across the room. "All in God's timing." That remark gave me goose bumps.

Katie smiled back at Bob.

"What brings you to our event?" I asked.

"I like to support a worthy cause. I heard about your gathering from the consulate general from Sri Lanka. I work at the Greek consulate," he explained.

I noted the Mediterranean accent. "That's very nice," I said.

"And what is your barista's name?" he prompted.

"Her name is Katie."

"Katie," he said softly.

"And what's your name?" I asked.

"Bob."

"Bob?" I nearly laughed.

It couldn't be . . .

"Yes, plain ol' Bob, I'm afraid." He paused. "My mother is half English."

I took a breath. *God certainly does work in mysterious ways, doesn't he?*

"I'll let you order your own coffee," I said, escorting the handsome stranger to the counter.

Katie took one look at his closeup form and nearly swooned.

"This is Bob," I said, fluttering my eyelashes at her.

"Bob!" Katie swallowed hard. "And what would you like . . . Bob?"

"A cappuccino, please."

"I think I can handle that," she said.

"Bob, what is your last name?" I asked as Katie tried to pour without spilling.

"Uh, it's Datsopoulos."

Katie froze like a statue.

"Do you have a paper and pencil?" he asked.

I grabbed one from behind the counter and set it in front of him.

"It helps to see it in writing. It is a challenging name, I'm afraid."

Datsopoulos, he wrote.

"It looks dreadful, doesn't it?" He smiled again, this time revealing a set of pearly whites. "It's a Greek name."

Katie eyed the paper.

"If you stare at it long enough, the letters reverse on you. But that's OK, because it has three *O*s."

"Wow!" Katie said.

"Ah, a dyslexic joke," he continued.

"What is?"

"Wow!" he said again.

"I get it now," she said, appearing embarrassed.

"Don't mind me. You have to laugh or cry," he joked.

"Laugh or cry?" Katie didn't get it.

"I'm dyslexic," he stated and smiled.

Katie's blue eyes lit up in wonder. "And so were Albert Einstein and Thomas Edison."

I felt it was safe to walk away.

Life is a richly embroidered piece of cloth, I thought.

Whoever would have expected such a happy ending?

About the Author

Debbie DiGiovanni is the author of two previous novels, *Concessions* and *Tight Squeeze*. She and her family live in Southern California, where she is hard at work on her fourth novel. She and Reality TV icon Mark Burnett are not accepting Reality TV ideas from the public at this time, and she is turning down all the major networks that have approached her about producing a Reality TV show centered around her faithful cat, Miss Kitty.

Enjoyment Guarantee

If you are not totally satisfied with this book, simply return it to us along with your receipt, a statement of what you didn't like about the book, and your name and address within 60 days of purchase to Howard Publishing, 3117 North 7th Street, West Monroe, LA 71291-2227, and we will gladly reimburse you for the cost of the book.

9 781582 294872